WICKED VILLAIN

CRUEL KINGS

WICKED VILLAIN

KELLIANN NELSON

978-1-958110-29-4
Published by Black Hearts Press LLC
hello@blackheartspress.com
Cover design by Damonza

CONTENT INFO

Some scenes and dark themes in this book may not be suitable for all readers. Visit kelliannnelson.com/content-info for specific content notes.

*For the girls who know
some villains are worth the fall.*

FOREWORD

This isn't just a book. It's destruction with elegance, sensuality wrapped in razor wire, and love that claws at your soul. This is a story you don't read. You survive it.

You're dragged into a world where desire is dangerous and love is sharp enough to leave scars. Every line is a challenge. Every scene burns. The characters aren't meant to be loved. They're meant to be obsessed over. He's merciless. She's wildfire. And when they clash? Nothing is left standing.

It's not about who wins. It's about who burns first.

"On your knees. Show me how sorry you are..." —it's not just a command. It's the heartbeat of this book: submission, shame, dominance, and trust colliding in one brutal, intimate moment. Power shifts. Walls fall. Pleasure cuts deep.

This book is too much for some. But for those who crave dark desire, brutal romance, and lovers who break each other just to feel something real, it's pure, addictive fire.

It scorches. It wrecks. And it leaves you begging for more.

— darkreadgirl

ONE

STEFANO

I should have fucked her again.

And again, until she carried my baby inside her. I should have stopped her from leaving me. I should've gone back and forced her to marry me, but I allowed her to stay in her innocent little world too long. I had to let her go.

My second-in-command cleared his throat for my attention.

I stood, leaned over the top of my desk, my hands pressed flat on the wood surface, and glared at him.

Fear flashed in Tony's eyes. He'd crossed the line.

And yet he repeated his question.

"I said, are you taking the wrong bride, boss?"

I'd been asking myself the same question for weeks, but that didn't mean I would tolerate being questioned about it by Tony or anyone else in my organization.

"Excuse me?" I asked, the edge in my tone making it clear he would get only one chance to explain.

"It's just that, well, the Capaldo girl... she..."

I turned to the French doors and watched the landscapers preparing the courtyard below for my wedding celebration.

"She what, Tony?"

"She isn't right for you, Stef," he said to my back.

"You're wrong. Benedetta was bred for a man like me. She'll know her place as my wife and do what she's told. And she comes with a fortune—her father's empire as well as her mother's family business."

It had taken some work, but I made sure she became the only remaining heir to those two tri-state area families. Our marriage would triple the number of men under my control and make me the most powerful mafia boss in not only the tri-state area but on the entire East Coast.

"But..." Then Tony's words fell silent again.

"But what? You wanted to speak, so fucking speak. You've gone too far to take it back now, so make your point and be done with it."

"She's a kitten. You need a lioness by your side. Your plans are ambitious and dangerous. Yes, boss, Benedetta's gorgeous, but she can't be the other half you need. You need a stronger woman to raise the sons you'll have to carry on your line."

"That's enough," I snapped.

I forced myself not to turn and look my second in the eye.

Talking about heirs was pointless because I would never have one. I wasn't building an empire meant to last. I wanted an empire capable of waging war to get my revenge. And after that, I would burn it all to the ground myself.

Telling a man his life would culminate in a suicide mission was considered unwise. Tony didn't need to know my plan. He just needed to follow my orders.

It seemed he might, but then he opened his mouth again.

"It's just that—"

"No woman is strong enough to stand by me," I said.

My own lie tasted bitter.

I moved my gaze from the window to a polished wooden box on the mantel above the fireplace. That box contained my truth, the real truth, and it mocked me and my lies even now.

My heart belonged to a woman who could have stood beside me, but she'd walked away long ago.

A man's heart held his weaknesses, and I'd never give anyone that kind of power over me. Benedetta was no Valerie Salera, and she never would be, so she could never have my heart.

Our marriage wouldn't carry any risk in that regard, and that was precisely what I needed. No emotional attachment.

I turned my back on the box.

"It's happening. Benedetta's exactly what I need, and you better get on board with it."

"Yes, sir..."

He stopped just short of the door and stood there without saying anything more, keeping his back to me.

"Is there something else, Tony, or do you just enjoy wasting my time?"

Someone knocked on the door before he could come up with the right answer.

"Enter," I said.

One of my enforcers came in, clasping his hands together.

"Sir, the rat. We got him chained up downstairs waiting for your judgment."

"Good. Then let's go to the cellar and get to work."

After taking off my jacket and draping it over the back of the leather chair, I left the comfort of my office for the less-than-luxurious underground level of my estate house.

The stark difference between the upper levels of the house and the basement had always struck me as poetic.

The perfect representation of mafia life.

On the surface, nothing but old-world glamour and luxury, while below the stairs an entirely different world existed.

A world of pain and blood so thick the stains would never wash away. All hidden by thick slabs of Italian marble paid for by death.

TWO HOURS LATER

The bloody mess chained to the brick wall in front of me could hardly be called a man anymore.

I had cracked his nose, given him two black eyes, even knocked out a few teeth, and still he hadn't broken. I hated to admit it, but the bastard's resolve impressed me.

He probably would've been a good soldier. Too bad he preferred spying on me.

Empty threats wouldn't scare the man now. Not after the beating he'd taken without uttering a word. Maybe an unexpected show of civility. With bottom feeders like this one, that usually threw them off enough to give me what I wanted.

"This can end for you right now, Mark," I said. "You know that. Just tell me what I'm waiting to hear, and I'll put an end to all your suffering."

"Go to hell," he said, blood spattering from his mouth onto my white shirt.

I sighed. "Suit yourself, Mark."

Turning to the small wooden table beside me, I studied the tools laid out before me.

The Beretta M9 was new, but I preferred the power of the Colt forty-five next to it. A bullet would shut him up, not make him talk.

I could deliver a hell of a lot more pain with the Bowie knife or one of the other tactical blades, but I hadn't gone down there just to cut him up. Mark would only focus on not dying rather than on opening his mouth.

Dead men kept their secrets, and I wanted to hear those secrets before I let him go.

A man who still drew breath could still be broken.

No, this called for maximum pain with minimal damage, so when I slipped the set of polished brass knuckles on my fingers, it felt right.

The situation would get messy, yes, and it would take a little more effort on my part to get what I wanted, but using the brass didn't run the risk of hitting an artery or slipping between a few ribs if I got a little overzealous.

After all, this kind of work was for patient men. While I rarely had an issue with patience, that morning had made me question how much I could spare.

This specific set of shiny brass had been made for my dead older brother, the man born to lead this family. But at some point, I had grown into them, and now they fit me perfectly.

My mother would have gone on about it if she were still alive and could see me now, some bullshit about it being a sign I had grown into my fate.

She would say it proved that running the family business was the life I was meant to lead, that it was God's plan all along for me to stay and fulfill my destiny as the head of the family.

Instead of leaving it all behind as I had planned.

I tried not to listen to her voice as it echoed through my head, because her words no longer mattered.

When I conducted interrogations and worked in the cellar, I lost my humanity, left it waiting for me at the top of the stairs.

Any thoughts about the life I had wanted, about the woman who left me, about the family taken from me—it all disappeared in the cellar.

Only the monster remained.

Rolling back my shoulders, I stepped in closer to Mark and his mess of a face.

"You sure there's nothing you want to tell me?"

"Go to hell," he repeated.

I bet he thought he was brave. He wasn't. He was stupid.

I nodded. "I'll see you there in due time."

Then I threw an uppercut into his ribs, followed by a striking jab into the exact same spot. The chains rattled, his body sagged, and he coughed up more blood than the last time.

"What happens next is up to you," I said, stepping back to collect my breath. "Just a few of the right words, Mark, and then your pain will end."

"If I tell you anything," he panted, "they'll kill me."

A stream of blood trickled from the corner of his mouth.

I let out a low, dark chuckle—a pale imitation of my father.

"I think you know you're dead either way. We both know what happens after this, Mark, and it doesn't include you walking out of here. If I were you, I would put more thought into how fucking painful you want your last minutes to be.

"And it will be painful if I don't get what I want. Or you can accept what you can control and finish this with at least a little dignity. So what do you say, Mark?"

The man glared at me through his swollen lids.

"I say if I'm dead either way, why tell you a damn thing?"

I stepped in again, looming close enough to smell the hot stink of his breath, grabbed a fistful of his sweat-drenched hair and jerked his head back, giving him no choice but to look me in the eye.

"Because if you tell me what I want to know, I won't hunt down your family and kill them too," I said.

His eyes got wider.

"I... I don't have a family."

"Really? Because when I found out you were spying on me and lying to my men, I didn't only have them drag you down here. You should know better than that.

"No, I had them follow you for a week. And now I know about your girl living in Queens. I know about her child, the one with your dark curls and your brown eyes."

"No, please..." he begged. "Please don't hurt them."

I shrugged, let go of his hair, and then landed one more solid punch on his body before turning my back to him.

"Start talking, Mark, and I'll have no reason to harm them."

Bile rose to the back of my throat, burning it. I swallowed it back down. Threatening a man's family turned even my stomach, but if that was what it took, then it had to be done.

No doubt I had become a monster. Same as my father.

That didn't mean I liked it or liked what my ambitions forced me to do. But if I slipped up now and went soft on the guy, I would lose the power I'd already worked so hard to gain.

Not power over Mark, he was nobody.

The power of my reputation.

No man in this business respected a don who went easy on anyone, not even with a nobody like Mark.

Respect, more than anything else, became the one precious commodity among men with enough drive and steel to fight their way to the top. Men like me.

I had already come so far, earning the respect, the reputation, and by the end of the week... hell, by the end of the day, I would be the most powerful man in New York.

So no matter how distasteful I found my work or how much I reminded myself of my father in those moments, the option for choosing a different path didn't exist for me.

I took a second to recover my resolve.

With that last blow to Mark's battered body, I knew something in him had snapped, physically and mentally. Even so, I turned to face him again, ready to get back to it, because I still meant business.

And business was fucking business.

But I didn't have to hit him again...

He slumped forward, hanging by the chains, hardly able to lift his chin and make eye contact with me as he gave in.

"Okay, okay," he gasped. "Fine."

"What's fine, Mark?"

I grabbed a white towel from the table with my tools and used it to start casually cleaning up the brass on my fist.

He panted and grunted.

"I'm listening," I said.

"The Commission knows you're marrying the Capaldo girl. They know you killed her brothers too. And they're..." —he coughed up more blood— "they're looking at you for the disappearance of her uncles."

"Hm. I'm not seeing the value in your information, Mark. Don Capaldo broke with the Commission years ago. Everyone knows that."

Although my statement was true, and I had delivered it in a dead-even tone, my thoughts raced.

What he'd said wasn't all that wrong.

In two days, I would marry Benedict's daughter, Benedetta

Capaldo. And I had her brothers killed. Her uncles too, but no one should've noticed they were missing. Not yet, not until after the wedding.

I tossed the cloth and headed back over to Mark.

"I still need you to make this worthwhile for me to end your pain. So..."

"So they know you want more than just her father's men," he blurted. "They know you want to wipe out the Capaldos and the Maltas. Absorb 'em into the Vignali empire. They don't want that to happen."

I couldn't help but smirk.

"Ah, and here I thought weddings were supposed to be celebrations. You know, families bonding with families."

Mark shook his head with the last bit of his energy.

"Makes you too strong, Vignali. Threatens the balance."

I froze.

Balance? The Commission didn't want balance between the families. No, those fuckers wanted control of everything, control of the families. And that was something I didn't want to happen.

I flexed my fist and tightened it around the brass knuckles.

Tony banged through the door then, panting heavily.

"Hey boss, there's a large envelope upstairs that requires your immediate attention."

"Not now," I snapped, noting Mark's desperate expression. "I'm in the middle of something here with Mark."

"Yeah, boss, I know, but you'll want to see this right away."

A bitter laugh came from Mark as he stupidly taunted me.

"Better go find out who else dug up your secrets... *capo*."

Narrowing my eyes, I moved my gaze from the living sack of meat chained to the wall to get a good look at Tony. My second's lips had set in a grim line, eyes darkened, and he dipped his head toward me. That look hadn't been on his face since the last raid hit my organization.

I nodded at him and slipped off the brass, clunking it down on the wood table. Within seconds, I had the smooth grip of the forty-five in my hand. I raised the gun, sighted it on Mark, and fired two clean shots into the lying bastard's head.

He had given me what I needed. Probably not everything he had, but enough for me to honor my word and end his pain. Enough to earn his death. And while I wouldn't protect his family from the others he might have betrayed, I wouldn't target them either.

I put the Colt on the table with the other neatly placed tools. One of my soldiers would clean it. Then I looked at Tony.

"What's so fucking important about this envelope?"

"It came by courier, and you're going to want to see this before you do anything else."

I nodded. "Bring it to my office in five."

Before he could acknowledge my command, I'd already hit the staircase.

"Be right there," he called out.

I took the stairs two at a time.

Tony was a decent man and a better soldier, but there were things even a don's second-in-command didn't get to see. My confusion, for one, which I wouldn't be able to hide unless I had a minute alone in my office.

What kind of package would make Tony look at me like we were on the verge of a battle with one of our enemies?

Packages and envelopes came often enough, especially with the wedding so close. The families enjoyed outshining each other with the flashiest gifts and stacks of cash, all in a show of respect.

Not enough to warrant interrupting me in the cellar.

If the cops had been sniffing around one of my properties, Tony would have just said so.

No, this had to be something truly unexpected.

First thing, after stepping into my office, I stripped off my white Ralph Lauren shirt and dropped it into the trash can behind my desk. The crimson stains remained hidden from plain sight as long as no one rifled through my trash.

The office had been mine for a decade, but sometimes I still felt like a kid sneaking into my father's domain the way I did back when everything belonged to him.

Part of me expected my mother or nanny to come scurrying in and drag me out of my father's office while scolding me.

Both women were dead now.

Everyone was dead.

I shrugged on a fresh shirt from the armoire and went out onto the balcony, working at the shirt buttons while leaning over to inspect the yard work. The lawn had been perfectly manicured for the wedding reception.

Not a large wedding. But enough celebration to make it legal with the right witnesses, then no one could contest my right when Benedetta's father retired—or died—and I took control of his empire.

For this reason, marrying Benedetta Capaldo made sense. She came with everything a man like me needed. The picture of absolute perfection.

But I could only conjure up cold disinterest for her.

Yes, she was beautiful, smart, elegant, knew when to speak up, when to use her wit, and when to laugh at a joke.

She would have made an excellent mother.

That might have been us… in another life.

In the life we had, we wouldn't bring children into the world to carry on the Vignali name.

Any children of mine would be forced to be part of the Mafia without an escape, and I refused to create that situation.

In families like mine, fathers groomed their eldest son to take over the business. Daughters became bargaining chips to strengthen ties, and it didn't matter in which order they were born or what they wanted for themselves.

Second sons like me, or even third sons, well, no guarantee existed that we would have the opportunity or the means to design our own destinies.

I knew this all too well.

I should have left the family business. I'd had dreams of my own, so many plans, and I wanted more than this. But the Commission snuffed out my options the minute they decided they no longer wanted my father's involvement and stripped us of everything.

My entire family, all gone within twenty-four hours.

My father and my older brother, bound and beaten like animals, forced to their knees, executed with a bullet to the back of their heads. My mother, begging me to swear I would avenge them before she then took her own life.

In that one afternoon, I had gone from being a lovesick boy chasing the career of an English teacher while trying to woo the most beautiful girl I'd ever seen to the new head of my family.

The Vignali crime family of New York.

Only I could make things right by playing the long game.

And for fuck's sake, I would never do to another child what was done to me.

So yeah, there would be no Vignali heirs.

The creak of my office door opening made me turn around, and Tony came in waving a large yellow envelope.

"Here it is, boss. At first, I thought it was a fucking joke, but... well, see for yourself."

I took the envelope and dumped the contents onto the surface of the solid executive desk where my father, his father, and his father before him once conducted their own business.

Words in all caps stretched across the first page.

CALL OFF THE WEDDING OR ELSE

No signature. No real threat. Just a vague "or else" in what looked like the writing of a second or third grade child.

"Is this supposed to scare me?" I asked.

"Look at the rest of it before I answer that," Tony said.

The page whispered as I flipped it to find a series of photos beneath it. I immediately recognized the girl in the first photo.

The one I had tried so hard to forget.

She looked the same as she had ten years before, with the same striking pale blue eyes. The same beautiful dark hair. The same perfectly pouty lips.

Her face had become a little more angular, and she'd lost some of the youth in her cheeks, but she didn't look too different. Not even older, just less innocent.

The girl who walked out on me.

The one I would never forgive.

She appeared in the second photo as well, this time walking down the street in Brooklyn. The same street I'd walked down a million times during college. The same street she'd taken to work at that little café where I first met her.

The next photo showed one gut-wrenching difference. She wasn't walking alone. No, in that picture, she held a young boy's hand. The hand of a child with painfully familiar eyes and my mother's caramel hair.

"So this boy is supposed to be mine," I said.

"I believe that's the sender's message, yeah. More than fifty pictures there, Stef. Her and the boy. Different places, different distances, but all pretty much like that one. And a hair sample."

"A hair sample?" I snapped.

"Yes, sir. I had one of the boys run it to our guys at the lab. DNA test is the only way to know for sure. It'll take a few days. Probably no results until after your wedding."

I jerked my fingers away from the stack of photographs as if the glossy papers with her face and his on them had suddenly caught fire and burned me.

"He's not mine. It's impossible. She would have told me."

My mind reeled, and as I turned away from those goddamn pictures, I fumbled with the top button of my shirt.

When unfastening the first two buttons didn't relieve the stifling heat rushing over me, I gave up.

It wasn't the shirt suffocating me or even the temperature in my office. The open balcony door still flooded the room with an icy chill, even if I couldn't feel it.

No, the situation itself burned me up from the inside out. She did that.

"What do you want to do?" Tony asked.

I lifted my gaze and scowled.

"I'll tell you what we're going to do. Whatever it takes to find out what the fuck is going on and put an end to it."

I yanked at my shirt collar again.

"We're going to pay this girl a visit right fucking now."

TWO
VAL

The alarm on my phone buzzed, reminding me to pick up my son from school.

Grabbing my purse, I reached inside to shut off the alarm, then ran my fingers over the cold but soothing metal of the pistol I had stashed between my makeup bag and my billfold.

I hated carrying it.

I hated more that I might not be safe without it.

"Marcy, I have to pick up the kid," I called out. "Can you handle the line?"

I threw my purse over one shoulder and grabbed a small bag of freshly baked cookies for Enzo on my way to the door.

"No problem, Val," my very bubbly employee said.

She took my place at the register, helping the next customer with a sweet smile and her cheerfully casual demeanor that screamed middle-class suburban family from the Midwest.

Her constant cheeriness was literally a godsend for my café when we had to deal with arrogant customers. She handled them with much more patience than I could. Beyond that, her sunny disposition seemed a little over-the-top to me.

None of my employees ever stayed long, though. Most were students who could work for me only as long as it took them to earn their degrees. Once they graduated and moved on, I got the next fresh crop of college kids to break in all over again.

I must have promised myself a dozen times that when the next hiring cycle came around, I would only bring on college students from New York. Maybe Boston or Chicago if they were less sunny and more sarcastic like me.

On my way out, with a second thought, I turned back to grab my travel mug and fill it with the fresh fall blend I'd made, a blonde roast brewed with cloves and cinnamon in the basket.

The flavor trick came to me from my adopted *nonna*, the woman who had left me her café, Con Amore, when she passed. No one else knew her special recipes.

I topped my coffee with some pumpkin spice foam, and then finally pushed out the front door.

As I hit the sidewalk, I completed my daily ritual... one more check inside my purse before leaving the café to get Enzo. And like the day before, my pistol was still there, unregistered, serial numbers filed off, fully loaded, with the safety engaged.

During the last few months, the gun had become more than a precaution.

It had become a necessity... my last line of defense.

I hadn't been able to prove it, but the signs were there. Someone was watching me, following me, so I carried the pistol.

With everything in order, I headed off into the beautiful fall afternoon.

Brooklyn's tree-lined streets were bursting with the vibrant yellows, oranges, and reds of a New England autumn. As I made my way to Enzo's school, I noticed even the air smelled sweeter, scented with crisp earth and a hint of apple.

Most nine-year-old kids in Brooklyn walked themselves home from school. Many of them didn't have a choice. And though we only lived a few blocks away from the school, I made it my priority to schedule my day around being there for my son.

We had talked about him being old enough to walk home on his own or even with a group of friends if he wanted that.

But then I pushed out the date by several months, around the same time I started carrying a loaded firearm in my purse.

At the end of my ten-minute walk to Saint Christopher Catholic Academy, I spotted Enzo right away. Even if he hadn't been almost a head taller than the other boys, his dark golden curls and his olive complexion made him stand out.

His usual stern expression didn't help him blend in either.

As he pumped his legs to swing higher in a competition with two of his classmates, that stern, unwavering concentration never left his face.

My heart, though, seized up every time he pushed himself farther toward the sky—farther away from me—but I did my best to hide it.

Sometimes I worried I would never really understand what went on in his head behind that calm, stoic expression. My boy could be completely unreadable at times, hiding his thoughts and emotions with a meticulousness I found a little eerie for a nine-year-old.

It didn't help knowing where that part of him came from.

I hoped to keep Enzo safe from the details about his father for as long as I could.

A familiar and unwelcome male voice split my focus from Enzo's swinging competition.

"Ms. Salera, hi. I'm glad I caught you. I was hoping we'd have a chance to talk."

With a tight smile, I turned to Enzo's social sciences teacher while fighting the urge to storm away.

"Mr. Luka, hi. How are you?"

"I'm well, thank you. Beautiful day, isn't it?"

"You can say that again," I said.

Then I returned my attention to the swing set, hoping this "chance to talk" wasn't code for more of his attempts to flirt with me. Maybe he would just express his disappointment in me for having missed the last night of parent-teacher conferences.

The same thought must have gone through Enzo's head as he watched us. He didn't stop swinging, but a thin line darkened between his brows as he scowled at his teacher.

"I... umm... I wanted to talk to you about one of Enzo's recent assignments," Mr. Luka said.

Good. At least I could mark attempted flirtation off the list, though I tried not to look too relieved.

"Which one?"

"Well, the fourth-grade students have been exploring their personal genealogies in class. You know, their family trees."

"Mm-hmm... yes, I do know," I said.

It took more energy than I had not to tell the man to mind his damn business. I knew where the conversation was going.

"Yes, well, he put your name and the name of your grandmother on his tree. The grandmother who used to make me the best cappuccinos at that little café down the street."

My tight smile quickly soured, and all I wanted was to get out of that conversation.

"Con Amore, yes. So? I hope you're not about to tell me the history of inherited family businesses is part of the assignment."

Mr. Luka chuckled, his breath puffing out near the side of my face. He kept grinning while I watched Enzo.

The man stood way too close to me.

"No, nothing quite that detailed," he said. "But I couldn't help noticing the paternal side of Enzo's family tree was blank, and he's usually quick to complete his assignments in class—"

"His father isn't in the picture," I blurted to make him stop.

But as soon as the words left my mouth, I knew it had been the wrong thing to say.

Mr. Luka's gaze roamed down my body and then slowly came back to my face, like he was trying to memorize every curve to better imagine what I looked like without my sweater.

"Why is that?" he asked.

"What? I'm sorry, Mr. Luka, but—"

"Please, call me Donnie."

His thousand-watt smile probably sent many women down on their knees. But it didn't work on me. And it never would.

With his overly styled hair, waxed eyebrows, overpriced but poorly tailored suit, and his obvious veneers, he might as well color me unimpressed.

I guessed the man was attractive enough if you were into that kind of thing.

But something about him sent an alarm blasting through my bones, telling me to stay the fuck away.

This was not the type of man I would consider inviting into my life... or my bed.

Donnie Luka pretended to be strong and in control, but

from the moment I'd met him at the beginning of the school year, I marked him as a man who would fold under the pressure of any real challenge.

He would never understand me or where I had come from, nor would he be capable of protecting me and my son.

Enzo and I needed protection more than anything else.

So far, relying on only myself for that protection had been and probably would remain my best option.

As we stood there, him undressing me with his eyes, I pretended his disgusting behavior wasn't so obvious, that he might be capable of some level of protection and decency.

I knew, though, he would never be capable of that.

He was a weasel, not a good man with good intentions.

"Mr. Luka," I said firmly, "I doubt Enzo is the only child in your class who lives in a single parent household. Tell me, though, do the other single parents get interrogated like this?"

"You're right." His smile didn't change. "Your son isn't unique in that regard. Plenty of students here at Saint Christopher are being raised in a more... modern environment."

The way he said it implied modern was less than ideal.

I took a step back and folded my arms.

"Still," he added, "most of these children in single parent households do know who their fathers are at the very least."

Everything inside me screamed to make this man shut up, but a public display of rage and discomfort on my part would do me no good. And it wouldn't help Enzo.

But Mr. Luka just couldn't stop himself.

"Most have at least one line of contact open with their father, or if not with him directly, then with others in that paternal line. Grandparents are still involved. Aunts and uncles. Family. Enzo seems to have no one—"

"Because there is no one, Mr. Luka."

The second I interrupted him, I knew I wouldn't be able to hold back any longer. This conversation had already gone too far for too long, and it needed to stop. Now.

"My son's father had no living family before his deployment to Iraq. Which, by the way, was his last tour. So no, my son isn't fortunate enough to have even one open line of contact with his dead father who never got to hold his own son.

"And by the way you're talking about it now makes it sound like you think that's somehow Enzo's fault. Maybe you think he deserves to be punished for having only his mother to raise him. So I have to ask, Mr. Luka, is that what you're trying to say to me this afternoon? Are you going to fail my son over this?"

He gaped at me, blinking furiously, then cleared his throat.

"No. That's not what... I... I'm sorry. I... didn't realize."

In any other situation, I might have jumped in to save him from stumbling all over himself.

Not this time.

It wasn't the first time I'd been asked about Enzo's father, and it wouldn't be the last time someone forced me to tell the lie that had become as close to the truth as my son would ever know.

But Donnie Luka made my skin crawl, so he wasn't getting a pass like others might get.

He continued after clearing his throat again and reaching into his light overcoat to tug on the collar of his shirt.

"I... I can only imagine how difficult it must be for you. Raising such a smart and willful boy on your own. All I mean to say is, a boy like Enzo would really benefit from having a strong male role model in his life as well."

And after all that, the slimeball had the balls to settle his hand on my shoulder.

I quickly brushed him away and stepped back. My cheeks heated as I clenched my teeth together for a minute and tightened my hands into fists at my sides.

"Enzo and I get along fine as we are, thank you very much."

I thought most men might have taken my reaction as enough to move on, but this jerk was one determined bastard.

He nodded toward the swing set at Enzo.

"Oh, I'm sure you do. For now, anyway, while he's still a child. But he'll grow up, Ms. Salera, sooner than you think. And as strong as Enzo is now, and with the leadership qualities he's already exhibiting in the short time I've known him, the lack of a father figure comes with an incredibly high risk.

"Enzo could channel those strengths in the wrong direction. He needs someone to teach him what kind of man he should become."

Are you fucking kidding me right now?

"Oh believe me, Mr. Luka, I know exactly what kind of man I want my son to be. And what kind of man Enzo needs in his life. But so far, that man hasn't entered our lives."

Luka choked back his reaction for a minute.

"That's... Ms. Salera, you can't honestly—"

"I do but thank you for your concern. I really could have gone without your unsolicited advice, though."

Before I had to further test my ability to bite my tongue, Enzo appeared at my side and slipped his hand through my arm, pulling down, so he could lace his fingers through mine.

Looking down at him with a smile, I gave his hand a reassuring squeeze.

"Hey, buddy. Ready to go home?"

He looked at me with his gorgeous blue eyes and nodded. Then all the love and admiration I had learned to recognize in my son's gaze, despite his stoicism, disappeared when he shot his teacher an annoyed frown.

I wished I hadn't seen that look before in another person. In someone who had made it impossible for me to not see what he had passed down to my son, including that exact expression, with those matching eyes.

"You have a nice evening, Mr. Luka," I said.

And with Enzo's hand in mine, we walked away before his teacher could say anything else to me or to him.

The defensive mood and the bitterness that man had dragged out of me needed to be gone by the time we got back to the café. The last thing I wanted was for my customers to taste it in their coffee.

"How's work going today, Mama?" Enzo asked.

"Work?" I flashed him a surprised smile. "Good, buddy. It's good. We've been pretty busy today, and everyone showed up for their shifts on time. So that's a good thing too."

"Why's it so busy?"

"Well, if I had to guess, I would say it has a lot to do with college midterms this week. So there are a lot of students coming in, studying, and loading up on caffeine. Plus, the constant rush of deliveries from the college and the new fall flavors being a massive hit always helps."

I caught myself then, noticing how easily I slipped into talking to my nine-year-old as if he were one of those college students instead. Talking to Enzo certainly felt like talking to a young adult so much of the time, though when I flashed him another sly smile, he was nine again.

"And you know what that means, right?"

An excited jump broke the rhythm of his steps as he tugged on my hand.

"I get to wait tables and make tips while everyone else fills the orders?"

"Yes, but only after your homework is done."

He pumped his fist in the air and jumped again.

"Yes!"

Most boys his age probably preferred to ride their bikes or climb trees rather than work with their moms in a fast-paced spot like Con Amore.

My Enzo wasn't most boys.

It hadn't taken me long to recognize how much he loved it the first time I let him serve a single table just for fun. That was also the first time I'd seen him smiling and chatting up complete strangers, even laying on the charm with some of the women.

"Did you make the new lemon cookies yet?" he asked.

I held up the little brown bag.

"Sure did. And I saved you some for after dinner."

The bright smile he shot me made my heart melt. This little angel. My miracle. The one bright spot in a life that I'd thought would be dark forever.

"So how was school today, buddy?" I asked.

"Good. We learned about..."

He rambled on, talking excitedly about some new books they were reading and the science project his class had started. The way he talked about dinosaur bones and fossils, his eyes lit up, one free hand flailing around in his enthusiasm.

Watching him like that made everything worth it.

All my sacrifices.

All my lies.

Then he caught me off guard with another topic change.

"Mama, why was Mr. Luka talking to you?"

"Oh, no reason," I said. "He just wanted to tell me how well you're doing in class."

That familiar frown flashed across his face again, the single line creasing between his brows perfectly echoing his father's.

"Yeah, but he looks at you funny."

I tried to shrug it off as casually as possible.

"I wouldn't say that, Enzo."

"Well, I would. He doesn't look at other moms like that."

"It's fine, kiddo."

Mr. Luka didn't concern me. I'd dealt with plenty of men like him, and unfortunately would have to do it again.

What did concern me? His very personal questions.

Enzo knew the story I'd been telling others about his father for years. And he knew it was a lie. For now, though, he seemed content to know his father just wasn't in our lives.

But that wouldn't last forever.

Soon he would start asking questions.

The day would come soon, and it scared the shit out of me.

There was always the possibility that my past would come back to haunt me. I hadn't moved since separating myself from that past. I still lived where Stefano had last seen me.

He only needed to cross the river to see me again.

And to see that he had a son.

Running would've been the smarter thing to do, and I had considered it more times than I could count over the years. But seeing those two pink lines on a pregnancy test had terrified me.

I couldn't raise a child all alone, not on the run.

Staying put had its advantages too. I knew the city. I had a job. Enzo and I had as much family as was possible for us... him, me, and the woman he knew as my nonna who had helped me raise my boy.

After so many years, the idea of leaving Brooklyn now felt like someone else's dream from long ago.

Still, I kept a stash of money hidden in my apartment, along with current passports for Enzo and me.

Better to have them and never need them than to go without and end up wishing that somewhere down the line I had been more prepared.

We crossed the street, and Con Amore was in sight.

"Mama, I'll go get my uniform. Be right back," Enzo said.

"Sure. Go on upstairs and get changed."

I let go of his hand, and he ran inside the café, heading straight for the hidden staircase behind the kitchen that led to our second-floor apartment.

Plenty of empty cups and plates covered with crumbs sat around for me to clean up once I got inside. More dishes than usual, but not so many that I couldn't have the place cleaned up before the next rush of customers came through the door.

As I stood in front of the large picture window overlooking the street, an icy chill crept up my spine and settled on the back of my neck, refusing to let me go.

I couldn't put my finger on it just yet.

But something just didn't feel right.

The street looked the same as always, with cars parked along either side, neighbors walking their dogs, students hustling back and forth with their bulging backpacks and laughing with their friends.

Nothing stood out as dangerous or even oddly curious.

An eerie sensation stuck with me.

The same one I'd had for the past few weeks after living quietly for so many years, believing like a complete idiot that everything might really be okay.

I was wrong.

Someone out there was watching me again.

Following me.

THREE

VAL

I really disliked all the in-between moments at the café.

The lull in rushes, the minutes before the first customer arrived, the minutes after the last one went out the door. It was just too damn quiet, and those moments left so much space for intrusive thoughts to prowl through my mind.

You aren't good enough.
They will find you.
He will take his son.
They know you're alive.

After I'd locked all the doors, Enzo and I had a simple pasta dish for dinner and finished our evening chores. I lifted the last chair onto the table, and he wiped down the back counters, then we were officially done for the night.

I dreaded being done almost as much as the quiet.

Because with nothing left to keep me mindlessly busy, the thoughts would come back.

They always came back.

"So what are we reading tonight, kiddo?" I asked, hoping Enzo would take the bait and be the distraction I needed.

When he'd been about two, our nightly ritual became the best part of my day. Every night after closing the café, we went to the big leather couch in front of the picture window to read.

The streetlamp outside the window cast just enough light.

Enzo got to choose the book he wanted if he followed two rules... the story had to take place in Italy, and it couldn't involve any form of organized crime.

I didn't allow tales of the Mafia in my home. Never.

But that didn't mean I had to separate my son from his Italian heritage. We could still read fictional tales set in the same country where our family had come from without endangering him or causing him to ask too many questions.

"I wanna read one of the new books," Enzo said.

While whipping up some chamomile tea and hot chocolate with a dash of cinnamon for Enzo, he sorted through a stack of books on the coffee table.

"You mean the novels we grabbed from the bookstore last week? Yeah, sure. Pick the one you want to read first."

"This one," he said, holding up his choice. "I read the back, and it seems cool. Plus, one of the boys in class said it's good."

He handed me a beautiful hardbound book.

The Mask of Aribella.

I flipped to the back and skimmed over the summary. A little girl who lived in Venice, the daughter of a lacemaker. She had magical powers. The publisher compared it to Harry Potter and mentioned an award it had won.

"This sounds good, Enzo. Get settled on the couch, and I'll grab our drinks."

He raced for our spot by the window.

As he put out the blankets and adjusted the pillows, I added a nice splash of sambuca liqueur to my cup. After the day I'd had, a nightcap sounded so good. Then I topped Enzo's hot chocolate with sprinkles over the whipped cream and grabbed the cookies I'd saved for him.

I carried everything over on a tray and set it on the table, then settled into my seat.

"Okay, so do you want to read first tonight, or do you want me to start?"

"I'll read the first chapter," he said.

My son crawled under my arm, nestled down, and started reading the first page aloud as I followed along.

Almost immediately, the vividly described scenes portrayed by the author made me homesick for a land I'd never even seen.

No, not totally true.

It made me long for a person from that land who I would never see again.

Enzo finished his chapter and handed me the book. I started the next one, reading about the little girl's adventure. Her escape from danger hit a little too close to home for me, but Enzo was engrossed in the tale, so I pushed on.

When I finished my chapter, I gave the book back to him.

"Ready for bed, buddy?"

He stared at me with his intense, dark blue eyes. Eyes so much like his father's.

"Just one more? Please, Mama?"

"One more, then up to brush your teeth and bedtime."

I took a sip of my tea, then settled back on our couch, this time lying on my side with my arms wrapped around my son.

He'd gone through another growth spurt, I realized. It

wouldn't be long until he was too big to cuddle that way. The damn thought broke my heart, but I pushed it aside, so I could stay present in the moment with him.

And while Enzo read, I let my mind go back to my earlier conversation with Mr. Luka. I didn't want to admit it, but he might have had a point.

Maybe Enzo needed a positive male role model in his life.

Would he turn out differently without one? Would he eventually reach an age where he no longer listened to me but might listen to a father figure if one existed?

I just didn't know.

I couldn't see my sweet boy telling me no, not just yet, but he wouldn't be my little boy forever.

So was I robbing him of the chance to reach his full potential by refusing to have a life outside of this café? By refusing to date and bring a potentially decent man into our lives?

I had tried dating years ago, once or twice. Each time, it had turned out to be a complete disaster. Not because the men were disasters. Because I'd spent the entire time feeling like I betrayed a man who I could no longer claim. A man who could no longer claim me.

Once I'd learned who Stefano really was, about his family, keeping him in my life was no longer an option.

Not even with a baby on the way.

Even after ten years, a deep, relentless guilt turned in my gut. The type of guilt I imagined I might feel if Stefano and I had stayed together, and I cheated on him.

It didn't seem very fair to drag anyone else into my mess until I could finally release the pain of that nonexistent betrayal.

I was so fucking stupid.

And now I hated Stefano Vignali with everything in me.

He'd made it impossible for us to be together.

Enzo stopped reading, and his body stiffened in my arms.

I looked back at the book to search for a word he might not have known, but he wasn't looking at the book.

He stared out the window at the black Mercedes stopped in the middle of the street, right in front of Con Amore.

Enzo slammed the book shut.

"Mama, the car... who is that?" he asked as he jumped up.

I got up, keeping my voice calm, though my pulse raced.

"I don't know, buddy."

But a custom Maybach like that wasn't hard to recognize if one had been around that kind of money before. Longer, wider, with dark windows made of bulletproof glass.

"It's probably just someone stopping to take a phone call," I murmured. "Maybe they're looking for the business hours on the window. No big deal."

Oh, but it was a gigantic deal.

And then two large men in black suits got out of the car. One had a bald head, and the other had his dark hair in a top bun.

I didn't recognize them, but I knew the type all too well.

The two men walked around the car and talked to someone in the back before heading toward the café.

They tried the door handle and found it locked.

My body froze in place.

I hoped the locked door and closed sign would be enough to turn them away.

But no, the bald one grabbed the handle again and pushed down hard enough to make the lock snap.

My heart beat itself into a frenzied rhythm.

"Enzo," I whispered, "as quietly as possible, I want you to get upstairs and lock the apartment door behind you."

"No," he snapped.

I almost looked away from the front door to double check if my son was still there...

Because that word came out of his mouth not in the voice of my sweet, innocent boy but as the voice of a stern, confident man, or at least the beginnings of the man he would become.

Before I could say anything else, Enzo stepped in front of me and faced the door like he meant to be my shield.

"Enzo, get upstairs now," I said through my clenched teeth.

"No. I'm not leaving you, Mama."

Then the door creaked open, and both men came inside.

The first thing I noticed about them? The telling bulges under their jackets. These men were armed.

And my gun was still in my purse.

In the kitchen.

I grabbed Enzo's arm and pushed him behind me, putting myself between the intruders and my child, and plastered on the fake customer service smile I used for work.

"I'm sorry, gentlemen. We're closed. There's a diner about two blocks down the street. The coffee is decent—"

"Are you Valerie Salera?" the bald one interjected.

I shut my mouth and looked back and forth between them. After a minute of silence, I found my voice again.

"Yes, I am. But like I said, we're closed for the night. So I need you to leave now or I'll have to call the police."

My voice didn't waver, not like my traitorous heartbeat.

Enzo tried to come back around me, and I dug my nails into

his arm. I wouldn't let that happen. I wouldn't let my baby stand between me and these fucking men.

"Calling the cops would be very unwise," Man Bun said.

Then he spoke into his phone.

"All clear, boss. Come on in. She's here."

FOUR

STEFANO

I didn't want children. Didn't want to be responsible for another generation of death and corruption. Didn't want to create more pain for yet another Vignali.

But in my gut, I knew Valerie Salera's boy was mine.

And no one took what belonged to me.

Val had kept my son from me, and now there she sat, holding him in her arms, reading bedtime stories in front of the window, pretending like the boy didn't have a father.

I inhaled through my nose and tightened my abs to control the conflicting emotions raging inside me.

She had taken the dream I once had, living it happily without me as if I never existed.

And I fucking hated her for it.

When the car turned onto the narrow tree-lined street in Brooklyn, my thoughts had shifted back in time.

The area didn't feel like part of New York, despite its closeness to the Brooklyn Bridge. I used to imagine it as another world, a place removed from the rest of the city, transformed into a small, nameless town.

For a decade, I had stayed away, ignoring my desire to live another life outside the family business.

Even before my father and brother died, my dream had been nothing but a fantasy, an indulgence my family allowed.

After all, I wouldn't inherit the business.

They'd done us all more harm than good by allowing me to dream like that.

My life had been simple back then, school two blocks away from Con Amore, a community college that fed students into NYU. I'd planned to transfer and become an English professor who shared his love of literature with bright, eager students.

My fantasy had driven my actions.

The perfect plan.

I would spend my days exploring Shakespeare and Dickens, then go home to a beautiful woman and the loving family we'd created together, where the hardest decision might have been which book to read to our kids before putting them to bed.

Then I would spend half the night making love to my wife

That had been the life I wanted.

Con Amore had been part of the dream too, starting out as a haven for me, my preferred home away from home.

Until everything changed one brisk day about ten years ago.

The day Val started working at the café.

The most beautiful woman I'd ever seen.

Light blue eyes. Rich, dark hair framing her pretty face. Her tight little body, made for me to touch, taste, worship.

I scoffed and pushed my fingers back through my hair, remembering the first thought I'd had about her that day, that she must have been an angel.

Then she let out her devilish laugh, and later, when she took my order, I could see the mischief dancing in her eyes.

An angel alright... *e un diavoletta.*

And fucking intoxicating.

Everything had changed for me that day. The café became more than a quiet place to study and focus on my career. It became the place where I counted on seeing Val, where I watched her move around the room, chatting and laughing with customers.

I showed up every day, not for the best cup of coffee anymore, but to hear her throaty laughter when I flirted with her.

After meeting her, my dream evolved from having some faceless, ideal woman to care for my children and keep our home and love me for me to having Valerie.

Always Valerie.

Still Valerie.

In the beginning, she didn't know about my family. I'd used a fake name and never gave her any reason to question it.

Had I felt guilty about lying to her? Absolutely.

After a few weeks, being Stefano Salvatore became quite comfortable, and I didn't want to let him go. At college and the café, Stefano Vignali, second son of a notorious New York mafia don, my brother's spare, didn't exist.

When Val came along, she represented everything young, normal Stefano Salvatore wanted. A happy family. A quiet life without vengeance and violence.

Then, in just one day, when the Commission killed my father and my brother, I lost it all.

The sight of Valerie now, sitting where we once sat together, drinking her tea, and reading to her child, brought all the unwanted memories back.

I preferred to keep the past in the past. It helped me get

through each day as the man I'd become. But seeing Val again made it impossible to keep the memories at bay, impossible to not feel the agony burst inside my chest all over again.

Ten years had passed between us.

I squinted, staring harder at her through the window, and even with only the light from the streetlamp washing over her, she still looked as beautiful as the day I first met her.

The photos in that fucking envelope failed to do her justice.

From my angle in the back of the car, my view of the boy was impeded. I could only see the top of his head, tucked under his mother's chin. A book covered his face.

My men headed for the café first. Standard protocol. Safety and all that bullshit.

"Call me when it's clear and be quick about it," I said.

Val had already noticed the car and now my men heading to her front door.

She said something to the boy.

I had no time to get a look at his face. The boy was on his feet in seconds, and when my men stepped through the front door, Val grabbed the kid and yanked him behind her.

Definitely her son.

Instinct like that only came from a mother.

More memories flashed through my head, twisting and turning, bubbling up like nostalgic fantasies just out of reach. Warm and soft at first, loving, freeing, then nauseating, pulsing with a hot, permeating hatred.

I couldn't make it stop.

The muscles in my jaw tightened.

How dare she hide him from me but keep him close enough for my enemies to find? How dare she keep my son from me?

He had been so close his entire life, and I missed everything.

I don't even know his goddamn name!

How dare she hold my son like that in front of a window, where anyone could see him and hurt him or think of taking him?

The boy had been devastatingly vulnerable all these years, and she allowed that to happen.

Val knew danger would follow any child of mine. The day she found out about my real identity, she said she didn't want me anymore, said she refused to be with someone like me.

She'd been afraid of the Vignali way of life.

Afraid of me.

Yet there she sat with him, in front of a big fucking window, putting herself and my son in danger. Anyone with a rifle and a vendetta against me could take his best shot.

Clearly, being safe had been another one of her lies.

How little this woman really knew about my world, or even the bigger picture that spanned beyond my own expanding control.

I jerked my neck to ease the pressure, tugged at my collar.

Didn't she follow the fucking news?

The world was full of madmen, sick pedophiles, and lunatics running amuck in the city.

But she thought it safe enough to be on the couch in front of a window, practically lounging in the spotlight like she lived in fucking Mayberry.

No more waiting.

No one in that café could take me out.

I got out of the car and walked into Con Amore, using each step to focus on the rage simmering in my gut.

To rein it in.

My pulse pounded in my ears as I entered the building, and I flexed my clenched fists.

"All clear, boss," Tony said into his phone. "She's here."

"Yes, I can see that," I said behind him.

After glancing back at me over their shoulders, Tony and Bruce stepped out of my way.

The second Val saw me, her gorgeous eyes got wider, her pretty lips parted, and her face paled.

Fuck. Still so beautiful.

The boy wanted to step in front of her like a shield, but she yanked him back.

"Mama, who is that?" he asked, his voice calm and strong.

Either he didn't scare easily, or he knew how to put on one hell of a brave face.

"What are you doing here?" Val asked.

Even through that breathless whisper, her voice still shook. She couldn't pretend nearly as well as her son.

Despite the tightening grip I clenched around my entire being now, holding myself back from the worst of what I wanted to do, the anger in my voice slipped through on its own.

"I think you know what I'm doing here, Valerie."

The boy snatched his arm away to get back in front of her.

"Mama?" he asked again.

She gasped and lunged after him, but he had already stepped beyond her reach. Or maybe she had finally given in to the futility of trying to withstand me.

The boy looked me up and down, his brow creasing with a single thin line that made me feel like I'd glanced in a mirror.

He had my mother's golden curls and Val's chin. Beyond that, everything else was mine. Our eyes were exactly the same, the shape, the blue so dark it appeared almost black.

I didn't need to wait for DNA test results.

This kid was my son.

Everything I had sacrificed in my life, every solemn oath I swore to myself—all of it went out the window with that truth.

I didn't want children, not because I wouldn't make a good father, but because any child of mine could never fully claim his future as his own.

And now the boy standing in front of me, so brave and stoic, no longer had the options his mother believed she'd protected for him. The world might have been his oyster, sure, but this child could never leave the sea.

Not now that someone had discovered him.

"Why are you here?" Val asked again, a touch more stability in her tone.

I cut my gaze away from the boy and fixed it on her.

"You tell me," I said coldly. "Why would I be here after nearly a fucking decade? What could have possibly brought me across the bridge to this shithole neighborhood again?"

I moved toward her, and she instinctively stepped back, taking the boy with her.

My presence terrified her. Yet another knife in my back.

It had taken me months to stop seeing the horror on her face when she discovered my real name. And there I stood, seeing it again as if no time had passed, and I hated it.

It was probably for the best.

She should be afraid. I was a dangerous man, and she had crossed me in the worst way imaginable.

As the boy struggled to get between his mother and me again, his hands balled into fists, and he scowled.

A mirror image of me again.

"Leave now," he said. "I don't know who you are, but we don't want you here, and you can't talk to my mother like that."

"I believe I just did," I countered.

Pride welled within me, conflicting with my anger.

Pride caused by the sight of my son filled with such brazen courage and certainty in his role as man of the house. A certainty I would have to break all too soon, because it was the only way to keep him safe now that his mother's way had failed.

"And I have every right to speak to her however I choose," I added while staring into her eyes.

"You absolutely do not," Val said.

Hm. She'd recovered some of her own courage, or maybe she realized my men and I weren't there to harm her or the child. Whatever the cause of her fortitude, it wouldn't last long.

Not once we had the conversation I planned to have.

"Tony, Bruce." I jerked my chin at the door without taking my eyes off her. "Get out."

"Yes, sir."

The acknowledgement came from both men at the same time as they left us. Neither one needed to be told I wanted them to watch the building from the outside, effectively leaving me alone with a broken version of the family I once wanted.

The door closed behind them with a tinny jingle of the bell hanging from the top of the frame.

"You owe me a new lock," Val said.

I tilted my head. "You owe me an explanation."

"I owe you nothing!" she spat.

If that was how she wanted to have the conversation, fine.

My gaze drifted to the coffee table in front of that damn couch by that fucking window, then I headed that way, my shoes clicking across the wood floor.

"Who's his father, Val?"

"A soldier," she snapped. "Killed in Iraq before we—"

"Liar."

I grabbed her teacup, the wet tea bag clinging to the empty ceramic, and threw it against the wall. The cup shattered, shards ricocheting off the wall and bouncing onto the couch cushions.

Val jumped and grabbed the boy again, but I hardly noticed much more than that.

With my pulse roaring in my ears, my only option was to move and keep moving.

Otherwise, I didn't think I could stop myself from ripping the place apart with my bare hands before wrapping them around her throat and squeezing with all the fury I'd kept bottled up for ten years.

Sure, I'd had my heart broken before and my world turned upside down. But I had never in my life felt the way I did in that moment, there with her.

My guts almost reached my throat. A cold sweat sent hot and cold shivers racing across my overheating back, where the previous comfort of my shirt beneath the tailored suit jacket was now a stifling prison, holding me inside the cage of a body I could no longer control.

So much energy coursed through me, so much fucking rage and shame and regret. I could have sworn I saw goddamn red.

If I didn't move my body, it would move itself for me in all the ways I'd never allowed before.

The monster would break free, not in the cellar where he did his best work, but there... in Brooklyn... in the open.

In front of my son.

Pushing my hands through my hair, I paced by the window,

forcing my breath to slow and my mind to recognize the rhythm of my clicking footsteps.

Control was all I had.

If I lost it, what the fuck did I have left?

After more pacing, I turned to the boy.

The first question that came to my mind, which seemed most important in the moment, was to ask him for his date of birth. As if such a simple answer would settle the situation between the three of us.

I opened my mouth to do just that.

A loud pop erupted somewhere on the street behind me, and a split second later, the window shattered.

I leaped at the boy, then threw us both over the couch.

Pain seared through my arm.

And more bullets railed through Con Amore.

FIVE
VAL

Stefano paced around the room like a caged lion waiting for his moment to pounce, and I couldn't stop myself from staring at him as he walked back and forth in front of the couch.

He was no longer the same man I had known and loved ten years earlier, and not the man I believed he had probably become before the truth caught up to me.

No, the man now inside my café appeared to be even more dangerous than I could have imagined... and so full of rage. He'd completely transformed from being my Stefano Salvatore into Stefano Vignali, the ruthless mafia boss.

Though I knew it couldn't be the case, he seemed taller.

And he was more put together. Gone were the jeans and sweaters he'd always worn, now replaced with an expensive three-piece suit, black on black, tailored perfectly to fit his tall frame, narrow waist, and broad shoulders.

The bitter taste of regret filled my mouth.

I hated to admit even to myself, but Stefano had become exactly the type of man I wanted.

Powerful, dangerous, someone who made me feel safe.

And yes, sexy as hell.

If only I could forget about the terrible things he did as head of his family, the crimes he committed, his sins, everything that made him what he was.

In another lifetime, if I were alone with him, I might have let this predator take me, take all of me, everything. I might have let him treat me the way I knew he could, let him protect me, worship me.

But I wasn't alone, and men like Stefano Vignali came with too much risk. I no longer had the liberty to take those risks.

I had to think about my son first and always.

Of course, I knew why Stefano had come. I didn't know how he'd found out about Enzo, but he had. He finally knew about his son. What he would do next, I couldn't foresee. He made it crystal clear, though, that he intended to confirm his suspicions.

He continued pacing in front of us, his intense fury burning him from the inside out. His body heat reached out to me like the licking flames of a blazing fire.

And still, all he'd done was call me a liar and break a teacup.

Was that really going to be the extent of it?

He could have screamed at me. He could have had his men deal with me while he took my son away from me, all of which he probably thought fell within his rights.

A man like Stefano, well, the legal technicalities of breaking and entering or kidnapping wouldn't bother him. He wouldn't give it a second thought, not if he believed something or someone belonged to him.

He didn't do any of that.

One brief explosion of anger, but the only victim turned

out to be my teacup. He had even thrown the cup away from Enzo and me, so it would hit the wall instead of us.

When he pushed his hands into his hair and started pacing, breathing deeply and slowly, I understood what he was doing.

This man functioned on order and control. Thrived on it.

Now he needed to rein it back in, and I used those seconds during his loss of control as an opportunity to do whatever I could to protect my child.

I grabbed Enzo and pulled him behind me, so he wouldn't have to face the full impact of Stefano's outbursts, or worse, if it came to that.

But Enzo yanked his hand out of my grasp and stepped away from me, his steely gaze focused on the dangerous stranger pacing by the window.

Was Enzo angry at me too, for keeping him a secret from the man he had to know by now was his father?

Probably. A conversation for another time, though.

Right now, my child likely thought he was protecting me from the big man throwing tantrums in our home, proving himself to be the nine-year-old man of the house.

The sight of my boy that way became a moment of pride for me and breathtakingly terrifying all at once.

Then Stefano stopped moving and turned to Enzo.

His chest and shoulders rose and fell with his heavy breath.

I wanted to stop him before he said anything else, to intercede and keep this inevitable nightmare from playing out any further than it already had. But I froze, staring at the man I'd spent nearly every night thinking about for the past ten years.

At that moment, I even questioned myself.

Why had I done this?

How could I have truly believed he would never find out?

Nothing but pure luck had ensured it took Stefano so long in the first place. If I really wanted to keep Enzo from his father, I would have left Brooklyn and New York altogether.

If I had taken Enzo across the country as a baby, somewhere nondescript and boring, Stefano would never have known.

He would have never found us.

The window exploded.

Glass shards sprayed across the room.

I screamed, but I couldn't move.

Stefano grabbed my son and leaped over the couch as bullets pelted through the window, shattering more glass, and tearing massive chunks out of the walls.

Blood burst out of Stefano's arm and splattered all over Enzo's face.

Something burned my arm, but that couldn't have been what a bullet felt like, could it?

The next thing I knew, a warm hand gripped mine, dragging me behind the couch for cover.

Time slowed as bullets crashed into my café. Mugs and porcelain teacups shattered. Wood splintered. My mismatched tables and chairs ripped to shreds of kindling. The couch thudded against my clammy skin as the onslaught continued.

Someone out there literally shot the life I'd built into oblivion.

Fear kept me from doing anything more than staring at the destruction around me from where we hid behind the sofa.

Was this really happening?

When Enzo grabbed my hand, I snapped out of the shock.

I snatched him up with what little strength I had and pulled him onto my lap, wrapping my arms—no, my entire body—

around his. If I could be another layer of protection for him to keep the worst of the danger at bay, then I would be.

He buried his face against my shoulder, his trembling hands gripping the back of my dress as he held on for dear life.

Then again, I could have been the one shaking.

It was impossible to tell the difference between us.

I had never been so grateful for my decision not to replace that ancient leather couch. Its solid wood frame and metal coils might have been the only thing keeping us alive.

In the next moment, I remembered Stefano and finally noticed him there beside us. With his back against the couch, he sat on the floor, squeezing pressure down around his left arm where crimson oozed between his fingers.

"This!" I shouted. "This is exactly why I couldn't tell you."

His upper lip curled into a snarl.

"It's happening because you didn't tell me," he spat out.

I didn't know how to respond to that, so I just held my child and prayed. It was the only thing I had as the bastards opening fire on us from the street continued.

I prayed to the Virgin Mother, to my grandmothers, and begged them to protect Enzo.

When I squeezed my eyes shut, meaning to pray harder, I finally saw in my mind what Stefano had done. It occurred to me it could have been my brain trying to process what I'd witnessed but had yet to comprehend.

Not a trick of the mind.

An honest-to-God vision sent from heaven.

Stefano leaping in front of Enzo, his arm outstretched, to take the bullet meant for my son. If he hadn't lunged at that exact moment, the shot would have buried itself in Enzo's head.

The thought, the very idea of such a horror, crushed the rest of my reserves, and I burst into tears.

Then the rest of it played itself out in my mind.

Stefano reacting even after being shot, hauling Enzo to safety first before literally doing anything else.

He had saved my son.

Even if I couldn't admit it out loud, it wouldn't matter.

I knew what I had seen.

Stefano undid his tie with one hand, then tightened it with his teeth around his arm above the bullet wound. He reached across his body into his pocket for his phone and shouted above the rain of gunfire crashing through my café.

"Tony? Bruce? Are you hit?"

He grunted, tapped the speaker button, then tossed it on his lap, so he could reapply pressure to his wound.

I had the urge to help him, to tighten the knot in his makeshift tourniquet, to make sure the bleeding at least slowed, but nothing in this world could make me let go of my son.

"No, boss," his man said over the phone. "We went around back. Approaching your position now."

The kitchen door squeaked open and then Man Bun and Baldy rushed in, guns drawn as they crouched to avoid catching a bullet of their own. They knocked down tables to use as cover while more chairs shattered into splinters and sawdust.

It had been less than five minutes since Stefano walked through my front door. And in time, my once peaceful little life had become his mafia war zone.

"Did you get a count on the shooters?" Stefano called out.

Baldy popped up from behind an overturned table and fired through the nonexistent window over our heads.

"Not yet, boss," he shouted.

Enzo jumped with every shot. I tightened my arms around him as best I could.

"Val," Stefano barked as he shook me.

The way he stared made me think he'd called my name a few times, but it was hard to hear anything other than the popping burst of gunfire and the high-pitched ringing in my ears.

"What?" I shouted.

"When I give the word, you take the boy and run to the brick wall over there. This couch won't hold up much longer. I need you two out of the direct line of fire. Do you understand?"

I nodded.

"Good. On my signal, stay low and move quickly."

I nodded again and shifted to bring my feet under me.

Then I secured Enzo on his feet as well, both of us crouching behind the couch. I maneuvered him to my other side, so my body would be between his and the window when it was time for us to run.

Stefano reached behind himself and pulled a pistol from the back of his waistband.

"Are you ready?" he shouted.

Nodding again, I stared at the brick wall.

Stefano crept to the other end of the couch and fired.

"Now, Val, move!"

With all the adrenaline surging through me, it wouldn't have surprised me if I'd been able to throw Enzo over my shoulder and run with him that way. It wouldn't have been necessary, though.

Enzo popped up out of his crouch the second I did, and together we raced across the room to our safety zone.

A crystal vase my nonna had bought at a flea market shattered above my head, raining shards of blue glass as we passed, half-running and half-crawling through the destruction.

So many shots fired.

I couldn't tell where they came from anymore.

I just had to keep moving.

By the time Enzo and I got to the brick wall, my entire body shook, and tears streamed nonstop down my face.

The sting of multiple cuts on my hands and knees bit through the shock, and when I looked down at myself, I hardly recognized my own hair hanging over my shoulders, as coated as it was with shards of glass.

Without bothering to brush it away, I grabbed Enzo by the shoulders and patted him down, searching for blood, scratches, wounds of any kind.

He trembled as violently as I did, his eyes so wide above his cheeks reddened with fear and adrenaline. Tears spilled from his eyes, but physically, he was unharmed.

Then the deafening cacophony of open gunfire stopped.

The instant silence was almost as loud as the previous chaos.

Sirens began then.

Those sirens were the only thing I could think of that could possibly make the situation any worse.

I had IDs for Enzo and me, of course, but they would only stand up to so much scrutiny. Getting the police involved threatened everything.

Baldy and Man Bun barreled through the open front door and raced outside with their weapons still drawn as they searched for the shooters, only to return a few seconds later.

The sirens drew closer.

"How many?" Stefano barked.

"Just one, boss. He started with a high-precision rifle before switching to a semi-automatic."

"Then he's still close. Find him now. And I want him brought to me alive, goddamn it."

"On it."

Both men were out the door again in a blur, the mundane jingle of the bell almost comical over the sound of their boots crunching across the debris of glass and wood and plaster now coating my café floors.

"Are you hurt?" Stefano asked, whirling on us. "Did they hit you or the boy?"

"N-no." I couldn't say anything else.

He nodded, grabbed his phone again, and barked orders at whoever had answered on the other end of the line.

Man Bun and Baldy stepped back inside.

"Boss?"

Stefano straightened and returned the pistol to his waistband.

"Where the fuck is he?"

"Gone, sir. We pinned down his previous location. Shooter had a car waiting. Couldn't get a read on the license plate. The cops are close, they'll be here any minute. And in this part of town, none of 'em is on your payroll."

"Bruce, you stay. But keep out of sight. As soon as the cops leave, canvas the area. This is Brooklyn... someone will have seen something. Call for reinforcements, as many men as it takes. I want to know everything about this son of a bitch now."

Without another word, his men marched out of the café to carry out their orders.

After taking a moment to collect himself with a deep breath and a short, violent sigh, Stefano headed over to Enzo and me.

His every step crunched, grinding the shards of my life to dust beneath his designer shoes.

"Are you two all right?" he asked.

It seemed like the stupidest question anyone had ever asked me.

Shaking, I straightened fully to my feet but kept an arm outstretched in front of my son, holding him against the solid, tangible safety of that single brick wall. After a deep breath of my own, I faced the man who had done this to us.

The panic, the rage, my terror, everything I'd felt up to that moment coalesced into one blazing electrical pulse searing through my veins. There was nothing I could do but let it out, or risk going up in flames beneath the all-consuming heat of it.

"Are we all right?" I repeated. "Did you really just say that? You show up after ten years, no warning, and the next thing I know, someone's shooting up my café. Shooting at my son! Look at him, Stefano. He's covered in your blood, and he's terrified. And that's all you have to say? No! We are not all right."

Stefano blinked, then rolled his eyes and turned away to look around the café again, or what was left of it.

"There's nothing else to say, Val. So if you're done with the hysterics, we can—"

I didn't make the conscious decision to lash out, but then my fist crunched into his nose the very second he turned back to me.

Pain throbbed in my hand and wrist.

"Fuck you!" I screamed, "You want to know why I decided not to tell you? For this reason. Wherever you go, this violence follows. Like a fucking plague it follows you, and now you've brought it to our doorstep.

"We never had any trouble until you walked through the

door, and it only took five minutes before you turned everything to shit. So fuck you, Stefano. Get out!"

His face twisted into a sinister glower.

"Maybe you weren't paying attention. Or maybe all these years of playing house by yourself has dulled your mind. But I just took a bullet for the boy, Valerie. I didn't have to do that."

"Oh, fuck off. It's not like you did it on purpose. This isn't about you. You're not our savior. You're not a hero. You're the villain, Stefano Vignali."

"Well, this villain's life would have been much easier if I'd thought only about my own safety and let the two of you fend for yourselves, now wouldn't it?"

He growled, tilting his head as he stepped closer to me, his nose bright red but no worse for wear than that.

"You think you were being smart, is that it, Valerie? Sitting in front of the window with him, right out in the open, practically begging for someone to find him and do exactly what they did tonight? If you can't see your own part in this, then you've made an even worse mother than I expected."

White hot rage erupted inside me, and I lashed out again.

But this time, I aimed my fist right for the gunshot wound on his arm.

"Goddamn it!" he roared, gripping his biceps.

A second later, gritting his teeth and seething through them with a heavy breath, Stefano drew his pistol again.

He aimed the barrel at the center of my forehead.

SIX

STEFANO

I had my pistol sighted directly between her eyes.

"You forget yourself, Valerie. Strike me again, and I swear to Christ, it will be the last thing you ever do."

The boy ran to his mother and pushed in between us.

While keeping my gaze locked on hers, I dropped my arm, engaged the safety, and put the gun away.

I had done plenty of fucked-up things in my life, and I would commit many more terrible acts in the future. Still, I had to draw the line somewhere, and under no circumstances would I allow myself to aim a loaded firearm at a child.

My child.

The pain in my left arm flared to explosive, searing throbs after suffering first the gunshot wound, then Val's fist. Clenching my teeth, tightening my jaw, I tried to ignore it and focus on what the hell I needed to do next.

With the two of them.

With the three of us.

Because I had frightened her, she no longer made eye contact with me. But what else should I have expected after treating her like that? I pulled in a deep breath and lightened my expression.

"Val, please look at me."

After staring at me for a second, defiance lit up her eyes.

I shook my head in warning.

"Here's what's going to happen. You'll take the boy to my car, and the two of you will get in the back. You won't argue. You won't make a fuss. And you won't fucking hit me again.

"And you'll go quickly before the police get here. Otherwise, we'll have to explain what happened here, and I don't want to do that. This precinct isn't one of mine. Do you understand?"

"I'm not going anywhere with you. Neither is my son."

"You will go. Because you're no longer safe here."

"You did this to us," she fired back.

I focused on the aching in my jaw while staring at her.

All I wanted in the moment was to set my rage free. To grab her beautiful, delicate throat and pin her against the wall with my hard cock while threatening her life.

I wanted to hear her beg me for mercy.

I wanted her to have nightmares filled with images of me.

Only me.

I wanted to scare her without pause or apology to make her obey me, to make her get into my fucking car.

But I wouldn't do it, not in front of the kid.

Enzo, she had called him.

I would never make him stare down the barrel of a gun or knowingly terrify him the way I wanted to terrify his mother for what she had done to me.

He had no idea who or what I was. If I punished his mother

in front of him, the monster he would see would be the only thing he ever remembered about me.

That meant the one play I had left was employing one of my lesser practiced skills.

Reason.

Fucking reason.

I cleared my throat, reminded myself to keep my voice low.

"Val, listen to me. You aren't safe here or anywhere else you might go. You're not safe because you didn't tell me about my son, and one of my rivals found him first. An enemy who is now using him to hurt me. Do you understand? If I'd known about him, this never would have happened."

She folded her arms, maintaining our eye contact.

"I don't believe you."

Damn it, had she always been so stubborn?

Yes. Her willfulness had always driven her decisions, and that once charmed the hell out of me. It made her strong, independent.

Made her the challenge I needed.

But right then, it proved to be a pain in the ass as she wasted what little time we had before the police arrived.

With that thought, my patience snapped again.

"I don't give a fuck whether you believe me," I growled. "The facts are simple, Valerie. You would be dead if I hadn't been here tonight. You'll be dead tomorrow if you refuse to do as I say.

"You and Enzo will stay with me until I get this sorted out. When I have removed the threat, you may return to your happy little life. And after that, I'll provide continued protection for you both. Then you'll never have to see me again. But you must—"

She lifted her chin to present herself as my equal and cut in.

"Who tried to kill us tonight, Stefano? Who did you piss off so much that they would come after two people who aren't even part of your life—"

"We need to fucking go," I shouted.

"I'm not going anywhere with you," she screamed.

Her scream shot into my face, almost drowning out the approaching police sirens. The cops were only blocks away, and we didn't have time for her disobedience.

I lunged at her, hovered over her, forcing her to bend her neck back to see my eyes, then I lowered mine to her throat.

She swallowed hard.

"You're getting in that car, Valerie. You can walk out of here on your own, with your dignity and the kid by your side, or I will carry you to the car. I suggest you make your choice quickly before I make it for you."

Her nostrils flared as she exhaled slowly. She said nothing.

"If you're so fucking convinced this is on me, then you know I'm the only one who can fix it. And I would prefer to do that before either of you loses your life."

My thoughts, my demeanor walked a fine line between desperation and anger and moving things along before my problems doubled over the next five minutes.

Val let out a sharp little laugh, maybe to buy herself more time. Then she redirected the point of her argument.

"Listen to yourself, Stefano. Do you honestly expect me to believe you care about us? You don't even believe it—"

"Get to the fucking car now," I roared.

I leaned in, prepared to put her over my shoulder despite the pain. It seemed she insisted on giving me no other fucking choice. The boy would follow us out.

Just as I gripped her waist, she let out an aggravated grunt and tossed her hands in the air.

"Okay, fine. I'll go."

Then she took the kid's hand and marched across the broken glass with him, through the busted front door, and out to the car.

I stood there with my eyes locked on her until she made it outside, expecting her to turn back and spear me again with all the pent-up hatred she'd clearly amassed for me over the last decade.

She didn't turn around.

Releasing a shaky sigh, I followed in her wake.

I let my eyes rest on her swaying hips.

There was no help for it. No help for me.

At the car, I opened the door, and she and Enzo slid into the back seat, and I piled in after them. Tony got behind the wheel, then Bruce took the front seat beside him.

I would have liked to have driven Val and our son myself, but I feared I'd lost more blood than I could afford to lose and still operate a vehicle safely.

Beyond that, Tony excelled at shaking the red-and-blue tail coming our way.

We peeled away down the narrow side street.

Muted flashes of red and blue hit the car's rear window.

Blaring sirens shrieked.

Two of the four squad cars followed us while Tony took them for a ride around Brooklyn without breaking a sweat.

Tony's nonstop grin made me wonder for just a second if he was showing off now that he had an audience.

I redirected my focus to the boy while bracing myself for the next sharp, high-speed turn, ignoring the spiteful glare from his mother sitting between us.

He said nothing and hardly moved. He blinked out the window and held his mother's hand.

Catching his expression proved difficult with all the jostling from Tony's maneuvering, but I caught it a handful of times.

This child wasn't scared.

His visible scowl hinted not at fear or concern but at anger instead, his brow furrowed around that single thin line along his forehead that echoed my own.

With his jaw tight and his back straight, he seemed determined not to let the mask slip, and after everything he'd been through, I couldn't have been more impressed by how he successfully achieved that aim.

Once Tony put enough distance between us and the police tail, he pulled the Mercedes into an alley just wide enough for the vehicle. He killed the engine and the lights, and we waited.

Val breathed slowly but heavily as she stared through the front windshield. With one hand squeezing the boy's, she clenched her other fist on her lap and almost succeeded in hiding the trembling of her body. Almost.

"Be smart for once," I said.

The last thing we needed was her trying to make a break for it with the car stopped.

She seemed to realize the same thing. Her fist relaxed, and she stayed put without starting another argument between us.

The cops passed by, chasing their own tail, probably without even noticing the difference.

That trick never got old.

The boy must have thought the same when a flicker at the corner of his mouth caught my attention.

Tony inhaled loudly through his nose.

"Back to the house?"

"Yeah, but call ahead first. Make sure the doc's awake and ready for us the second we walk through the door."

"Sure thing, boss."

Then Bruce passed back a familiar yellow envelope.

"Hey boss, this is for you. Left behind at the shooter's initial position."

Tony started the car and rolled us carefully out of the alley.

I couldn't open another one of those envelopes, not yet.

I didn't want the contents to strike up another flare of contention between Val and me, especially in such close proximity in the back of the car, where neither of us could walk away to avoid crossing a line that couldn't be uncrossed.

Where I couldn't walk away.

My conviction lasted all of three minutes before I needed to know what the envelope contained. I opened it and peered inside, thumbing through the items without exposing them to nearby prying eyes. Val's mostly, but also the boy's.

The top sheet of paper had a note written with the same red marker as the first one.

END THE ENGAGEMENT OR WE END YOUR
BASTARD AND HIS PRETTY WHORE MOTHER

Behind the note were several new photos, each more detailed than the last. The first showed the boy on what looked like a school playground, surrounded by classmates and two teachers.

The next shot captured him at a desk in the classroom, his

head bent low over his work, lips pressed together in concentration, a pencil gripped in one hand.

The bastards had followed him to school—the one place he should have been safe while neither of his parents were around.

I swallowed hard and examined the images printed on the next pages. My son walking through the park with his mother, my son sitting at a table inside Con Amore, and again my son at the park just down the street while his mother watched him from her seat on a bench.

More photos zeroed in on Val by herself, shopping or tending to customers at the café or approaching the boy's school.

All those unsettled me enough on their own.

But the last photo made my blood run cold.

A picture of Val and the child lying on the couch, her holding him, echoing the exact view I'd caught myself earlier from the back seat of this very car.

A book propped up in front of them. A teacup and a mug on the table. The most intimate details captured.

A sweet picture on its own.

In context, a living fucking nightmare.

Over the next few minutes, I considered keeping it all to myself. But this was no longer about just me, so I reluctantly handed the envelope to Val.

She had the right to know about any threats made against her and her child.

Maybe a glimpse of this one might help her understand how dangerous it had truly become for them.

With trembling hands, she lifted the envelope flap and peeked inside. A wince contorted her face as she sifted through the photos, but she said nothing.

The next ten minutes of the ride to my estate passed in silence, despite the night we'd all just had.

I breathed in the surrounding scent. Hers, the one overwhelming my senses. Something sweet and flowery, like orange blossoms, with a warm vanilla base.

The same perfume she'd worn back then.

Then and now it took me back to my summers on the Amalfi coast, so beautiful and carefree. Like Val when we first met.

The way she looked at me now told a different story.

She sat between the kid and me, and the dirty looks she shot at me, even over the top of that yellow envelope, showed it was intentional.

Before long, she and I would have one long, incredibly uncomfortable conversation about what came next for us, but it had to wait. It couldn't happen in front of her son.

My son.

The wrought iron gates rolled open as Tony got us close in the Mercedes. After clearing the stretch inside the gates up to the house, we pulled to a stop beside the wide front steps that led to the front door.

I exited the car first, ignoring the lightheaded waves making things spin. The bullet hole in my arm throbbed with my pulse, although the sharpest pain had dulled some.

Doc needed to get the wound patched up, and soon.

Still, being cared for by my physician in my home didn't seem as important as the other pressing matters I needed to handle immediately.

That included making sure Val and the boy made it safely inside my home and then remained safe.

I waited until they climbed out of the car before heading for the front door.

"Both of you, follow me," I ordered.

The maid greeted us first, just inside the door. Pretty little thing, quiet as a mouse, obedient to a fault. She'd proven to be one of a kind, which allowed me to trust her.

She held her eyes downcast, stepped aside, and gestured to the staircase.

"The doctor's waiting for you, sir."

"Thank you, Bella. Show my guests up to their suite."

"Yes, sir. Right away."

The girl said this every time I asked her to do something, but now with Val and the boy behind me, Bella's answer caught my attention differently.

What would it feel like if Val called me sir?

The alluring thought didn't come as any surprise.

I looked over my shoulder at Val.

The corner of my mouth twitched. I frowned to suppress the smirk and to stop my cock from getting hard.

As if she could read my mind, she shot back a spiteful glare before following my maid up the staircase and down the main hallway.

The guest suite and my suite were at opposite ends of the house, and for the first time, I realized the inconvenience.

I didn't like that she would be so far away.

After Bella, Val, and the boy disappeared, I headed up, going right instead of left. The doors lining the hallway all remained shut. I passed by them and went into my office.

The doctor waited there for me.

And with him... Benedetta's father. Benedict Capaldo.

Fuck. The night just kept getting better and better.

"You have some explaining to do, son," he said.

He'd already helped himself to my whiskey and stood at the bar to fill his glass again. Then he sat his fat ass in my father's chair, his impeccable Brioni suit and perfect posture the embodiment of good health.

But I knew better.

He'd failed to hide the smear of makeup on his collar, the makeup he used to cover up the pale gray pallor of his skin.

It hadn't helped alleviate the dark circles under his eyes.

The antiseptic they used to prep his skin for the chemo he received in the privacy of his home burned the lining of my nose.

Images of things I'd seen—like the young nurse sneaking into his house dressed as his favorite prostitute to hide the fact that he needed medical intervention—wormed their way into my mind with the acrid odor.

If he had been anyone else, I wouldn't have allowed him to sit behind my desk. Such a blatant challenge of my authority and the lack of respect wouldn't have gone unpunished otherwise.

But I knew he went to great pains to hide his illness, and he'd taken the only chair with a back high enough to keep him from slumping over.

I didn't have the energy to berate him for maintaining his facade while inside my home.

He successfully maintained the ruse, just not with me.

The man would be on his way out soon enough.

For the second time that day, I stripped off a white shirt ruined with bloodstains, this time my blood, and sat in another chair, so Dr. Avery could get to work.

Then I responded to my future father-in-law's daring

comment and ignored the sting from the doctor's poking and prodding around the bullet hole in my arm.

"I'm surprised to hear you think I owe you anything."

"Do you think my daughter deserves to be treated with such disrespect?"

He paused before continuing, still unmoving in my chair.

"You're to marry her in two days, Stefano, and no one knew about the bastard you've been hiding in Brooklyn. Now you have him and his mother in your home, and everything's supposed to carry on as usual, is it? People are going to talk.

"And it won't be about how lovely the wedding was or what a wonderful couple you and my daughter make. You owe me quite an explanation, especially since you clearly intend on housing your own shameful secret under the same roof you intend to share with your wife once—"

I spun too quickly toward the dying man sitting behind my desk to cut him off, forcing the doc to scramble to keep up with my arm.

"Who I choose to house under my roof is not your concern."

If I didn't need the medical attention, I probably would have been on my feet, towering over this small, ailing man, reminding him exactly who he was dealing with.

The threat of violence wasn't necessary with Capaldo anyway. He was too weak.

"You have some secrets of your own, Don Capaldo," I added. "Maybe that slipped your mind while you've been so interested in my affairs. We both know why you're eager to marry off your daughter as quickly as possible. If I were you, I would rethink your attempts to lecture me or renegotiate our arrangement."

I gnashed my teeth through the pain from the doc digging around in my flesh with a metal instrument to find the slug I'd been carrying around in there.

Then I refocused on Capaldo with a biting glare.

"And don't ever call me 'son' again."

"Do you think you're worthy of my daughter?" he asked.

I shrugged my shoulder.

"You're about two years too late to worry about my worth. But if you're changing your mind about our arrangement now, then call it off. I won't hold you to our contract."

Muffled choking and wheezing came from the living skeleton sitting in my chair.

"What? That's not... I..."

"It's fine," I said. "I'm sure you can find a suitable replacement for Benedetta's hand before the cancer finishes what it started. Of course, that won't mitigate all your problems. People will still talk. Only in this scenario, they'll be talking about the bride and what she must have done to disgrace herself so badly.

"Very few things are worth calling off a wedding at the last minute. Unfortunately, the families have always been quick to blame the bride in situations like this. That hasn't changed. It isn't fair, and it won't change as quickly as you need it to, now that you've changed your mind about me."

I shifted again in my seat to face him more fully, almost smiling at the simplicity of how easy it was to silence him.

"So tell me, Don Capaldo, do you think you can find another suitable man for Benedetta in time? More importantly, I think, what will happen if you don't?"

Capaldo looked me up and down for a few seconds, then slammed the crystal whiskey tumbler on the desk. The liquor sloshed over the side, splattering across the wood surface, but he paid it no mind.

I thought maybe I heard his bones creaking as he threw himself out of the chair and marched across the room without a word or even a glance in my direction.

Throwing a tantrum wouldn't change anything about his situation, but at least he'd mustered enough physical strength to make it look somewhat convincing.

On his way out, with all his blustering and fuming, Capaldo almost crashed into Tony. My second-in-command narrowly avoided bowling the man over before stepping into the room and pulling the door shut behind him.

"Do you think he's behind the threat?" Tony asked.

I'd already considered it.

Capaldo needed this wedding to happen. No better match existed for Benedetta, especially not since her father's life became shorter by the day. And who knew, maybe the old man had grown a conscience as he drew so close to his death.

I pushed the doctor aside and went to the bar to pour myself three fingers of whiskey. I threw it back in one long swallow, hoping to take the edge off the pain.

"No, I don't think he has anything to do with it."

Tony clasped his hands in front of himself.

"So then who could it be?"

"I don't know. Not a clue at this point."

Noting the smooth aftertaste lingering on my tongue, I eyed the whiskey bottle again, a thirty-four-year aged Macallan, but then decided against having another.

"The Commission?" he asked.

"It goes against everything the Commission stands for, but it wouldn't be the first time they've broken their own rules. No, seems like there's another player involved, which would make more sense in the long run.

"Suspecting the Commission is the obvious reaction. But not mine, if you can believe it. Part of me wonders if this is a power grab from a smaller outfit trying to play with the big boys. Find out who else Capaldo considered for Benedetta before me."

Tony nodded but didn't move to leave right away.

"Is there something else, Tony?"

"Yes, sir. Bruce called a few minutes ago."

"And?"

"The cops got a tail on the shooter but called it off after he put two of 'em down. Whoever this guy is, he's reckless enough to brand himself a cop killer, Stef. He's going to bring more attention down on us than we can afford right now."

I poured myself that second glass after all.

"Fuck."

SEVEN
VAL

I blocked out most of the ride to Stefano's house, my mind reeling and distant, only able to hold on to enough awareness to keep myself physically between my son and his father.

At the moment, it seemed like keeping them apart kept Enzo away from the life I had tried so hard to protect him from, like one last barrier.

Such a stupid thought.

At the back of my mind, though, I took in all the flashing lights and police sirens as they chased us, and I felt the jolting high-speed chase as Stefano's man maneuvered us through the streets of Brooklyn.

I knew enough about Stefano's life to understand he had become a competent mafia boss, at the very least. The telling signs were right there in plain sight.

Signs like his confident mentions about the precinct's beat cops who probably made it to Con Amore first. And how little he or his man behind the wheel worried about getting away from the police by being faster and smarter on the road.

We pulled into a narrow alley to wait them out for several

minutes, and it felt like a damn eternity, but that was when my rational mind returned bit by bit.

My heartbeat raced again.

I had to do something, though I knew without a doubt that trying to escape from the car with Enzo would be nothing more than a futile attempt. Stefano could easily overpower me, even with an injured arm.

And he would threaten me again in front of Enzo.

So I kept my mouth shut and focused on my contingency plan instead.

Much like the pistol I carried in my purse, I'd hoped I would never have to put in play these mental escape routes, but tonight was the last straw.

Enzo and I would have to run now.

I had the money saved for it, locked up with the fake documents I'd had a forger make that gave us totally new identities.

And I'd had the new records updated every two years, keeping them untraceable and above suspicion.

Now that was our only way out.

I just had to get back to my apartment without Stefano catching me, grab the documents, the cash, and some clothes. Maybe two or three of Enzo's favorite books. Then I could take my son and leave this nightmare behind without looking back.

We would abandon this dangerous life and build a safer one somewhere else.

I knew how to do this. I'd been planning it for nine years.

I just hadn't expected it to become our reality, not really. And now that it was, I felt unprepared to actually make it happen.

What the hell would I tell Enzo?

How would I explain to my nine-year-old that he could no

longer be Enzo Salera? That his new name for the rest of his life would be Angelo Salvatore, and he could never go back to the only home he'd ever known?

How would I explain the importance of never mentioning Brooklyn again, the importance of never telling a soul when or why we had moved to Arizona?

How the hell would I tell him he had to forget about our life in New York, quickly and forever, because it was the only way to ensure we would have any kind of life at all?

How could I make him understand he needed to leave behind the child he'd always been, the young man he was becoming, as we ran for our lives?

The running would never be the hard part.

I had all the logistics covered, including half a million dollars cash in a lockbox at a small bank with the hundred thousand hidden in my apartment. I knew what I had stashed in my apartment wouldn't be enough to live on for very long.

So my new identity already had bank accounts in a different state and funds in an offshore account for good measure.

I had prayed it would never come down to it, or that if it needed to happen, Enzo would be too young to remember his old life or old enough for me to tell him the whole truth.

He was neither.

Still, it was happening, ready or not.

When Stefano's car pulled through his estate's iron gates and up to the house, I got out of the car and pulled Enzo with me, keeping him snuggled tightly at my side. I never once let go of his hand.

He didn't fight me. He held my hand and just stared at everything with his mouth closed, his eyes wide.

No fear. No terror.

It wasn't the first time I wished my son wore his emotions on his sleeve like so many other children his age. Sometimes I knew exactly what he was thinking, but those moments were becoming the exception.

Enzo's face might as well have been etched from marble.

I'd seen his stoic expression enough to understand it, though.

Like some kind of machine, my son gathered data, cataloging, and analyzing, trying to understand the facts of the situation before deciding how to feel about it.

Then again, he could have also been in shock.

Stefano led us into the house and brusquely dismissed us by instructing his maid to take us to the guest suite. Enzo and I quietly followed her up the staircase.

I'd been expecting a moderately large guest room, something more like what we would have found at a four-star hotel. Ha. Not even close.

The maid led us through what she called my room first. The second we entered, I instantly understood what Stefano intended for the room to be. A gilded cage—beautiful, decorated in rich golden ochers, warm whites, and hints of delicate sky blue.

The room was large and airy and would have been more than suitable if someone hadn't forced it upon me.

As if to emphasize my new captivity on her employer's behalf, the maid went straight to the balcony doors and locked them with the set of keys pulled from her apron.

"If this room is satisfactory," she said, gesturing with an open arm at Enzo, "I will show the boy to his room."

"No," I half-shouted, then cleared my throat and attempted to smile. "We'll share this one. Thank you."

"Oh…"

For all her efficiency, the maid clearly didn't know what to do with a guest who argued—with her or with her employer.

"But… I was instructed to make up the adjoining room as well. There's plenty of space for you both, with a shared bathroom in between. You're welcome to leave the pass-through doors open whenever you like. That's up to your discretion, ma'am. The entire suite is yours."

Enzo stepped forward and intervened before I could argue any further.

"Adjoining rooms are fine," he said.

The maid blinked at him, probably as surprised as every other adult who didn't know my son when he let out an unexpected comment like that far beyond his years. Then her eager-to-please smile returned, and she dipped her head at him.

"Wonderful. It's right this way."

Enzo let out a big yawn and rubbed one eye with the back of his hand before following her.

He looked exhausted, yes, but there was more to it. The way he'd snapped out his last words signaled his growing anger, and when he got angry, he needed space. He had always been like that, sitting by himself for an hour or two before moving on to deal with whatever had upset him.

Mainly, that anger had stemmed from watching a customer being rude to me or because he had some kind of argument with another kid in his class. This was on a whole new level, though. But it made sense he would want to process this unexpected experience.

If he was angry with me, well, I couldn't blame him.

Sure, I could argue against Enzo having his own room, since we shouldn't be here in this house. And yes, I wanted to insist that he and I sleep in the same room. In the same bed even. That was the only way I could know he was safe every second we spent in Stefano's house.

I really wanted to insist.

But I also realized how unfair that would be. My fears were my own, not his, and while keeping him at my side like that would have made me feel better, it wouldn't have been a decision made with Enzo's best interest as the top priority.

More than that, as much as I hated to admit it, Enzo and I really were safe under Stefano's roof.

Stefano wouldn't have taken a bullet for my son if he had wanted to hurt him.

Mafia men did not hurt their own children.

In this world, any child was useful, even illegitimate ones.

Little boys were raised to be soldiers. A bastard could rise to the ranks of lieutenant or even a don's second-in-command if he was smart enough.

Girls, though, were raised as the property of everyone else but themselves, sold into marriage to solidify business deals.

In the Mafia, no one was free.

Men were expected to bleed for their families, die if necessary. Women were expected to go along with it all if they wished to be honored, expected to live in obedience, opening their legs and keeping their mouths shut.

I had worked so hard to keep Enzo away from this life, yet here we were.

At least he was safe. For now.

I would stay close to him, be there whenever he needed me. But without literally saying the words, he'd asked me for a little space, and I would give him as much as I could.

His slightly smaller room would be just fine since it still

connected the two of us. I didn't like it, but I could live with it for his sake.

As the maid led us through and pointed out various things to Enzo, I propped the doors open and ensured all the locks were disengaged.

When it came time for Enzo to go to bed, I knew it would be an entirely sleepless night for me. I would be up all night without even trying, listening for any sound or disturbance.

No big deal, though. Because that provided me the perfect opportunity to solidify my plans for our future, including how my son and I would leave this beautiful cage and run to our new life... where no one would ever be able to find us.

Not even Stefano.

Just before the maid left us, I touched her arm to stop her.

"Hey, I didn't get your name."

She smiled. "Bella... I'm Bella."

She shut the door behind herself, and Enzo sighed.

"I want to go to sleep, Mama," he said with the faintest whine curling the end of his statement.

I nodded and pointed at the bathroom behind us.

"Okay, buddy. At least brush your teeth."

He nodded back and did as I asked without another word.

I wanted to talk to him. And cuddle him. I wanted to explain everything, but I didn't know where to start. I doubted he was ready to listen. I'd kept secrets from him, and now he knew it.

Once I had him tucked in beneath the luxurious down comforter, I headed through the bathroom to my own room, but stopped to draw myself a bath instead. I closed the door between my son and me, thought better of it, then cracked it open a little. Then I turned on the faucet and stripped down.

As I sank into the large clawfoot tub, quickly filling with steaming water, everything I'd been holding in burst out of me without warning.

Maybe it was the roar of the faucet masking all other sounds that made my letting go feel safe. Maybe it was the instant burn of the hot water melting into my tense muscles. Maybe I'd just run out of strength to keep it together.

I sobbed in the bath, releasing all the frustration, anger, and fear from my body, mixing it into the hot water. Then eventually, it would all drain away together.

I knew even before the first tears fell, it wasn't sadness for the life I'd lost that night or grief over the childhood stolen from my son. No, the sadness would come later, when it was time to mourn what we'd left behind.

And mourning could only happen when we were safe.

In this life, Valerie and Enzo Salera were dead.

Angelo and Victoria Salvatore could grieve for them when it was all over.

That night, I cried to purge all the excess emotion I couldn't let Enzo see. To clear my head, so I could think.

When the tub was full, I turned off the tap, stopped crying, and put myself back together. That was all the time I gave myself to cry—only until the bath was full, hiding it beneath the sound of rushing water. My nonna had taught me this trick, and I used it more times than I could count.

More times than Enzo would ever know.

We must never let the men see us cry. They view it as our weakness and use it as a weapon against us.

I could practically hear my sweet nonna's accented, almost

musical voice whispering those words to me, just like when I was a child.

But no longer would I worry about the men in my life using my tears against me, even though her words would never die. It made me feel close to my grandmother, like she shared my grief, my frustrations, my anger, even from beyond the grave. So I never had to carry the burden alone.

Near the tub sat an assortment of bath oils. I grabbed one in an expensive looking glass bottle and sniffed its contents— warm vanilla and flowers.

For a moment, I wondered who it belonged to before realizing I really didn't care. I poured some into the water, leaned back, and took long, deeply cleansing breaths.

The bathroom was quite beautiful, the walls a soothing earthy yellow with green millwork and little pops of blue accents here and there. Italian stone tiles covered the floor, and the tub, toilet, and sinks matched each other in their soft, gleaming white.

The color scheme evoked the Tuscan countryside, with no expense spared in bringing a bit of the old country into the new.

Both bedrooms in this suite of ours shared the overall scheme, though mine had lighter, airy accents like a vase of white and yellow roses, while Enzo's room boasted darker wood and flowerless plants.

Clearly, this suite was made to be shared by a man and a woman—the masculine and feminine aspects of the same color scheme and theme throughout. Whoever Stefano's decorator was, the grandmothers would have been proud of their work.

With one more deep breath, I sank under the warm, fragrant water, submerging my entire body to my nose.

Tonight, all I needed to do was process our current situation. I couldn't leave, not yet. Returning to the apartment wasn't safe until we dealt with the threat.

But the second it was, Enzo and I were gone. Stefano had said he would respect my choices, that he would ensure our safety, and that we would never have to see him again.

I didn't believe him for a second.

A man like that, a man in power, would never let his only son grow up outside the family business.

Even if Stefano was a rare breed on his own and intended to keep his word, I couldn't risk it. If he got to know Enzo, if he saw in his son what I did, the man would suck my innocent baby boy into his world like a sinkhole opening beneath our feet.

I had to leave. It had to be done.

If I had my way, I would buy plane tickets to Italy and get on a train to anywhere after that. The idea of international travel had always tugged at me, but our documents weren't anywhere close to passable for getting them through TSA security. We probably wouldn't make it to the gate.

No, the second it was safe, Enzo and I would head north. Boston maybe. Or Maine. It wouldn't be a bad idea to get out of this cold climate and head south either. Georgia looked pretty. Louisiana had culture and character.

Then again, there seemed to be fewer people out west, where the cities were larger and not so closely packed together.

While the warm water soaked my weary bones, I let myself fantasize about what life might look like for Enzo and me in Albuquerque, Denver, or Seattle. I had enough money. I might even rebuild Con Amore in another city.

Either way, whatever move I made, it would take time I didn't have. So I needed to decide right away and make what preparations I could before our window of opportunity closed forever.

In the morning, I would explore the house, create a mental map of the layout. Once I found the fastest, easiest path from our suite back to the café without being seen or followed, we could make our move.

After that, I figured I would need fifteen minutes, thirty at most, to get into the apartment, gather what we needed, and get out again to be on our way.

I reached over the rim of the tub for my pile of clothes and fished my cell phone out of my dress pocket.

It took a few tries to unlock it with my pruney fingers, but then I opened the encrypted banking app and made the transfers from my offshore account to another one under the name on my new passport ID, moving it in one-hundred-thousand-dollar increments at a time.

The cash would only last us so long.

Maybe only long enough to get out of the city and hide our tracks until I found the next best place for Enzo and me to call home. After that, legitimate bank accounts and plastic and the paper trail they left would draw far less attention.

Whatever I did, I had to be sure no one followed us.

Not Stefano.

Not my own family.

EIGHT

STEFANO

The doctor finished stitching up my arm while Tony and I talked about possible suspects in the campaign against me and how I wanted to proceed.

The bullet had lodged itself deep in the muscle, which hurt like a motherfucker when the doc got a grip on it and pulled it out. The pain would continue for a while, I knew that as well as the fact that it would take some time to heal.

Doc assured me the wound would fully heal with no permanent damage.

Once we got a good look at the bullet, my opinion about the shooter changed. We originally thought someone had fired high-powered rifle rounds, but a low caliber round came out of my arm, not something meant for a precision rifle.

An experienced hit man wouldn't make that kind of mistake.

Whoever made the hit certainly wasn't a professional.

He couldn't have been very far away from Con Amore. Probably holed up in a tree less than two blocks away at best. Setting up like that had been a stupid mistake. A branch might have broken, a dog could have barked, or a pedestrian could have seen him.

Too many unreliable variables with the potential to give away his position.

Yes, he knew enough to pull the trigger all right, but that was about all he knew.

Dumb fucker.

And when I found him, he would be a dead fucker.

Since the job had been so messy and disorganized, that helped us rule out most of the people, I thought I might have pissed off enough to pull a stunt like this.

The list was a long one.

I had been reckless the past few years, living and working like I had nothing to lose, because I thought it was the truth.

I hadn't known I had something to protect all this time...

Tony interrupted my thoughts while pacing by the fireplace.

"I don't get it, boss. Who would know how to find a kid you didn't even know about? And I mean, well, shooting up Con Amore is one thing, but killing those cops? Everyone in the business knows that draws more heat. Looks to me like the bastard panicked."

"The whole thing was weak," I said, "even for a rookie. Maybe he was just sent to deliver a powerful message, and he got caught up in it more than he should have. I don't know. That doesn't feel right either."

I poured myself another drink, then waited as the doc finished up with my arm.

He tied off the stitches, applied gauze, and then wrapped a linen bandage tightly around my biceps.

I clenched my teeth and flexed my jaw to keep from grunting.

No one in the room would blame me for expressing my discomfort, but my father had instilled the habit of hiding my pain at a young age.

Real men didn't show their weaknesses to others.

Being strong meant you suffered in silence.

A knock came at the door. I motioned for Tony to answer it. He drew his pistol and slowly opened the door, positioning himself between me and whoever stood on the other side.

Overkill. No one unwanted would get past my enforcers and enter the house.

My first thought was that my soon-to-be father-in-law had returned to improve the terms of our agreement for his daughter's hand.

But then Tony holstered his weapon and stepped aside, giving me a clear view into the hallway.

It was the boy.

His gaze swept around the room. He ignored everything until he settled his eyes on me.

"Can we talk? Alone?" he asked.

I met his gaze and held it, then flicked my wrist at Tony and the doc.

"Give us the room."

Doc quickly finished with the tape, repacked his bag, and headed for the door.

"I'll come back tomorrow, sir, to change the dressing and examine you again for any signs of infection."

Tony went to the door, holding it open to usher the doc out while gesturing for the kid to step inside.

"I'll get started on those leads," he said.

As he and the doc left the room, the boy kept his eyes locked on me.

I motioned for him to come closer and take a seat on the antique couch my mother had picked out for my father when I was about this boy's age. If she'd known a child would be sitting on it now, grandson or not, she would have killed me.

"Do you want something to drink?" I asked.

I didn't know if we had anything appropriate for his age. What the hell did a kid his age drink?

"I might have chocolate milk or something more suitable for you in the kitchen."

"Just water," he said, taking a seat.

I walked over to the stocked bar in my study and poured him a glass, dropped in an orange slice and a cherry, and then mixed myself an old-fashioned.

After handing him his glass and taking a seat in the chair opposite the couch, we sat there for a moment in an oddly comfortable silence, taking each other in, gathering our thoughts, and sipping our drinks.

He looked so much like the pictures of me as a child, but with the added stoicism that reminded me of my older brother Anthony.

"Where does your mother think you are right now?" I asked.

"Asleep," he said, "She's taking a bath. That's where she likes to think. She'll be there for probably an hour."

No sign of shame or any other indication that he thought he might have stepped out of line.

The instant image of Val soaking in the bathtub entered my mind, but I quickly pushed it aside.

"And why are you here if you should be in bed sleeping?"

"I have questions," he said with a shrug. "I'm pretty sure you have answers."

To a child, I supposed that would make perfect sense.

"I think I have more questions than answers myself, but I'll tell you what I can," I said.

"You won't just lie to me, will you?" he asked. "I want the truth."

The way he said it sounded nothing like an attempted insult or insinuation that I was some pathological liar. His question was genuine. The boy simply wanted to know beforehand whether I would choose to be up front with him or to treat him like the child he was.

All things considered, his question was more than fair. He didn't know me, my name, my face, or my reputation.

"I will answer as honestly as I can, boy."

He nodded like that was an acceptable answer.

"Are you my dad?"

Nothing like getting straight to the point.

"I think so," I said. "We can do a DNA test to make sure."

He shook his head without breaking eye contact.

"We can, I guess. But I don't think we have to."

I finished my drink and set the crystal tumbler on the coffee table between us.

"No, neither do I."

"She has a picture of you in a drawer at home. She thinks I never saw it. You look different in the picture. Younger or happier or something. But I still think it's you."

I was confident I knew exactly which photo it was. The day we had taken it, Val and I were on the same couch I used earlier to shield us from bullets. She'd made a joke I couldn't remember now, but I remembered how surprised I was to hear her making dirty jokes at all.

Then she pulled out her camera and snapped the candid

photo of us together. It had perfectly captured her beautiful smile, aimed directly at the lens, and my face turning away mid-laugh.

She'd said she would send it to me, but she never did.

"So what are you gonna do about all this?" he asked, pulling me from the memory.

"I don't know. I didn't know about you until a few hours ago. I don't even know your name. I mean, she called you Enzo earlier. Is that right?"

"Yeah. My name is Enzo Salvatore Salera. Why didn't she tell you about me?"

I pulled in a deep breath, trying to figure out the best way to answer. I knew I should tell him to ask his mother instead of me, but the boy deserved answers from us both, didn't he?

He deserved whatever truth I could give him.

I couldn't help but wonder just how intentional his middle name had been.

Val had known me as Stefano Salvatore before she discovered the truth—the fake last name I'd given her to hide who I really was. Was that where the name had come from? Was that her way of admitting to the world who Enzo's father really was?

"Your mother and I weren't together very long," I said. "I wasn't completely honest with her back then about who I am, and when she found out on her own, she left me."

"Well, who are you?"

That question shouldn't have thrown me as much as it did. How could I answer that honestly? How could I tell the child I was a criminal, a mafia boss? That I ran one of the most vicious family businesses on the East Coast? That my family traded in arms, drugs, extortion, and bribed city officials?

I cleared my throat and settled for the middle ground.

"I'm a man whose family obligation dictates his life more than I would have liked."

"That's why Mama left and hid me from you? Because of your obligations?"

"I believe so, yes."

We stared at each other, and I couldn't bring myself to leave it at that. This boy, however clever he thought he was, however strong, still needed to understand the type of world he'd just entered. The type of danger that now defined his very existence.

"You should know that being my son comes with risks. A significant number of them. More so if you were legitimate, if your mother and I had married before you were born. But the fact remains, a lot of things are going to change for you. There are significant benefits, but also sizable drawbacks."

"Is that why you didn't want to marry her?"

The lump in my throat urged me to turn him away, cast him out of my study this very fucking second, end this conversation before this child's uncanny ability to draw these truths out of me like water from a faucet undid what remained of my composure.

But I couldn't.

"That's one of the reasons, yes," I said.

His questions just kept coming.

The more the boy talked, the more he reminded me of my brother—blunt, direct, straight to the point. He wasted no time with pleasantries or asking questions to which he truly didn't care to know the answer.

A trait like this could serve Enzo well if he learned how to apply it properly. If not, he might end up like Anthony. Dead before his twenty-eighth birthday.

"Your turn to answer a few questions for me, Enzo."

"Okay. I'll tell you what I can."

After parroting my own words back to me, a sly smile curved his lips. Good. He was smarter than Anthony.

"Most kids your age wouldn't know how to deal with any of this," I began. "Sometimes even I don't know how to deal with this. But you're sitting there, so calm after all the violence tonight, and finding out your mother's been hiding you from me all these years. How do you do that?"

Enzo took another sip of water from his crystal glass, then set it on a coaster on the wooden table.

"It's always been just me and Mama and the café. Well, her nonna too. I don't think she was Mama's real grandma, but she loved her like that. Before Nonna died, her mind got sick and started falling apart.

"She told me stories about her kids and how they died and the Mafia. It made her so sad, but she didn't stop talking.

"One day she was telling me about her last son and how he got in trouble. How he died because powerful men used him as a pawn. That was when Nonna told me why my mom has her secrets too.

"I don't think she knew what she was saying, but she still knew a lot. That my mom was keeping a secret from me. After Nonna died, I was going through some of her things and found where Mama keeps her secrets. Some of them anyway."

"What kind of secrets?" I asked.

Enzo looked me in the eye with one brow slightly raised, the same way my mother had whenever I'd acted up and earned her disapproval.

"The kind I shouldn't be talking about," he said. "If you really wanna know, ask her."

The way Enzo seemed to look through me and yet see absolutely everything was more than a little unnerving.

My father had been able to do the same thing, especially when someone tried to hide a certain truth from him. He could sniff it out like the best bloodhound on a trail.

Now I could practically see the wheels turning in this boy's head as he pondered his next moves, as if he were calculating all the outcomes of every scenario and then choosing his actions accordingly.

"My point," Enzo continued, "is that I know Mama had to make really hard choices in her life. I know her choices have always been to protect me. So when she keeps a secret from me, I know Mama has a good reason."

I nodded, searching his face for clues, but there were none.

"I understand. And you don't want to tell me what those reasons might be."

"I think what happened tonight is one of them. Something she was trying to keep me safe from."

Again that eyebrow arched, reminding me of my mother and her silent warnings that I knew better than to act in whatever way she disapproved of so much.

"Maybe it is," I conceded. "In that case, why don't we talk about a few things your mother won't object to?"

That seemed agreeable enough to him. Enzo asked me questions about my family, which I answered as honestly as I felt was appropriate.

I told him I was the last one of us, that I had a sister who was married into another family. I told him my father and brother had passed and that my mother had followed shortly after, though I didn't divulge how.

I got the impression that Enzo learned more from my

conversational pivots and strategic silences than he did from my answers.

I asked him about school, what subjects he liked, which he didn't like, and what his goals were.

The boy lit up when he talked about how much he enjoyed reading and exploring new worlds, fictional or otherwise, and watching the movie that played out in his head whenever he dove into a good book.

I understood the feeling at a surprisingly profound level.

"You obviously read at an advanced level for your age," I said. "And you enjoy it, which is half the battle right there, if you ask me. It makes me wonder, though, why your mother still reads to you.

"I'm sure you could blaze through those books yourself in less than half the time. So why keep indulging her with bedtime stories? I would have expected you to outgrow something like that by now."

Enzo finished his water and set his empty glass down in the exact middle of the coaster. Then he looked me in the eye in a way that most grown men didn't have the balls to do and replied with a simple answer.

"Because it makes her happy."

I nodded slowly, trying to mask the unfamiliar tightness in my chest at his words.

"I should go back before she finds out I'm gone," he said.

We both stood.

"Do I need to show you back to your room?" I asked.

"No, thanks. I can find it."

Enzo headed for the door, reached for the handle, and paused before turning back to face me.

"One other thing."

"What's that, Enzo?"

"If you ever point a gun at Mama again, I will come at you no matter how big you are, and I won't stop until you kill me."

I suppressed a grin and nodded.

Then he opened the door and stepped through it as if he'd said nothing more threatening than a casual goodnight.

That said more about the boy than anything he'd told me in that last half hour.

Plenty of grown men who'd lived their entire lives inside the Mafia didn't have the nerve to pull off something like that, let alone do it with such unwavering bravado.

It didn't matter that Val had tried to keep my son from me.

Even if she had succeeded, Enzo was born to lead. It was in him just as surely as it had always been in me.

Politics or business, criminal or otherwise, he would grow up to occupy whatever position of power he wanted.

And he would have the strength to keep it.

Yes, this boy belonged to me.

And not just because he carried my blood.

He carried my name.

My legacy.

NINE

VAL

The exotic blend of a rich woody scent layered with a pleasant floral scent rose from the bathwater, soothing the tension in my muscles along with my anxiety.

The relaxation cleared my head, helping me focus on what really mattered.

Floating in that big tub, I'd come up with several contingency plans, all ready to put into motion at a moment's notice.

The secret to success would be simple enough. I had to be prepared for anything and everything, starting with the worst-case scenario.

If it turned out that Enzo and I could get away in the next twelve to twenty-four hours, then yes, I definitely had a plan. And if we had to wait longer and bide time, I still had a plan.

These plans unfortunately hinged on when Stefano would deal with the threat that had brought us here. After watching him earlier, something told me it was already at the top of his list. Perfect.

If Stefano tried to lock us up or take my son away from me,

or even if Enzo told me he wanted to stay here, I'd already decided how to deal with that as well.

Every contingency had to be considered.

Even the unthinkable.

Though I'd already considered it, I wasn't nearly as worried about what Stefano would do as I was about how Enzo would react, the possibility I might not be able to predict my own son.

Enzo wouldn't stay with a man like Stefano, not even if he thought it was what he wanted. Not on my life. If I had to explain to my son the hard truths about his families—Stefano's and my own—before he should really hear them, then so be it.

Any mother on the planet knew the hard choices had to be made sometimes to protect her child. Nothing in life was so precious to me that I wouldn't sacrifice it to ensure Enzo's safety, not even if it changed the way he saw me or meant he would never love me the same way again.

I hoped beyond hope it never came to that, but there would always be a chance. And if that chance became my reality, I would meet the challenge head on like I had every other one.

The only thing I couldn't decide was where we would go after leaving Brooklyn and New York altogether. That decision had to be made in the moment, or I would end up spending too much time researching a specific place beforehand.

Even internet searches for apartments, neighborhoods, and schools left their own virtual paper trail that couldn't completely be erased by simply clearing a browsing history. Not if someone with the right means really wanted to know what I'd been up to.

Stefano totally had the means, and now that he knew about Enzo, he would never let his son go without a fight. No matter what he'd said.

That kind of planning, looking ahead at that level, came with too much risk. Once Enzo and I got away, I had to be sure we couldn't be tracked in any way.

Long after the heat of the bathwater had cooled, I stepped out of the tub, wrapped up in a fluffy towel, and collected my dirty clothes.

The dress I'd worn got covered in plaster, sawdust, and slivers of glass, and I couldn't bring myself to put it back on.

So after heading back into the bedroom, I opened the closet and found a brand-new robe from the Neiman Marcus Collection, recently purchased but never worn, the tags still attached.

Whoever this robe belonged to before me, it didn't matter. The damn thing belonged to me now.

The soft fabric hugged my body, wrapping me up in a warmth that rivaled even the steamy bath water. Just light enough and thin enough to stuff into a suitcase or backpack. I'd be taking it with me when we finally got out of here.

Stefano could consider it payment for my pain and suffering.

The finer details of my plans still needed to be locked down. More circumstances to consider. The weighing of pros and cons against staying until it was safe or leaving sooner while Stefano was distracted.

With all the rattling around in my head, I wouldn't sleep. Not even a wink.

I sprawled out on the soft chaise lounge with the beautiful blue throw pillows, closed my eyes, and ran through the scenarios in my mind over and over, looking for weak points or potentially unforeseen circumstances that might hinder us. Or help us.

So many variables. So many things I didn't know. How

many people occupied this house at any given time? If Stefano left the house, how many men did he take with him? Could I sway the loyalty of one of his employees?

The men wouldn't lift a finger to help me, that I knew. They were Stefano's men through and through.

What about the maid? Would she see another woman in need and lend a hand, or did she value her resume more and the paycheck that came with it? Was she the only female in Stefano's employ, or were there others?

I just didn't know.

And I couldn't say how long it would take Stefano to solve our problem with whoever had started this private war with him.

Then my thoughts turned to the yellow envelope he'd handed me in the car and everything inside it. The note on the top had mentioned an engagement, and that introduced even more variables.

Did I need to worry about his fiancée as well?

If she'd somehow discovered Enzo, she could also be behind the attack, wanting to get rid of any potential future claims to Stefano's empire, claims that might come between her own children and their inheritance.

Stefano hadn't even known about Enzo, though. The existence of a bastard son living so closely in Brooklyn seemed like something a bride-to-be would discuss with her future husband, even if only to warn him that she knew and expected him to clean up the inconvenience.

The more I considered this mystery woman, the more I thought about her on a more personal level. Had he put me in her room? Was I wearing her robe after having bathed in her scented bath oils?

The idea of it all turned my stomach, not with jealousy but with a strange eerie feeling.

Then again, this suite could have been stocked to accommodate any other women Stefano brought home regularly. Everyone knew mafia men often didn't uphold the morals of chastity or monogamy.

But a cashmere robe seemed a little much for one of his whores. It made more sense that it had been purchased for his fiancée. Then I realized it really didn't make sense.

Mafia princesses didn't have sleepovers with their fiancés before the marriage. Their families usually made sure they remained virgins until their wedding day.

I squeezed my eyes shut. None of that mattered.

If Stefano had a problem with me wearing the clothes stored in this suite, he would just have to deal with it. He hadn't exactly given me an option about where I was going to stay or what I was going to wear.

With a sigh, I pressed my thumbs against the bridge of my nose to relieve the pressure building behind my eyes. I would have killed for a glass of wine to calm my nerves and take the edge off. I couldn't do anything else while waiting to see what move Stefano would make first. So yes, a delicate glass of red.

Waiting was always the worst. It offered too much time for nerves and overthinking.

The door to the bathroom whispered over the floor as Enzo entered my room.

"Mama?"

I sat up and looked him over, instantly recognizing the potential for having missed some smaller injury during the earlier chaos of this never-ending night.

"Yes, baby, I'm right here. Why aren't you sleeping? Is everything okay?"

"I never went to sleep, Mama. I went to have a talk with Mr. Vignali while you were taking a bath."

He said it like a grumpy old man complaining about having to chew someone out over something annoying but trivial.

I might have laughed if his confession hadn't caught me so off guard. Now I didn't know what to say. I took a deep breath, shut my eyes, and nodded.

"Enzo..."

He had questions. Of course he did. And I couldn't be upset with him for that. After all, it was my fault, all of it. I had to tackle his questions. Who knows what Stefano told him.

I opened my eyes and met his.

"I'm sure you have even more questions now, huh? Do you want to talk about it?"

"Yeah... in the morning. I'm tired, and I just wanted to know if you would read me another chapter."

He drew his hands out from behind his back to reveal the book we'd started reading before our quiet little life had literally been shot to pieces.

I hadn't even realized he grabbed it.

The fact he wanted something so simple and calming at a time like this overwhelmed me with relief. All I wanted was to pull him into my arms, hug him so tightly, and never let go.

"Sure, buddy. Let's go to your room. I'll tuck you in again and we can read one more chapter. Sound good?"

"Sounds good. Thanks, Mama."

He turned on his heel and marched back to his room, hugging the book to his chest.

Once I pulled back the covers for the second time, Enzo

crawled between the soft sheets beneath the thick down comforter. I tucked it all around him, then lay down on top beside him, opened the book, and picked up where we'd left off earlier.

A little girl running from her powers, from her destiny, from the people who would hurt her for simply being who they made her to be.

Despite the chapter's action scene, I kept my tone low and even, hoping it would lull him to sleep while I absently played with his soft curls.

His body relaxed within minutes, followed by the gentle, steady rhythm of his breath.

Worked like a charm every time.

After everything that had happened, the sound of a child surrendering to a deep sleep, unaware of what horrors waited just around the corner, comforted me more than I'd expected.

I considered staying, falling asleep beside him, just like I always had whenever a nightmare woke him, but movement on the other side of the room caught my attention.

I looked up and froze.

Stefano leaned against the open doorframe, watching us.

He hadn't changed his black slacks from earlier, but he had replaced his shirt, tie, and jacket with a white tank top that clung to muscles he hadn't had the last time we were together. A bandage covered his upper left arm.

I raised a brow at him, silently asking what he wanted.

He answered by tilting his head and holding my gaze.

A request for me to step outside so we could speak.

That was the last thing I wanted. But if my plans were going to work, Stefano couldn't suspect a thing.

I nodded, took my time kissing Enzo on the forehead, and

tucked him in before walking out of the room to face whatever Stefano planned to do to me. At the very least, he would want answers too.

Everyone wanted answers.

As if the robe could shield me from whatever rage, hurt, anger, or indifference he was about to unleash, I tightened it around my body, and then gently shut the door behind me.

"What?" I asked, keeping my voice just above a whisper.

"I already know the answer," he said, "but I want to hear you say it. Is he mine?"

My cheeks burned, possessive fury overwhelming me.

"He's mine," I snapped.

The same level of vitriol filled Stefano's eyes.

He clenched his jaw and snapped back at me.

"Am I his fucking father?"

There was no point in lying about it. I sucked in a deep breath and blinked.

"Yes."

He nodded. "He and I spoke tonight. Did he tell you?"

I folded my arms, pulling the robe tighter when his gaze dropped lower.

"My son doesn't keep secrets from me," I said.

"No, I suppose he doesn't. But he knows you keep secrets from him. He doesn't know exactly what they are, or if he does, he wouldn't tell me."

"Okay..." I pretended like that wasn't news.

Enzo and I would talk about my secrets when the time came. But that conversation would happen when I was ready for it. Stefano had no say about the timing.

His gaze narrowed, his eyes so dark.

"Why didn't you tell me? I would have been there for him. And for you."

I had known this conversation would have to happen, but that didn't mean I was looking forward to it. With a frustrated sigh, I tilted my head.

"You know why. Same reason I couldn't be with you."

That was mostly true. He just didn't know why those reasons were so important to me, and I wasn't about to volunteer that information.

His eyes darkened even more if that was possible. I could see his anger seething within the tight grip of his composure.

"It didn't work, did it? Keeping my son away from me did not keep him safe."

"No, it didn't," I admitted. "Now you know about him. You've met him. Talked to him. So tell me, Stefano. Tell me what you're prepared to do to keep my son safe. Because I will burn this entire city to the ground if it means even a single hair on his head is never harmed. Do you understand me?"

I expected him to fight me. I expected him to belittle my conviction or scoff at the whole idea.

What I did not expect was his startling lunge at me, or his hands wrapped around my throat as he shoved me against the wall. He squeezed hard enough that I knew he could hurt me if he wanted to. But he didn't.

"Our son," he snarled. "Ours."

The next thing I knew, Stefano's lips slammed against mine, his kiss pinning me against the wall as his hands left my throat to run down my body and inside the robe.

I should have fought him. My mind screamed for me to shove him away, to tell him no. But my body was a traitor and melted into his hands.

Stefano was the first man I had been with. The only man.

I'd already known from our first night together that no one could ever compare to what I felt when I was with him, so I never bothered with anyone else. I'd considered a few men, gone on a handful of dates, for Enzo's sake, but no one ever seemed good enough.

No one had ever been strong enough, fiery enough, perfect enough. And now I remembered why.

Because they weren't Stefano.

The instant chemistry between us overpowered my self-preservation the same way this man overpowered me and held me against the wall.

It wasn't normal.

No average man could make me feel that way. Then it occurred to me, maybe not for the first time, that my reaction to Stefano had everything to do with who he was.

What he really was.

God help me because the fact that he was a powerful mafia boss attracted me to him.

Mentally, I recognized his intelligence, his strength, his loyalty, and even his arrogance. Physically, instinctually, I recognized his power.

In my heart, I understood this man's ability to save me from my demons... or to sacrifice me to them if he so chose.

Either way, he could do whatever he wanted with me, take whatever he wanted.

To feel this again, to see it, taste it, and exist in it, melted away my resistance and turned my soul inside out.

No ordinary man, no matter how sweet or loving, could ever truly meet my needs. Not the way Stefano Vignali did.

He made my heart race.

Only he could send heat rushing through my blood and make me forget everything else.

With one kiss, he reignited a hunger inside me.

The passion I thought had died the day I left him.

TEN

STEFANO

Val returned my kiss with furious passion.

And I fucking hated her for it.

She didn't want to share her life or my son with me. Yet she didn't fight me. Didn't shove me away. No, she opened her sweet mouth and kissed me back without hesitation.

As our kiss deepened, I pushed my way inside her robe, exploring her body, remembering every one of her curves like I'd just had her the night before.

She dragged her fingertips up my arms, softly, over my chest, and then she dug her nails into the back of my neck.

This woman still intoxicated me after so many years apart.

So easy to believe she was meant for me.

This spunky little barista who couldn't have been any more my opposite if she wanted to be. Innocent, filled with light, thoughtful, a loving mother. A woman who wanted nothing to do with my money, my lifestyle, or my influence.

But she couldn't deny wanting me.

Val opened herself to me like she'd spent the last ten years waiting for me to come back, waiting for my attention, longing for my touch. My touch, only mine.

Despite the shit storm between us and all around us, the secrets, and the lies, her body responded to mine with just as much greed and hunger.

Twenty seconds into kissing her, and I wanted to take her right there against the wall, even with our son sleeping on the other side. Just a kiss with anyone else could never make my cock so hard. Val owned that.

I wanted her with a desperation too dangerous for a man in my position, even after everything she'd put me through when she left me, kept my son from me, and put him in harm's way.

True, I didn't want children.

But Enzo had come along, like it or not, and he was my flesh and blood, my heir, a Vignali.

Val had robbed him of his father and his family.

She let me believe I didn't have anything to live for, nothing to lose, while she hid the boy who should have been my reason for getting up in the morning all along.

Despite that, after one fucking kiss, for Christ's sake, I was ready to give up the ship.

My plan for vengeance, the rage that fueled my every move, it seemed almost insignificant with this woman in my arms and our son under my roof.

But then her mouth fell away from mine, and she pushed me away. I stared at her, working to catch my breath, watching her catch hers. A few seconds later, I caught something else... the full force of her open palm slapping my face.

Before I could react and punish her, she buried her fists in my hair and pulled me in for another kiss. I pushed her against the wall again with my body and let her kiss me with everything she had, everything she would ever be.

All of it, mine.

Her familiar scent, the sweet taste of her tongue, and her warm skin touching mine overwhelmed me. I needed more. I needed to have her in my bed.

I slid my hands around to grip her ass.

She had filled out so perfectly over the years.

With a growl, I squeezed and pulled her harder against me while letting her continue kissing me, tasting me. It took everything in me to bring myself to break away.

I rested my forehead against hers, giving her a minute to calm down and myself time to re-engage my brain and think.

"We need to talk," I said. "About a few things. I don't want to wake the boy."

She nodded with her lips parted, her breath still rapid but her grip on me loosening.

"I know. Where should we go?" she whispered. "To talk I mean, and nothing more."

I nodded to reassure her.

"Your room works. It's the closest."

Val shook her head. "Somewhere without a bed."

Under different circumstances, I would have told her she was being ridiculous and insisted. But considering my unrelenting erection and how I'd almost taken her right there in the hallway, she made a valid point.

I grabbed hold of her arm to drag her along with me... I didn't want to stop touching her.

"Come with me."

I took her to my study without letting go until I closed the door behind us. Even then, bed or no bed, I had to force myself to keep my hands off her.

The temptation was strong, and I had to turn away for a minute. I could have easily lifted her, put her back against the door, and fucked the hell out of her.

"What is wrong with you?" she hissed. "You can't just drag me through your house like a caveman."

Then I caught her full-length reflection in the window, and I could only think about how she looked under the robe, betting it was as beautiful as when we were kids.

Val noticed my stare and grabbed the edges of her robe, pulling them tighter to hide herself from me.

There they were again—the mental images of our past, her lying naked in my bed, inviting me closer, calling me to her.

I shook them from my head and went to the bar to make another old-fashioned for myself and an amaretto sour for her.

We'd only gone on one proper date, and I still remembered the drink she ordered.

It would have been better if I could say the memory had just then come flooding to the forefront of my mind. But it had always been there.

Every moment of that night existed on repeat in my mind. The best night of my life and the worst. The last night of the life I'd wanted before it died forever.

"What are you doing?" she asked.

"I'm making us a drink. I know I could use one. We'll have a sit-down and talk like rational adults."

"Rational went out the window the minute you stepped back into my life, Stefano. Immediately followed by a storm of bullets. You put my son's life in danger, and now you want me to behave rationally?"

No other woman on the planet could turn arguing with me into the type of seductive strength I saw in her now. It only made me want her more.

That pissed me off more.

At the end of the day, though, it didn't matter how much I wanted her or that she was my son's mother, because no one talked to me like that.

No one.

Val would show me the respect I had earned.

Then there was the matter of that slap.

"Our son," I corrected. "And you'll watch how you speak to me."

I pulled long from my glass with my eyes on her, warning her to keep her mouth shut.

"I'm not the one who put our son's life in danger. You did that," I said. "Whoever is behind this didn't have to work hard to find him, since they knew about him before I did. You forget, Valerie, I could have let them kill you both."

"No," she snapped.

"No what?"

"Enzo is my son, only mine, and you don't get to change that now. You weren't there for his first steps or his first words. You didn't take care of him when he was sick or teach him how to read."

Her voice rose in volume and pitch as she continued.

"You have never been there for him, not once did you—"

"Whose fault is that?" I yelled.

I would have been there. Maybe not for everything, but I would have been involved. She'd robbed me of those moments, the first steps, first words, and now she had the fucking balls to blame me for missing them.

"Yours," she said. "It's your fault for lying about your identity. If I'd known the truth, I wouldn't have talked to you. But no, you had to make up some fictional character to get off on. You obviously have a thing for roleplaying."

I clenched my teeth, once again forced to keep a tight grip on the rage burning through me.

"Stop it, Valerie."

"Was that fun for you?" she asked. "I deserve to know the truth now that we're here. Did you enjoy your game? Did you have a good laugh behind my back? Did you tell all your serial killer friends about the idiot woman who trusted you and fell for the act?"

Her last words faded, and I had to look away for a second.

Even now, she was still heartbroken over the whole thing. Finding out my real name and what it meant had shaken her to the core. Then she'd clearly made up her own story about me and what had happened between us.

She made me the villain.

It couldn't have been further from the truth, not with her.

I pushed out a heavy breath through my nose, feeling the need to explain, though I didn't know how. I doubted she would believe me anyway.

"That's not what happened, Val."

"That's exactly what happened, Stefano. Then you waited ten years to show up again, waltzing back into my life with a small army on your heels, bringing gunfire and literally blowing up my café. This isn't a fucking John Wick movie. This is my life. An innocent boy's life."

I flexed my fists, my self-control waning, and fired back.

"You're not turning this around on me. This is on you. I can't protect what I don't know about. If you'd told me about my boy, I would have kept you both safe. I don't understand why you are so stubborn and pigheaded and insist on doing everything on your own.

"You not wanting to be with me is one thing, Valerie, but this is something entirely different. I would have helped you. Yes, I would have been there. And I would have paid for him to have a safe home, for his clothing, his education…"

She scoffed, but no way would she dismiss me so easily.

"I could have protected you, made your home secure. I would have provided for you both. Provided stable, consistent employees for Con Amore, giving you more time off, so you didn't have to work as hard day after day, so you could focus more on raising our son."

I bit my tongue for a second.

"I would have given you everything to make your life easy. But you had to do it on your own without me. And look where that brought you, *mia bellissima diavoletta*. Right back to me."

She drained her drink in one shot, then threw the glass. It hit the wall behind my head and shattered.

I slammed my glass down on the table.

"I swear to Christ, if you hit me or even so much as think about it one more fucking time…"

She took a step toward me, her shoulders back and her chest pushed out, ready for a fight.

"You'll do what?"

"You will regret it," I warned.

Hatred made her light eyes glow as she dared to get closer.

"I already regret everything with you, Stefano Vignali."

Lust flashed through her eyes.

"No, you don't," I said with a smirk.

Then I moved in and closed the last bit of distance between

us, looming over her. I didn't know if I wanted to grab her by the throat and actually strangle her this time or kiss her again."

"You're right," she whispered.

The malice in her eyes melted, revealing something more. Regret? Fear? Both. Then she went on.

"Not everything. I love my son. I just hate that he's no longer safe... because of you."

Her gaze darted to the side for a second, then returned to my face like she had to force herself to look me in the eye.

Definitely fear.

She was scared. She had almost lost her son earlier, and then I dragged her into a life that she knew nothing about...

Val had probably watched one of those old gangster movies, and then convinced herself that was how shit would go down, how something bad would happen to our son if they had anything to do with me. I might have laughed if I hadn't already been so pissed.

It didn't have to be like that, not for my boy.

I had to make her understand things could be different for him. I was among the strongest. I had the greatest resources. I could protect them both.

How many times would she make me repeat myself?

"Just because you don't want me, Val, doesn't mean I'm not his father," I said. "I would have accepted him and done everything necessary to protect him if I'd known about him."

"From others, but what about you? Who would protect him from you? I'll tell you who... me. And that's what I was doing. He needs protection from who you are and what you do. And I need protection from the corruption and power and violence and all the heartbreak your life would bring. I need..."

A sobbing gasp escaped her. Her eyes filled with tears. And for the first time, I saw her complete truth reflected in them.

She hadn't left me. She'd rejected my family, the business.

"Why do you think you need to be protected?" I asked, studying her face. "What is it you think you know about my life, about my family, my business? What makes you so afraid?"

There was plenty for her to fear, sure, but I needed to understand what she really thought. Or at least what she thought she knew... it might even have been close enough to the truth.

If I understood what exactly scared her, maybe I could show her how I would protect her from that very thing. Maybe I could convince her that her fears were based on lies.

She swallowed hard.

"I know enough. I see the news reports about the shootings in the streets. I see what happens with drugs. Gun trafficking. Crime is running rampant throughout this city. Every day there's another tragedy.

"Someone missing. Someone found floating in the river or in a landfill. This street or that street, people killed in drive-by shootings. It all leads back to one thing."

"Val, it's not all—"

"Are you really going to tell me you don't know about every corrupt deal taking place in this city?" A bitter laugh escaped her. "That you haven't put money in the pockets of crooked politicians, police officers, and whoever else is willing to sell their souls to men like you?"

"I—"

"This is a city of widows and grieving mothers, Stefano. Victims of your family and families like yours. You can't choose the family you're born into, I know that. And I know being a Vignali isn't your fault.

"But me not keeping my son away from your family legacy, seeing him become part of it, that will be my fault. I have to make sure blood never stains his future the way it has yours."

When she stopped, it took her a minute to catch her breath. Good. My turn.

"If you don't let me protect our son, he won't have a future at all. I won't claim him as my heir if that's what you want, but that doesn't mean I'm going to abandon him. Or you."

Her eyes filled with tears again, and she paced the room.

"You just don't get it, do you? Just being your son is enough to put him in danger, even though he's a bastard, as your people so kindly call him. I tried. I tried so hard, but I don't know how to protect him from your life.

"And even if you aren't the danger, even if you loved him, especially if you loved him, your rivals would keep trying to hurt him. You all play by the rules only when it suits you. A monster in a three-piece designer suit is still a monster, no matter what he pretends to be. At his core... he's always that monster."

I had the strangest feeling in that moment that Val could see into the depths of my heart to pull out exactly the right words that hurt me the deepest.

What the hell did she know about the beast living inside me?

It had nothing to do with her or the boy. Yes, it was part of me. A piece of me I would keep away from them, locked up where it belonged.

But her words.

She'd used her own metaphor without realizing how closely

it hit home for me, without knowing I often thought of myself that way.

So yes, I got it. I understood what she meant about my life inside *La Cosa Nostra*.

At one time, I'd felt the same way. And that was why I had tried not to father any children. Hell, I still felt that way.

But what was done was done. Enzo was here. He was ours.

I couldn't change the fact that he was my son, and I would never turn my back on him.

Val stopped pacing, crossed her arms, lifted her chin. She didn't have to say anything. I could read the words on her face.

I told you so.

Fuck.

I'd run out of ways to tell her I would protect them both. And judging by the tired look in her eyes now, she probably didn't have it in her to listen to anything else until she rested.

I had to come up with a plan that would convince her.

"We can talk about our son's future later," I said. "First, I'll handle this threat. Once I deal with whoever's behind it, I'll make it clear to all the families that no one will ever use him against me again. This will not happen again, Val."

She met my gaze. A tear trickled down her cheek.

"I don't know what I would do without him."

Seeing her like that, scared, hurt, vulnerable, it unlocked something inside me that I didn't know existed.

And I couldn't handle it.

I pulled her to me, slid my hands into her hair, and kissed her. Softer this time, sweeter. This one not meant to control her or own her but to show her that she wasn't alone.

Not anymore.

She pressed her palms against my chest, her heat burning me

right through my undershirt. She didn't pull away. She opened herself to me, let me kiss her the way I chose to, with want, need, holding nothing back, and holding everything back.

When she stepped back, I thought we were done, that the night had ended.

Then she untied the knot in her robe.

The cashmere fell open, revealing her breasts, larger than I remembered, her stomach softer, hips rounder. My younger Valerie looked different now, even more beautiful.

I pulled her into another kiss, a harder, more intense kiss. Her hands dropped to my stomach, dragged over my abs, and then she moved lower to unbuckle my belt.

She'd pushed me too far.

I didn't have the will to stop her.

I didn't have the will to stop myself.

There was no fucking way back for us.

ELEVEN
VAL

Sweet mother of Christ, I wanted this man.

I slipped my hands inside Stefano's pants, but he grabbed my wrists in one of his hands and raised them above my head before letting go. Before I could even think about my next move, he lifted me and carried me to his desk.

Then, with one swipe of his injured arm, he cleared the desk of everything. Everything flew off the edge and clattered to the floor. A lamp, his laptop computer, countless papers.

He lay me on the cold wood and loomed above me.

At the onset of his swift tantrum, my robe had dropped to the floor, leaving me open and exposed. Vulnerable.

At his mercy.

The heat of his gaze burned into my body.

When we'd been together years before, I let him take the lead. I let him spend as much time as he wanted exploring my body, and we learned together what I liked, what I didn't, what made me moan, and what coaxed the most exquisite pleasure from deep inside me.

In a very short while, Stefano had mastered my body.

But this was nothing like that. Or it wouldn't be, because I wanted to overwhelm him now, the way he had done to me.

I might not have been as experienced as he was, but I wasn't the naïve girl in my twenties anymore. And besides, I'd devoured so many spicy romance novels over the years after reading to Enzo and getting him to bed.

I had a few ideas, thanks to those spicy romance books.

Stefano would soon find out I'd grown into a woman who knew how to take what she wanted, and now... I wanted power. Control. I wanted to make him feel as helpless as I did every time he kissed me.

This time I wanted him to be the one overwhelmed and lost. And I wanted the loss of control he experienced to come from me, my fingers, my tongue, my body. Even just this once.

He stood over me at the end of his desk, his hand on his jaw as he stared at me, drinking in my naked body with his eyes.

Everything about me had changed since he last saw me without my clothes, but if the weight of his blazing-hot stare was any sign, he still found me appealing.

Biting my bottom lip, I cupped my breasts and lifted them in a little tease. Then I pinched my nipples.

He watched me, his cock so hard it tented his black slacks.

I began caressing myself, my curves.

A trail of goose bumps raised over my skin.

Stefano's gaze met mine, and I held it, matching him stare for stare while bending my knees to put my feet flat on the desk.

His dark eyes got wider as I spread my legs so slowly, letting them fall open and expose every inch of me. I slid my hands down between my thighs and touched myself.

"Do you still want me, Ace?"

A term of endearment from our past.

No words from him. He growled.

His eyes followed my fingers as I circled my clit.

In the back of my mind, I had to wonder how I'd suddenly become so shameless and daring. I'd only ever revealed my naked self to Stefano, yet something inside me that I couldn't define made me feel like I'd done this a million times.

His eyes filled with hunger.

He needed me as badly as I needed him.

Just once, I wanted to be the sort of woman who could have a man like Stefano and meet his bravado step for step. Just this once, I wanted to do whatever the fuck I wanted.

Including him.

If my plans to escape worked, I wouldn't have to deal with him for very long anyway. I would never see him again.

That thought made the moment even more exciting.

I arched my back and moaned. I'd already been so wet after the way he kissed me.

"Say it," I said. "Tell me."

Stefano flattened his hands flat on either side of my hips.

"Yes, I want you, Val. But you can't really think I don't know what you're doing."

Unsure if it was his ability to stay so focused or the pace of my fingers, but I involuntarily sucked in a sharp little breath.

"What am I doing?" I asked.

His eyes flashed from dark to dangerous. He licked his lips.

"You're a silly little girl, Valerie. You think you can seduce me and make me believe you can handle everything on your own? You think you don't need my help? That you're smarter than me. Stronger than me. That I can't provide for you or take care of your needs."

"I'm taking care of things just fine on my own now, aren't I?

I've been doing it for ten years, and I'm getting damn good. Do you want to see?" I teased.

He growled again, then gripped my thighs and yanked me to the edge of the desk.

"There are many things I want to see," he said, watching my fingers work. "But right now I'm going to show you something, then you'll understand that I'll always do everything better. Everything, Valerie."

Forcing my hand out of his way, he dropped his face between my thighs and sucked hard on my clit. And then, with each flick of his tongue, he sent wave after wave of intense pleasure through me.

"Oh... fuck..." I breathed.

I reached for the edges of the desk to hold on.

His mouth on me was so much better than I remembered. This time, he fucked me with his tongue harder and faster to prove his point.

He drew more pleasure from my body faster than I thought was possible. He slid his hands over my stomach, up to my breasts, where he pinched and stroked my nipples while continuing his hot oral assault.

A warm, tingling flush raced through my body almost as quickly as my heart pounded. I knew even my cheeks burned bright red by then.

The pressure inside my core rose higher as he pushed me closer to the edge. My thighs shook, and I was so close to shattering when he stopped and straightened, wiping his mouth with the back of his hand.

No, no. Why did he stop?

I raised my head and immediately wanted to slap the smirk right off his face.

"Are you ready to admit you're wrong?" he asked. "Everything is so much better—and safer—when you're not trying to do it all your way like some stubborn little brat."

"Absolutely not," I said. "I know how to finish the job—"

He lunged and grabbed my throat, pressing my back against the desk again, pinning me there while his other hand swept down between my thighs. Two of his fingers filled me.

"You know I won't put up with such poor behavior," he snarled. "You're going to show me that you can be a good girl, Val. And you're going to admit things will be better with my involvement."

His fingers curled inside me, pressing up and right into that sweet, sweet spot.

I moaned. My eyes might have rolled back.

Stefano's hand on my throat tightened. He wanted to make it clear he was the one in control.

I could breathe, yes, but my breaths were shallow. The intensity of my other sensations flared to unimaginable heights. My lips tingled, my head swam, my core tightened as he set a steady pace, pushing into me, and teasing that spot inside me.

"Admit it," he said. "Admit your life would've been much easier if you hadn't cut me out."

I gasped for more air and pushed through the waves of pleasure flooding through my body. I managed two words.

"Fuck you."

"Ah, I see time hasn't cleaned up that mouth of yours. I hope for your sake our son doesn't hear you talk like that."

I wanted him to let me orgasm. I wanted to let him. I wanted to give in, to feel him completely control my body, to keep holding me down while knowing I hadn't given him my submission, because he'd taken it.

I knew he was strong enough to overpower me. And deep down, I knew he had the strength and the means to protect me and our son.

If I let him.

I wished I had the luxury of making that choice.

But he'd had to bring our son into it.

So I arched my back, still loving the way my body tightened for him, and then I kicked him. My heel hit the center of his chest, and just like that, his hold on me broke.

No hand on my throat. No fingers inside me.

Stefano staggered back a few steps.

"What the fuck is wrong with you?" he roared.

I slipped off the desk and strode toward him, exaggerating the sway of my hips with every step. I was already naked. No reason to be shy about it now.

A red flush covered his face, and his lips curled into a furious snarl. I grabbed the back of his head before he could retaliate, pulling his hair, and brought his mouth to mine.

Still kissing, I pulled him toward the desk and pushed him down into the chair.

To take back control, he shoved his hands through my hair to pull my mouth harder against his. Then he broke our kiss.

"What the fuck do you think you're doing?" he demanded.

I slid my hand into his slacks and took hold of his hard cock. Such a beautiful cock.

"Just proving things are better when I handle them myself."

Part of me had wondered for years if I let my imagination get the best of me, but now I had proof in hand. The memory or my imagination or whatever hadn't done him justice... Yes, Stefano was quite a big boy.

My fingertips and thumb didn't even come close as I stroked him.

He grunted and pushed into my hand.

"You're playing with fire, little girl," he warned.

"If you say so, daddy."

A serious groan vibrated in his throat.

Preparing to align my body with his and ride him until I got my orgasm, I moved up on his lap.

"Uh-uh... I don't think so."

He got up, taking me with him, and slammed my ass down on the desk so hard it would probably leave a bruise.

"Only good girls get to ride my cock. Here's what happens to goddamn brats like you... you get fucked like one."

He dug his fingers into my thighs and flipped me around so fast, putting my feet on the floor, my ass in the air, and my chest on the desktop. He used his foot to spread my feet apart.

He pressed himself against me, grabbing a fistful of my hair. When he pulled it, I couldn't help but arch my back.

"Are you going to admit it and tell me you know everything would have been better if you hadn't fucked it up?"

"I didn't fuck up anything," I said. "I did what I had to do, and I took what I wanted, and that hasn't changed."

I shoved my hips back, impaling myself on his erection, taking it as deep as I could with that one thrust.

Stefano groaned with pleasure, and I moaned, burying my face in my arms, overwhelmed by how much he stretched me. It felt amazing, better than anything—like coming home but with the smallest bit of pain.

After a few breaths, I arched my back again and pushed against him, riding him while he had me bent over his desk.

"See? So much better my way," I muttered.

"We'll see about that."

He pushed me flat against the desk again, this time pinning me down with one hand pressed on the center of my back.

Then he smacked my ass.

Hard.

He pulled out halfway, smacked the other side of my ass, and then thrust back inside me in one strong motion. I had to bite my lip to stop from screaming while he fucked me and spanked me.

"See? You even like being punished by me. I can feel your tight little pussy squeezing my cock, pulsing with need."

"Oh fuck," I groaned.

What else could I have said?

He was right.

I hated that he was right, but I couldn't deny it.

The more he spanked me, the more he took control and fucked me, the closer I drew to what had to be the strongest orgasm I had ever had.

I was about to lose our little game. I couldn't let it happen.

So I tried to stand up, but his hand on my back kept me down. I had to get creative... I reached between my legs and grabbed his balls as he kept fucking me.

"Fuuuck. Don't do that," he snarled.

"Just proving it's better my way," I said over my shoulder.

Stefano abruptly pulled out of me and stepped back.

I stood up, not wanting to waste the opportunity, but he pushed me back down on the desk, onto my back. He grabbed both my wrists and pinned them above my head before angling his hips and thrusting into me again.

"Why do you have to make everything so difficult, Valerie?"

I couldn't move. And I didn't want to.

This was even better. I could still feel every single inch of him sliding in and out of me, brushing against the most sensitive parts of my body, but now I could watch him. I got to see the focus and determination in his wicked, dark eyes.

He transferred my wrists into just one hand and slid the other down to my breasts and tweaked my nipples a few times before continuing down to my clit.

"I wanted to be sweet with you. I wanted to be loving. I wanted to show you that you don't have to do any of this alone, that I'm here for you and our son. But you always have to be such a stubborn little bitch.

"I could have taken you on a bed of feathers and silks and made love to you for hours, but you had to be a damn brat, didn't you? Now you've reduced it to me fucking you like a whore on top of this desk."

The pressure in my core built higher and higher, taking with it all the stress, all the frustration, all the fear, all the worry. All of it replaced by my muscles tensing, preparing for the explosion Stefano was about to draw from my body.

I gasped. "Don't stop."

"You don't give the orders. I'll tell you when you can come."

He ran his thumb in tight circles as he thrust inside me, harder and harder, over and over.

Sweat beaded on his brow, his jaw tight with concentration as he made me feel things I didn't know were possible.

"Now be a good girl and come for me," he growled through his gritted teeth.

My body obeyed him. As my vision faded, the most incredible release of my life overtook me. Wave after wave of pleasure licked up my spine and radiated through my limbs.

Stefano's roar of satisfaction followed me over the edge.

I closed my eyes to ride out the waves. The next thing I knew, I lay stretched out over Stefano's body, both of us on the sofa in the sitting area of his office.

He kissed the top of my head, and when he spoke, his voice got softer, becoming almost a whisper.

"I'll break you every time, Val. Tell me what I want to hear."

"Tell you what?" I asked, not wanting to be fooled by his docile tone.

Even lions could be docile when not stalking their prey.

"That it's better when you're not alone."

"Fine," I sighed. "It feels better when you fuck me than when I masturbate."

I rolled my eyes at him, and when he laughed, I couldn't help but laugh with him.

Somehow, I felt lighter. All my problems were still there. They still needed to be dealt with. My plans hadn't changed, but at the moment, that didn't have to be my priority.

For the first time in I didn't even know how long, I could just be in that moment, not looking over my shoulder or worrying about what or who waited around the next corner. I could just be a woman enjoying the carefree afterglow of sex with a man.

"I hate how good this feels," I admitted as I traced the patterns on his chest.

He'd had a lot of ink added over the years.

His fingers played absently with my hair. How nice it felt to be the one being taken care of for a change. I couldn't remember the last time someone held me like this.

Actually, I could. It was the last time I slept with Stefano.

"Why do you hate it?" he asked. "This is what I used to

dream about. Just being with you like this, all our problems on the other side of the door. I fantasized about this for the longest time. The only reason I stopped is because it hurt."

Surprised, I looked up at his face to find a slightly panicked expression as he stared back at me. I didn't think he'd meant to say all that out loud. I rested my head on his chest again and listened to the steady rhythm of his heartbeat.

Since he'd given me a truth, it only seemed fair for me to give him one too.

"That's why," I told him. "Because I know it can't last."

He answered with a non-committal rumble in his chest.

I took it as a request to change the subject, so I did.

"So what else did you and my..."

I cleared my throat and tried again.

"What else did you and Enzo talk about?"

"Not much. He told me a little about school. I told him some stuff about my family but kept it vague. Not sure what you would want him to know."

I nodded, appreciating his efforts to defer to me.

"He mentioned you haven't dated."

"That's true. Enzo comes first. And dating as a single mom isn't very easy, especially when I don't trust other people to watch him."

Another low grumble in the back of his throat was Stefano's only reply while his fingers slid through my hair and down my back.

"This isn't the life I wanted either. When I was with you, and I told you my last name was Salvatore, it wasn't because I wanted to lie to you. I was lying to myself. I was giving myself a moment to live the life I wanted. For a while, it looked like maybe I could."

I knew no one ever escaped the Mafia. Not really. But I also wanted to keep him talking, because in the morning, everything would be different again.

"Really?" I asked.

"Yeah. I was the second son. I fought for the ability… for the luxury of living my life the way I chose to. But after you left me, everything changed."

"What do you mean?" I asked.

I was afraid to move or say too much and risk him changing his mind and clamming up again.

"I wasn't going to just let you go," he continued. "I was going to fight for us. I was going to explain that my father's world wasn't my world. It didn't need to be. I had an older brother who would follow in my father's footsteps and take over the family business.

"But my father made a play for a seat on the Commission. He would have been the king of kings in New York. The don of dons. Turned out somebody else wanted it more."

My heart broke for him. I knew his pain. I knew how it felt.

"The night you sent back the necklace with the letter telling me you didn't want to be with me… was the same night another boss decided they wanted what my father was about to have. So they abducted him and my brother. Beaten and executed together, they were left dead in the middle of the street.

"My mother made me swear to avenge them after that. It was one of the last things she said to me before the grief became too much and she… joined them. In death. I knew then there was no escape from this life. So I decided instead to focus on the revenge I promised my mother."

My lungs seized as the agony in my heart sharpened. I heard the pain in his voice, how it wasn't his father's execution or even his brother's that hurt him so much, but the knowledge that their deaths had broken his mother.

And that his mother had abandoned him in her grief.

I wondered for a moment what would have happened if I hadn't sent him that letter, if I hadn't abandoned him too. Would his life have turned out differently?

It didn't really matter anymore, I supposed.

What had happened had happened. No amount of daydreaming in a post-sex haze was going to change it.

"Is that who's after Enzo now?" I asked.

"I don't know. It's possible, but it doesn't make much sense. I'll do everything I can to find who's targeting you two, but right now I just don't know. I explained to Enzo that being my son comes with risks. He was amenable to taking precautions to protect not only himself but you as well."

I nodded. That sounded like Enzo.

Stefano let out a deep chuckle.

"You know, that kid sees more than most people. When I told him about that, he asked me if that's why I didn't have a wife and any legitimate children."

"Is it?" I asked, looking up at him.

"Yes," he admitted. "I wouldn't have agreed to marry Benedetta if she didn't agree children were off the table for us."

The reminder that he was engaged to another woman hit me like a bucket of ice water.

The soft warmth of our afterglow disappeared, and I remembered I was lying naked on a man who didn't belong to me.

"Could it have been her?" I wondered aloud.

"What?"

"Your fiancée. I know you said she didn't want kids or whatever, but could she be lying about that? Maybe she thinks things will change between you two, and with Enzo in the picture... that makes him a threat."

"It's not her," he said.

"But are you sure? Are you sure she's not looking for a way out of your engagement? I mean, that's what the note demanded, right? Given your position, I'm assuming she's a mafia princess, so she didn't really agree to this wedding. She was informed. Could she be trying to get out of it?"

"No, I don't think so."

Still reclined on the sofa, he reached out and tried to pull me back into his arms, but I was already on my feet, then pacing the room, my mind going a million miles an hour.

I grabbed the robe—another woman's robe—and slid it over my naked body.

"Look, this was a mistake. It shouldn't have happened."

"Val, calm down," Stefano said, sitting up.

"Calm down? You're engaged to someone else, and I'm not a home-wrecker. I'm not this kind of person. Please forget this happened between us. Just find out who's after my son and take care of it."

"Our son," he corrected.

"God, just find out who's trying to kill him, Stefano. You can start with your fiancée and anyone else who would benefit from your wedding not happening."

I turned on my heel to leave him.

Again.

TWELVE
STEFANO

Val had gone from the blissful state of a freshly fucked and satisfied woman to a neurotic banshee in seconds.

I jumped up and slammed my hand against the door to keep it shut, caging her inside my arms.

"Listen to me," I said.

She kept her back turned, refusing to look at me, and pulled on the door handle.

"I've heard enough. I need to go make sure Enzo's okay."

I leaned in close to her ear and lowered my voice to help calm her.

"The boy is safe, Val. This house is completely secure. Security sensors on every door and window. My enforcers have everything locked down. If anyone comes onto the property, I will know."

Her body relaxed against mine, and I wrapped my arms around her waist and held her.

"I don't think this is coming from Benedetta," I continued. "But you're right. She didn't have a choice, and she knows it's a contract. I don't love her. She doesn't even like me, but we have an understanding. I understand it isn't what girls dream about for their future, so I'll look into it."

It couldn't be.

She wouldn't betray me.

I walked Val back to the sofa, pulled her down on my lap. Then I slipped my hands into her robe to press her tighter against me, needing to feel her skin against mine again.

"You'll look into her specifically?" she asked.

"I will look into her, her closest friends, her security staff, and her father," I promised. "Just in case that shady bastard gets tricky. I don't think it's her, but it could be someone inside her inner circle."

"I don't know if I can believe you..."

Her voice sounded small now. The fight had finally left her.

"Do you think I would lie about something this serious?"

"There's too much on the line for me to take that risk, Stefano. You're on a path of blood and vengeance. I get that. You made a promise to your mother, and you're seeing it through."

I nodded.

"Is your marriage to Benedetta in service to that debt?"

"It is. And for no other reason."

I grasped the back of Val's neck, wanting to bring her lips to mine, but she held firm, grabbing my wrist and wrapping her fingers around it. She raised her gaze up to meet mine.

"Then I need you to make me a promise," she said. "A single promise that's just as important as the one you made to your mother. Can you do that for me?"

"I can, of course. But if I will, well, that depends on what it is you want."

"No, you need to agree before I tell you."

Her narrowed eyes burned into mine. She was dead serious.

"I'm not promising to stay away from my son," I warned.

"That's not what this is about," she snapped.

I nodded.

"Then whatever you need, Val. It's yours."

"What I need is for you to find the man threatening our son. And when you find him, end him. Make an example of him. Make everyone terrified to come for Enzo."

An understandable request. But the increasing intensity in her expression as she asked me to murder someone unsettled me a bit.

I'd already planned to do that. This attack could not stand. I knew this situation could end in only one way. But to have my innocent little barista ask me to kill a man...

There was a darkness in Val that hadn't been there before. Or maybe it had been, and I never wanted to see it.

I was no longer the young dreamer she had fallen for years ago, and I realized she wasn't the lighthearted woman I once knew either.

We had both changed, grown darker, more twisted.

Or had we both had the darkness in us all along?

I dismissed the thought as quickly as it had come. Val had been an angel back then and still now. She didn't want to be tainted by my world. Motherhood had strengthened her, and the attack at Con Amore frightened her. That was all.

Still my angel.

I refused to believe she could be full of malice or burn for vengeance like me. Fear. It had to be fear, and I hated that someone had caused her to be so afraid. Val shouldn't feel anything other than comfort and love.

I took her chin and tilted it, so she could meet my eyes.

"Anyone who even thinks to lay a finger on our son will die a slow, painful death, and the others will whisper about it in the back alleys of New York forever. No one touches what is mine, and that includes you and now our son. I will keep you safe."

Giving my word meant something to me. I took my vows seriously. Always.

"Thank you," she said, touching my face.

I pressed my cheek against her palm, taking comfort from whatever contact I could get.

"Fix this, Stefano. Show them who you are. Make sure no one ever dares to touch him. Then Enzo and I will go back to our life, and you can go on with yours. I promise."

"What?"

I took her hand away from my face and held it, running my thumb over her soft skin.

"Val. That's not what I want. I want to be in his life. If you don't want me to be actively involved until he's older, I can live with that. And I won't name him my heir, not unless he chooses this path when he's grown.

"But I will start paying for his education and everything else. I'll make sure neither of you want for anything. I have power, money, and influence. I want to do something good with it for the people who deserve it, the people I owe it to. For my family."

My family.

My words made my chest ache. I didn't realize how alone I'd felt until saying them.

"I'll think about it," she whispered.

Val's gaze dropped to the floor. She was lying to me.

Then she leaned in and placed a small kiss on my cheek

before getting up. She nodded as she walked away, and the room suddenly grew cold.

I should have been used to the loneliness.

I'd been numb to that dull ache for so long. But Val reminded me what it felt like to be touched by not just another person but by someone who mattered to me.

The hollow space in my chest was her fucking fault.

And it would get worse when she took my son away.

She tightened her robe, still avoiding eye contact.

"It's been a very long day, and I'm exhausted. I do need to check on Enzo. He has always slept at home, and this is new for him. I need some sleep too, and so do you. I mean, you got shot earlier tonight, so you should get some rest."

I nodded.

"Check on him but come back and stay with me. I want you in my bed tonight."

Pressing her lips together, she headed for the door.

"I'll see you in the morning," she said.

Then, without as much as a glance over her shoulder, she stood still for a second before walking out on me.

"It's you, Stefano, who will be king of kings one day."

What she'd said, words signaling that she believed in my strength, caused an overwhelming need for me to claim her.

Fuck. I wanted to grab her arm and pull her back to me, to carry her to my bed, to have her sleeping next to me, so I knew she was real. And safe. Then again, the last time she'd slept beside me, she was gone the next morning.

I needed something to get her in my bed, to make her sleep where I could protect her. Where I could make up for lost time by sinking into her tight little cunt over and over.

Ah, but I would have her in my bed soon, so I let her go back to her own room.

I had work to do.

The day had started with me not wanting children, and the evening ended with me being a father and fucking the barista who had stolen my son.

Worse, the city wasn't safe for my child. That couldn't stand. The threat against him had to be rectified swiftly... a brutal message to all the other families to keep my son safe.

I grabbed my phone and called Tony.

He and Bruce were still canvassing the Brooklyn neighborhood, looking for other clues left behind by the shooter.

"Hey, boss. We're not finding much else down here," Tony said right away.

"No, I don't think you will," I said. "I want you to redirect your efforts now."

"Sure. What do you want me to do?"

"I want to know where Benedetta was tonight. And I want her inner circle included in the search. Don't forget her security team. Anyone she had contact with in the last forty-eight hours.

"Check them all. And I want a convincing answer about how her father already knew about our close call tonight before I found him waiting in my office."

"Actually..."

I pictured him standing there as he stared at his polished shoes and rubbed the back of his neck. He was about to apologize for screwing up something.

"Yeah, that was a coincidence, Stef," he said. "Don Capaldo showed up to talk about something else, but then he overheard the maid taking my orders to make up the rooms. She came clean when we got there. She panicked, thinking she would get in trouble. I'm sorry."

I rolled my eyes.

"She's not, but you will be if you keep that shit up. Stop giving her so much info. And fuck off with that... loyal maids are too hard to find... she doesn't want to be your old lady."

Bella had turned him down countless times.

"Yes, boss. So do you think the Capaldos are involved?"

"No, not Benedetta anyway, but we must investigate her father. Maybe he's on some power trip, some last hurrah before the devil comes to collect him. We'll see about that. Go on, Tony. Investigate all possibilities, including Benedetta, just to be sure, and report back in the morning."

I ended the call and hit the bar for another drink.

Val was right... the day had been too long. I had a feeling the entire week would feel the same. I was supposed to get married in two days, and now I had a son, a woman in my house that still made me crazy, and a faceless enemy to hunt down.

Never a dull moment.

I slid into my slacks and picked up my laptop from all the shit strewn across the floor. I had plans to make. I had to find out who targeted my son. And I needed to figure out how to make sure he stayed with me.

What Valerie wanted didn't matter.

I knew what I'd said to her, to win her over.

If not her, then I had to win the boy, had to find out what he wanted, what his goals were, and how I could provide for him in a way he'd want to stay with me, where he now belonged.

The kingdom I'd inherited and turned into one of the strongest on the East Coast would be his if he wanted it.

So fucked up how quickly my mindset had shifted.

Rage and pain no longer fueled the growth of my empire.

No, my new desire for a legacy fueled it now.

For Enzo.

No other Vignali child would ever come along, not from me. Enzo was it.

He'd inherited everything good about his mother, and with my ferocity, his grandfather's bravery, and his uncle's intelligence, the boy was born to rule my kingdom.

And I wouldn't let his mother stand in the way.

THIRTEEN
VAL

Once I was finally able to crawl into bed, of course, I couldn't get to sleep.

I'd hoped the vigorous work out with Stefano would help, hoped to be out cold as soon as my head hit the pillow.

But no. I had tossed and turned most of the night.

Every time I'd closed my eyes and thought I might be ready to let go, I heard the creaking of a floorboard or wind blowing against a window, making my mind race. Then I just lay there with my eyes open again, wondering if Enzo really was safe.

At some point, I had finally given up, gone to Enzo's room, got into the bed with him, and wrapped my arms around him.

Having him safely protected in my arms had done the trick.

The next morning came, and we woke to someone banging on the door.

I stretched, feeling like a Mack truck had hit me. My body ached in so many places. Some of it was annoying, and some of it was kind of delicious.

My head pounded from the lack of sleep, and I was

nowhere close to ready to deal with all the problems waiting on the other side of that door.

Suppressing the urge to yell at whoever waited at the door, I jumped up and opened it, finding no one... just a large silver tray holding coffee and lots of breakfast foods.

Not what I expected.

I carried it into the room as Enzo sat up, yawned, and wiped the sleep from his eyes.

"What is it, Mama?"

"Breakfast in bed, baby. Are you hungry?"

He nodded.

I set the tray on the bed, and Enzo lifted the domed lids to reveal a feast of pancakes, waffles, eggs, bacon. A little French coffee press, cream and sugar, and a tall glass of orange juice were also on the big-ass tray.

Watching Enzo quickly dig into the waffles, I took the press and poured myself a cup. As a café owner, I was a little embarrassed to admit the coffee might have been some of the best I'd ever had. I made a mental note to find out where it came from.

Not that it would matter. We were leaving soon.

A thought about Enzo's school popped into my head. I hadn't yet detailed in my plan how to handle his absence. Shrugging, I grabbed my phone and called Saint Christopher to let them know he would be out for a couple of days.

Instead of speaking to a human, a voicemail prompted me to leave a message on the attendance line. I let them know everything was fine and he would be back soon.

I lied.

The family emergency part of my message was true, though, technically speaking. It seemed perfectly logical that Enzo's back-from-the-dead father getting shot counted as one.

It didn't matter anyway. Enzo wouldn't be going back to Saint Christopher once we got away from Stefano and on our way to our new life.

But the last thing I needed was to have the school call the police or do something equally stupid because they hadn't seen him or heard from me. That would complicate things more.

An AMBER Alert for my son would make escaping nearly impossible.

Soon after ending the call, my phone rang with an unfamiliar number. I thought it might have been a barista from Con Amore, so I answered, slipping into the bathroom to keep Enzo from hearing whatever lie I would have to tell.

"Hello?"

"Hey, Ms. Salera... Valerie. It's Donnie."

I moved the phone away from my face and stared at it for a second, like it had pulled a prank on me.

Are you fucking kidding me right now?

"Valerie," he repeated.

"Yes, Mr. Luka. How can I help you this morning?"

"I saw the attendance report. Enzo isn't coming in today?"

"That's correct," I said. "We have a family emergency, so we need a few days."

"Anything I can help with?"

"What? No, but thanks."

Why couldn't this guy just take a hint?

"Are you sure, Valerie? I'm a great listener. Maybe you'd like to grab some coffee with me? Have someone to talk to."

"Really, Mr. Luka, I appreciate the offer, but I'm busy."

"Is everything okay?" he asked before I could end the call.

"I'm sure it will be," I said through my clenched teeth.

"Well, if there's anything I can do to help... I know it's just you and Enzo, and—"

"You know, Mr. Luka, I'm so sorry, but I have to cut you off. I need to go, but don't worry. Enzo's looking forward to being back in your class soon."

I hung up and tossed the phone on the marble countertop.

Who the hell did he think he was?

When I went back to the bedroom, Enzo hit me with one of his knowing looks, but no way would I try to explain that call.

"Hey, you saving me any of those yummy-looking waffles, buddy?" I asked.

"Nope, but the eggs are all yours."

I couldn't help but laugh at his syrupy grin.

"And this is for you too, Mama."

Enzo waved a white envelope with my name on it, and I snatched it playfully from his hand.

Stefano had left me a note.

God, he had beautiful handwriting.

Val,

Most of the men will be with me today, but I left my two best enforcers behind to protect you. The household staff know you're not to be disturbed.

You may go anywhere in the house you'd like other than my office. Kitchen is on the ground floor. First floor has a theater and game room.

Do not go outside beyond the protection of this house. The enemy has high-precision weaponry, and I don't want them to get a shot at you or my son. Not even for one second, Val.

And keep Enzo out of the cellar.

Stefano

Well, okay then.

I stuffed the note into my pocket, making sure Enzo didn't see the letter. The last thing I needed was for him to ask questions about the cellar.

Cellars in mafia houses were all the same. Cold, dark, often soundproofed, and strictly on the Do Not Enter list.

Matters of a very specific type were taken care of down there. Issues far too sensitive to be handled aboveground and in plain sight. Issues that mob bosses often handled themselves because they required a certain, well, personal touch.

Just thinking about it made my skin crawl.

"If I'm not going to school, then what are we doing today, Mama?" Enzo asked.

"You know, buddy, I'm not so sure. But how about this? We start by reading a few more chapters in your book."

As good a plan as any.

His eyes lit up, and he nodded, reaching for the book on the nightstand. Then he crossed his legs and balanced the open book on his lap.

"I'll read the first chapter while you eat, then you read the next one while I finish the waffles."

I smiled and ruffled his hair, taking a seat beside him.

"Yeah, okay, sounds like a plan."

He stopped flipping through the pages to look at me.

"Just don't touch my waffles."

I couldn't help but laugh at his unexpected seriousness.

"Absolutely not. I promise."

After a curt nod, he went back to flipping through the book to find the page where we'd left off. The second he started reading, he became engrossed, as if nothing else in the world existed.

So hungry, I hardly listened, focusing more on eating what I had to admit was a pretty good breakfast.

We read until we both became a little stir-crazy. I hated not knowing what was happening out there in the world beyond this house. Hated that I didn't know Stefano's plan. Even more, I hated leaving everything up to others.

Enzo got fidgety near the end of our last chapter. He was a nine-year-old boy with natural energy plus a sugar high from the half-bottle of syrup he'd poured over his waffles.

We both needed to get out of the suite, and I needed to find the info to support my contingency plans when the time came.

So much still had to be done.

If Stefano's note contained the truth, Enzo and I had the run of the house with no one to interrupt us. And no one to catch me investigating the layout and gaining as much understanding about Stefano's current staff as possible.

"Hey, apparently there's a theater somewhere on the first floor," I said. "What do you think about watching a movie?"

"That sounds fun," Enzo said, but I wasn't convinced.

The boy had sat enough already. He tried so hard to behave, but I had to give him something physical to do now.

"Awesome. Before we do that, let's say thanks to the men helping us. I think a few batches of cookies might be the perfect way to do that. We can find the kitchen on our own, right?"

Enzo nodded, his curls bouncing.

"Perfect. Go wash the syrup off your face, kiddo. Then we'll go downstairs and see what we can find."

He ran off to the bathroom, and I followed, remembering I'd left my dirty dress there on the floor after my bath.

The dress wasn't where I left it, though, so I went to the closet in my room, hoping to find something else to wear. Instead, I found my dress hanging there, freshly laundered, with no trace of the stains or the tiny shards of glass left.

Totally a little creepy, but still appreciated.

TWENTY MINUTES LATER

The ground floor of Stefano's house seemed mostly deserted.

The two men he left behind walked around talking on their phones, pretending to be uninterested in Enzo and me while still following us. I appreciated their wide berth.

Bella and another maid turned the corner, heading to a back hallway just as Enzo and I found the kitchen. I wasn't sure if we'd chased them out or if it might have been a coincidence.

No worries. They would either come back or they wouldn't.

Enzo went straight for the fruit bowl on the counter and snatched up an orange in each hand.

"Let's make some orange cookies, Mama!"

Then he ran to the refrigerator to gather some other ingredients he knew by heart.

I should have known he'd picked up on my stress, which meant I would inevitably want to bake some of the classic recipes my grandmother had taught me.

While my son searched the fridge and kitchen drawers, I found all the dry ingredients we needed in the pantry, everything available, neatly labeled, and well-stocked on the higher shelves.

All-purpose flour, sugar, a red mixer.

And my nonna's secret ingredients.

Then I laid it all out on the massive kitchen island while Enzo searched for the cookie sheets and mixing bowls.

Between the two of us and the perfectly organized kitchen, we had everything we needed ready in under five minutes.

Stefano's kitchen almost made me reconsider running away. Every chef dreamed about spaces like this, and it was so hard not to appreciate it.

After so many times making these cookies with me at the café, Enzo got started without the need to even peek at a recipe, measuring out the dry ingredients on his own before dumping them into the mixing bowl.

I almost suggested we stick with half or even a quarter of our usual batch size but fuck it. Worst-case scenario, they didn't all get eaten. There were greater tragedies.

It wasn't like we had anything else to do either.

I preheated the double ovens and mixed up the dough. Once I had it rolled into little balls and laid out on the cookie sheets, Enzo and I sat for a minute while they chilled.

"Should we make some chocolate ones too, Mama?"

"Let's bake these first and see how we feel."

But with my anxiety returning and unraveling my nerves with every second, I was already certain we would make more than enough cookies to feed everyone who worked for Stefano.

We had our entire system in this new kitchen worked out and streamlined by the time I pulled the third and fourth dozen out of the ovens and put them on the cooling rack.

As Enzo finished getting the next batch ready to bake, I noticed how my nerves had calmed and my heartbeat settled.

Doing something my grandmother had taught me always gave me the strength to persevere, just like she always had.

"Hello there," a soft voice said behind me.

I spun around.

A beautiful woman dressed in a classic sheath dress came into the kitchen. Her caramel hair spilled in loose waves over her shoulders.

I held my breath to avoid panicking.

Stefano was marrying a woman named Benedetta, I knew that. But I didn't know it was Benedict Capaldo's daughter.

It had been fifteen years since I last saw Benedetta Capaldo, and I prayed she didn't recognize me.

My heart thundered in my ears as I pasted on a smile.

"Hi. I'm Valerie. This is my son, Enzo."

She stared like she was trying to place my face, shrugged one shoulder, then gave me a warm smile and introduced herself.

"I didn't mean to interrupt. I came by to see Stefano for a minute, but this amazing smell distracted me, and I just had to see what was happening."

"It's our orange spice cookies," Enzo said with a big smile. "Do you want one?"

He extended the platter to her, and Benedetta stared at his face while picking up a cookie.

What did she see?

Stefano's unmistakable eyes?

His smile?

"Thank you," she said before taking a bite.

I noted the way she covered her mouth while she chewed, as if being seen with food was a punishable crime. Or maybe she really was just that polite.

"These really are amazing, Enzo," Benedetta added.

Then they talked about the cookies for a minute, and I couldn't help but wonder if this woman was behind the attack.

Stefano had said he didn't think so. Now I could see what he meant. Benedetta didn't seem like the type.

So engaging and friendly, her smile genuine and warm.

Enzo seemed to like her instantly, not something that happened with him very often.

He talked to customers at the café, and he was always polite, but it took a different sort of person to get him to open up to this level of friendliness and acceptance.

My son was a great judge of character. Always had been.

It made sense. When I'd known Benedetta as a girl, we weren't friends. More like acquaintances with mutual friends, and even then, she was always very sweet.

The type of girl who followed her father's rules. The type of girl my father had tried so hard to shape me into.

The perfect mafia princess.

Beautiful, demure, and a little weak.

But that was the thing about those princesses. They were always strongest when being underestimated.

Their mothers taught them very early how to put on a sweet smile and use impeccable manners to make people believe the facade while secretly stabbing them in the back simultaneously.

I would know.

Was that what this mafia princess was doing now? Smiling at my son while plotting to kill him?

My hands reflexively balled into fists.

I hid them behind my back.

This bitch would never get the chance to touch a single hair on my son's innocent head.

She would have to kill me first.

FOURTEEN
STEFANO

I paced the floor in my study, head down, eyes on the floor, my hand raised in warning for Tony to shut his fucking mouth for a minute.

My patience hung by one last frayed thread.

We had searched the entire city, checking out alibis, looking for clues, doing more detective work than the entire police force in the state of New York.

Still, my men and I came back with nothing.

Soon I'd have no choice but to act.

I knew better than to do anything without the necessary information first, but the clock was quickly running out.

As I took a seat behind my desk, I pushed my hand through the top of my hair. My mind dropped to an image of Enzo, his hair, those little curls. I pounded the side of my fist on the desk.

"How the fuck is this possible? Everyone knows the lengths I'll go to when I want something, when I protect what's mine. And yet, nothing. Not a word."

I had promised Val that our son would be safe, and I wanted to deliver on that promise right away.

She wanted to get back to Con Amore, and while I would restore her business, I needed her out of my house.

In less than twenty-four hours, I would be a married man. Having the mother of my bastard child—who I couldn't seem to keep my goddamn hands off—under my roof seemed like a terrible idea.

Benedetta might use it to pitch a fit and give me the cold shoulder, delaying consummating our marriage, but in the end, she would live with whatever I told her to.

Her father would use it to threaten me.

Don Capaldo wouldn't break our contract this late in the game, with no alternatives lined up. He would fuck with me, though, making threats and interrupting my business with all his bitching while his dead ass sat in my chair.

But then again, I couldn't underestimate Benedetta. She had listened and learned from her father over the years, and her motivations for our match were less clear.

I never asked her why she'd been so agreeable because I didn't care what she wanted. Her dowry and the power it gave me were all that mattered.

After giving me a few minutes, Tony cleared his throat.

"We're trying to uncover any new angles, boss, but nothing's turning up. I checked out Benedetta myself. Nothing suggests it might've come from her. Her trusted circle of friends, family, and staff... all accounted for.

"Her security men still belong to her father, and they don't take orders from her. So all we know at this point is someone wants the marriage contract broken, and that's it."

I flicked my wrist at his words.

"Listen, Tony. I want you to take a good, hard look at the

Capaldo situation. Ensure I'm not being biased or underestimating Benedict."

The bitter taste of regret hit my tongue.

Admitting bias meant admitting weakness.

Capaldo had only one option left to ensure the survival of his legacy anyway, and that was me. Under normal circumstances, if the man hadn't been on his deathbed with no living sons or brothers, I wouldn't have put much stock in that idea.

And after meeting Enzo, I understood his commitment to our marriage contract.

Benedict Capaldo knew his name wouldn't live on after his death... he was ensuring the future of his only living child, his beloved princess.

He'd chosen me to lead his family not for my leadership ability or for my intelligence and strategic planning expertise but because I was the only don without illegitimate kids running around the city who might take his empire away from Benedetta's heirs.

He didn't know there wouldn't be heirs. And he didn't know about my son, not when we executed the contract.

"I suppose it could be him," Tony said. "We can't take anything off the table right now. But it makes no sense to me. Capaldo's soldiers are top marksmen, and even their personal sidearms are more advanced than the shooter's.

"Even if one of 'em owned a shitty rifle, any of 'em would've been a much better shot. Besides, the dons don't miss."

I released a heavy breath through my nose and nodded.

"Right. That's true."

"I hate to say it, Stef, but with that big window, not hitting anyone but you, and only in the arm, no less, it had to be an intentional miss or we're dealing with storm troopers."

I rolled my eyes at the reference and let it go.

"Who would shoot up a window like that and try to not kill anyone?" I asked.

"Take your pick." Tony shrugged. "The only thing we know for sure is the guy knew how to get to the boy and his mother. They had to be watching her for a while."

Thinking out loud, I shook my head.

"Let's circle back to the Capaldos. I don't think Benedict would be behind this," I said. "He wouldn't go through all this trouble just for the embarrassment of a broken engagement. He knows that would affect his daughter's reputation.

"Maybe if he weren't dying, sure, but he and I both know he'll be gone in a few months. If we broke the contract now, it would destroy his dynasty, leaving Benedetta unprotected. She might get some money, but she would no longer have the protection of his men. They would die before following a woman."

"Right," Tony said. "But what if he arranged another match?"

"There isn't a better one out there. Even if it were the case, he would give the kill order right out the gate to take me out. I wouldn't have made it out of that café alive."

"Who else then, boss?"

"Accusing Benedetta still doesn't sit right with me, even though Val made a good point last night. Benedetta clearly does not like me, and she never had the option to say no to this marriage. Although she agreed to the no children thing, I don't think she's crazy about that either."

Tony shrugged again. One more time, and he'd be picking himself up from the fucking floor.

"I need to talk to her myself," I snapped.

Something undefined stuck in the back of my mind. I was missing an important piece of information that could lead me straight to the shooter.

Maybe Benedetta could shed some light on it.

I grabbed my phone and sent her a text, telling her to get to the estate as soon as possible.

She immediately replied. From my kitchen.

Not wanting it to be true, I stared at my phone.

"Tony, find out if Val's still in the kitchen with my son."

Nothing good could come from the two women meeting without me there, though I had given no thought to what I might say to keep the peace between them anyway.

Tony texted one of Val's guards and received an instant reply.

"Yeah, she's in the kitchen with the boy, baking cookies. He says you told him they had the run of the place."

"Yes, I did. Who else is in the kitchen?"

Tony sent and received another text, then met my gaze with his "oh shit" expression.

"Benedetta's down there," he said.

"Fuck!"

I threw my phone. It shattered against the wall.

"Get that replaced... and stay out of my sight until you have a lead. I don't care how small... just get me something we can use to find this asshole and put him in the fucking ground."

Then I quickly headed for the door. The second I opened it, the familiar scent of orange spice cookies hit me—the addicting cookies Val used to make every morning at Con Amore.

She had always set aside a handful for me each day.

My mouth watered, and my stomach rumbled.

The sweet smell instantly took me back to those anticipated stops on my way to school in the morning, hoping to see her.

Back to where I'd gone during my breaks to study on that old couch. Back to where, if I leaned the right way, I could see Val in the kitchen with her nonna.

She'd be standing over the counter, her expression relaxed and happy as she rolled out the cookie dough.

That was what she'd been doing when she agreed to go to dinner with me. I had stormed into that kitchen to stand face-to-face with her, my foul-mouthed little barista with powdered sugar on her cheek.

I hadn't even asked. I told her she would go.

Her grandmother had shouted at me.

"It's about damn time you got off that couch!"

Others laughed and applauded.

Val's cheeks had turned the prettiest shade of pink. Then she nodded and gave me her beautiful smile.

Goddamn it, that memory still left a hollow place in my chest. I shook myself out of it and marched downstairs, bracing myself for what waited for me in my kitchen now.

When I got there, I stopped short in the doorway and stared, watching Val hand an espresso to Benedetta.

Benedetta glanced at the child, at my child. A sad smile hit her face, like she knew she was missing a vital part of herself but couldn't hold a grudge against another woman who had it.

Her expression and body language revealed no anger at all.

Val rolled out more dough, and just like in my memory, she had powdered sugar on her cheek. She handed the little balls of orange-and-spice goodness to Enzo.

He tossed them into the sugar, then placed them in neat rows on the baking pan.

What other skills did he have? What other bonding moments between mother and son had I missed observing all those years?

If she had told me about him, would Enzo and I have bonded in our own way? Would my son and I have done special things together too?

We might have gone to the shooting range for target practice. I might have taken him to his first football game, or maybe boxing lessons.

Heat rushed through me, burning up my chest, my neck, my fucking face.

Val had stolen that from me.

Seeing her and the boy doing something together as simple as baking made the whole thing look so normal. Not the normal I knew... the normal my younger self had wished for.

Watching them brought back the painful loss of the future I had planned out as a younger man. The dream I'd given up and locked away inside me.

Now it all flooded back to the surface.

Val had kept more from me than my son. She'd taken the life I wanted with her, the late-night candlelit dinners, the arguments that ended in passionate sex, and even the lazy Sunday mornings in bed.

It wasn't just about the sex but everything that came with it.

The dates, the intimacy, and the companionship. Having someone there to listen after a rough day, to speak up when things had gone too far, to encourage me to push harder and strive for more, to find a better way.

I'd had none of it.

We could have had that.

Benedetta clacked her cup down on the saucer to get my attention. She'd been watching me watch them.

I jerked my gaze away from Val and my son.

"We need to talk," Benedetta said, void of emotion.

Then she got up and came toward me, everything about her as unreadable as glass.

We didn't know each other very well, so there wasn't much to compare to her stony behavior. I didn't know if seeing Enzo made her rethink not having my children, or if she was just pissed because I had Val staying in my house.

"In private," she added.

I searched her face, looking for a clue about what was going through her head and what I should expect.

She gave me nothing.

"Let's go up to my study," I said.

I led the way to what I fully expected to be an unpleasant conversation. We were supposed to be married in less than a day, but if I didn't have a handle on who was after my son before then, I couldn't risk it.

A sharp pain hit me in the gut, and I gritted my teeth.

The mere thought of caving to blackmail made me want to destroy everything and everyone. Once I got my hands on the son of a bitch, I could purge some of that rage.

In the meantime, I had to decide how to handle Benedetta. I wanted her father's men, her father's fortune.

But at what cost?

Suddenly, I found the idea of an arranged marriage distasteful. I didn't want anyone but Val in my bed.

Even if my marriage to Benedetta was a business contract, it would still have to be consummated, and I suspected that would tear Val out of my arms permanently.

Benedetta might refuse to marry me now that she knew I had a son with another woman and wouldn't give her a child of her own.

Though she had no choice in whom she married, she still had to stand in front of a priest with me. If she rejected me at the altar, things would become very complicated.

So yes, we needed to talk. We needed to understand where the other person stood and how we planned to move forward.

A great deal hinged on what this conversation produced.

If she turned out to be the one coming for Enzo, may God have mercy on her soul. I sure as fuck wouldn't. Being a woman and my fiancée would not save her.

But if not her, then maybe she had some ideas.

Or maybe she would refuse to help me protect my son.

Maybe she would lie to me.

There were a million ways for the conversation to go wrong.

FIFTEEN
STEFANO

Benedetta didn't say a word until we got to my office and shut the door behind us.

She turned on her stilettos and put her hands on her slender hips in her polished way. Then she stared at me as if inspecting my features. Or comparing them.

The woman was beautiful.

And not only beautiful but also approachable, very polite, and obedient too. Every don's perfect bride.

But something lacked between us.

Fire.

My fiancée didn't seem to have the fight in her that Val had. It wasn't her fault. Val had something to protect. Something to fight for. She had my son.

"When were you going to tell me about your bastard?" Benedetta finally asked.

I relaxed my jaw's involuntary clenching.

"Do not call him that," I warned.

She dropped her gaze for a second, then met mine again.

"I'm sorry. That was cruel. But why didn't you tell me you

have a son and moved him and his mother into your house the day before our wedding?"

Then she paced around the room, waiting for me to compose my response while mumbling something about the damn tooth-whitening gel and really needing more espresso.

I didn't bother to decode whatever the fuck that meant.

"We're not exactly close enough to share our deepest secrets with each other, Benedetta."

I motioned to the velvet armchair for her to take a seat.

She chose the sofa instead.

The sofa where I'd held Val after fucking her on my desk. I couldn't look at the desk without my cock stiffening. That made things difficult, so I took the armchair myself, facing away from the desk.

Benedetta crossed her ankles, folded her hands on her lap.

"We're supposed to be getting married tomorrow," she said.

"That doesn't mean I have to tell you everything. Standing in front of the priest and saying our vows doesn't make us equal partners. Do you understand that?"

Her eyes narrowed almost imperceptibly.

"Yes, I know that. I still think either you or my father should have told me about your son. I'm entitled to at least that much."

With this level of visible control over her anger, maybe Benedetta had some fire in her. If she did, it was buried deep, and I had no interest in digging it up with her or any woman other than Val.

Even if that woman was my future wife.

"You're entitled to whatever I say you are, Benedetta. Nothing more, nothing less. I can be a fair man, but I won't be if you push me."

"I don't think I'm being unreasonable here, Stefano. I understand what this is between us. A contract. On my part, there are no expectations of love or anything of that nature. I'm not walking into this under any illusion."

I scoffed. "Then what's the problem?"

The second I'd said the words, I felt like an asshole. Here I was, completely dismissing a kind woman who'd done absolutely nothing to deserve my ire.

"I think it's only fair you let me know why people will point at me and whisper. When you made this agreement with my father, you made an agreement with me as well.

"We swore to have a childless marriage. You made me promise to relinquish any future claims to motherhood, to spare other children from being forced into this life the way you and I were."

"And you agreed," I pointed out.

"I didn't have a choice."

Her words dripped with venom, even as the perfect line of her lips curled into a smile.

It took me a minute to realize it, but then I saw that smile for what it really was—pure hatred.

Now when I looked at her, really looked and considered her as a person instead of a means to an end, I believed she was far more capable of violence than I'd given her credit for.

Not enough to convince me she had arranged the attack on Enzo, but she certainly was capable of something like it.

This was a mafia princess sitting across from me, after all, and Benedetta presented herself perfectly that way.

Her parents raised her to accept only perfection before it came time for them to sell her to the highest bidder, to ensure the family's strength and position.

But this one had her own thoughts, ambitions, and desires.

That wouldn't affect my decision to marry her. I cared only about the power that came with her hand, the power I needed to fulfill a promise and avenge my family.

Had my ambition and my blood lust really blinded me so much that I hadn't seen the snake I had agreed to marry?

With a deep breath, Benedetta straightened her back, and like magic, the anger in her expression melted away, the mask of cold indifference sliding into its place.

"You still agreed," I said.

"I agreed because that's what's expected of me. I understood your reasoning too, don't get me wrong. It wasn't my choice, but I absolutely see the logic and even some warped form of mercy behind your decision. It made sense."

"Then what's the problem?" I repeated.

"The problem is, now you have a child, Stefano. That renders our agreement null and void, and I would be well within my rights to call off this wedding. But for other reasons, I can't. So what I want is to hear it straight from you. Why did you lie?"

I raised a brow. "You still think I owe you an explanation?"

Yes, I was being an ass, but the strategy I employed was to bait her into showing her true colors. Then, at the very least, I would have a better idea about the likelihood of her being involved in the attack on my son.

"You don't owe me anything," she said. "You've made that clear. But like I said, I think I deserve to know what people will whisper about me in the coming days, so I can adjust accordingly."

"Adjust how?"

"That depends on the situation. I need the facts, and I need to know the expected outcome."

Inhaling deeply, I gave myself a minute to think it through.

She wasn't being unreasonable. Considering the circumstances, her reaction could have been much worse, and if I wanted Enzo in my life, I needed her and Val to at least remain civil to each other.

For better or worse, my house would be under Benedetta's control, and I would need her to want to make it welcoming for Enzo. I decided to lay the cards she needed on the table.

"I didn't know about the boy until last night," I said.

She tilted her head, and the tiniest crease of confusion darkened her delicate brow.

"What do you mean?"

"I received an interesting bit of correspondence yesterday from an anonymous sender. A personal threat. The envelope contained photographs of a woman I hadn't seen in a decade. And her son. I recognized Valerie, of course, but not the child.

"There was, however, a lock of the boy's hair included with everything else. Before I saw DNA results for myself, I wanted to confront his mother first. I wanted to see it with my own eyes and hear it straight from her mouth."

"So you... what? Called her up and invited her to bring the boy over to make cookies in your kitchen?"

"That would be a gross oversimplification of this entire situation. I went to the café she owns. Like I said, I needed to see the boy for myself."

"And what about the mother?" she asked. "This anonymous threat could very well have come from her for a multitude of reasons...

"Because she wanted you back in her life. Or to extort

money from you. To force you to do her a few favors and make you think it was your idea all along. You must admit, Stefano, this is awfully convenient timing."

I gnashed my back teeth to stop from lashing out.

If I were viewing this scenario from the outside, watching this situation unfold for another man in my position, I would have thought the same thing.

Benedetta was being entirely practical, and I couldn't get past how little I appreciated what she was insinuating about Val.

I sat back and propped an arm over the chair frame.

"Listen, I was there for all of two minutes before someone opened fire on the place. Most of it meant to be a distraction, I'm sure. But the shooter intended to harm the boy. I took a bullet for him."

"You were shot?"

"That doesn't matter."

She looked me over, then her eyes widened in realization.

"Someone tried to murder that sweet little boy? The child downstairs in the kitchen right now, baking cookies?"

"Yes, so what concerns me far more at the moment is that someone out there was brazen enough to go after a son I didn't even know I had."

Benedetta stood to pace around the room again, her head dipped slightly forward as she pinched the bridge of her nose.

"Why would someone do this? Who would do something like that? I mean, the shooting is one thing. That's part of the life. But to go after a child? That's just evil. In its truest form."

"I agree," I said, observing her.

Now that I'd gotten this kind of reaction from her, besides the way she handled the first part of our conversation, I didn't think she had anything to do with it. Her response seemed genuine, but if I didn't confirm it without a shadow of a doubt, I would fail us all.

I couldn't trust my gut this time.

There was too much on the line.

Then Benedetta spun out of her pacing to face me.

"What was the threat?" she asked.

"Excuse me?"

"What do they want? You don't just threaten a child and his mother and actually attempt to go through with it without wanting something first. What do they want?"

I considered lying to her, giving her some unrelated response, so I could gauge her reaction to the lie, in case this was a ruse, and she was a more skilled actor than I imagined.

But in a few split seconds, I decided being blunt would give me the best reaction.

"They want me to call off the wedding."

Her eyes widened again, joined by the faintest paling of her flawless skin.

"What? But why?"

Her confusion seemed entirely authentic, as far as I could tell, but that still wasn't enough.

"I don't know. That's why I asked you to come here. I wanted to see what you thought. If maybe anyone came to mind when I told you, someone out there who doesn't want us to get married."

She shook her head, staring blankly across the room.

"No, I don't know. Everyone has shown nothing but excitement about the wedding. The few close friends I have. My family. Or what's left of it anyway."

"Think, Benedetta. Is there anyone in your orbit not wanting this to happen?"

"If you're referring to anyone who might have a more intimate understanding of my family's situation, Stefano, then no. Those who know about my father are happy to see I'll be protected. The line of succession for my father's legacy is already perfectly clear.

"And honestly, most of them are thrilled to know that his death won't cause a blood feud over the new boss."

"And the people who don't know about your father?"

"The people who don't know about my father's illness are equally excited. Blending the families will make us one of the strongest, if not the strongest, crew in the city. Most likely in all of New York."

Now she was only repeating back to me things I already knew, and that wouldn't get us anywhere.

I gave her a curt nod.

"So you can't think of anyone."

A statement, not a question.

"No, I can't. I've not heard anyone expressing anger over the wedding. And certainly not disapproving enough to shoot a child. I don't know anyone capable of such a thing."

After that, Benedetta resumed pacing and pinching the bridge of her nose.

I had hinted as much as I could and gotten nowhere.

Time to be direct.

"What about an ex-lover?" I asked. "A boyfriend who couldn't stand the thought of you in another man's bed?"

She froze near the far wall of my study, her back going rigid. Then she slowly turned to look at me over her shoulder.

"Are you really accusing me of being impure?"

"I don't give a fuck about your virginity, Benedetta. As long as you're not carrying another man's child and you ended all relations from before our engagement, as agreed, then it's none of my business."

"Well, you're in the minority with that," she seethed. "Stefano, I've remained untouched. I'm sure you understand the consequences of dishonoring my father like that before he decided who my husband would be."

Her eyes narrowed again with a twitch.

"And to imply otherwise is an insult to my family."

"My son's life is on the line. I must consider every avenue."

"Well, that avenue is a dead end," she snapped. "I can promise you that."

Leaning forward, I pressed my palms against my eyelids, hoping to mitigate the beginning of a headache.

"If it is, then give me an alternative. I can't link any of my rivals to this. And no ties between this botched job and the Commission either. There's just... nothing."

Benedetta hurried back to her seat on the sofa and realigned her perfect posture.

"The alternative is simple. Cancel the contract, Stefano."

"What?"

I dropped my hands and opened my eyes to stare at her.

"You want to break our marriage contract? Is that why you showed up here this morning?"

She shook her head.

"I came because my father told me to. He said I needed to ease your cold feet. I was supposed to dangle myself in front of you and act like the doting bride, concerned about my future husband after a shootout in Brooklyn."

A bitter chuckle escaped me.

"And instead of playing the part, you would rather go back to your father and tell him you're no longer marrying me?"

Don Capaldo would not take that well.

Another small smile flickered over her lips, this time with less fury and more wry amusement.

"Well, it won't be pleasant. But I think it's the best course of action for now."

"So you're willing to let me call off this wedding so late in the game? What about your reputation? Even if I take the blame, you'll still be the one damaged by it. And I don't think you have time for your reputation to heal before your father must find you another husband."

She shrugged a bony shoulder.

"I'm willing to call it off myself. I have grounds for it, even if you didn't know you had a child. You do now. I don't want to be a home-wrecker, Stefano. And I refuse to have that innocent boy's blood on my hands.

"Nor do I want to be the other woman in my own home. But we both know my father would kill me, so you need to do it. Oh, he'll be furious for sure, but his anger will be directed at you instead of me."

I wasn't too concerned about a dying man's tantrum.

Let the old fucker be furious.

"You'll be ruined, Benedetta," I said. "I can do many things, but I can't stop the rumors. It doesn't matter what reason I give, rumors will circulate."

"I'd rather that than hurt the amazing little boy I just met downstairs. Yes, it'll be hard. No doubt. But I'm sure my father can quickly make another match. It won't be nearly as lucrative, of course, but it'll be something.

"Who knows? Maybe it's for the best. Maybe I'll end up with someone from the old country and move to some beautiful vineyard for the rest of my life and have a dozen children."

She couldn't fool me. I could see the sadness in her eyes. We both knew that wouldn't happen. She would be lucky to end up with the third son of a second-rate family.

Why would she ruin her own life for my son?

"Are you sure, Benedetta?"

She was giving up a lot to keep Enzo safe. Me too. If our marriage contract ended, I would lose her father's men and his fortune and my chance to gain more strength than the Commission had.

Christ, I'd just met the kid. It made no sense for me to be so willing, not given my history.

But I was willing. For my son, my flesh and blood.

Benedetta got up, pressed her hands down along her dress.

"I'm sure. It's settled. I'll leave you to handle the details and get back to your manhunt."

She went to the door but paused with her delicate fingers resting on the handle before turning back to me.

"Please speak to my father and make the announcement right away. At the very least, you can save me the added humiliation of being left at the altar."

I nodded, holding her gaze.

"Of course. If there's anything else I can do to ease the situation for you, don't hesitate to ask."

She returned the nod and then Benedetta Capaldo walked out of my office and likely out of my life for good.

After she'd gone, Tony knocked on the open door.

"Come in and shut the door behind you, Tony. Do you have something?"

"Not enough, boss, not yet. But now I can prove Benedetta isn't part of this."

"So prove it."

He bobbed his head up and down while placing a new phone on my desk.

"Phone is charged. Data transferred. And as for your fiancée, well, she was out of town until about two hours ago. We confirmed using her credit card records. I applied pressure on her maid, and she swore it too.

"Don Capaldo's and his captains' whereabouts are also accounted for. The Capaldo family is clear. And their staff."

I'd already come to the same conclusion during my conversation with Benedetta, but having proof never hurt.

"Check out every member of the Commission again," I ordered. "Dig deeper into their finances this time. You'll need a professional hacker, so call in a favor from Hastings."

"You mean the British guy from Wall Street?"

I nodded. "That's right. I granted him access to one of my buildings... he owes me."

"Got it, boss. I'll get right on it."

When I didn't offer further instructions, Tony tore out of my study, leaving me alone to think.

I moved to my desk, forcing myself to block the memory of Val lying on top, and focused on what needed to be done.

There had to be another way to look at this.

I pulled the first yellow envelope out of the drawer and went through the pictures again. So many. Different days, different seasons, multiple locations. Some taken with a magnified camera lens. Some captured at close range.

The connection I'd been missing hit me.

"You son of a bitch."

Whoever he was, he had some kind of privileged access to get close without being caught. It had to be someone Val knew. Nothing else tracked.

I snatched up the photos and jogged down the hallway.

Inside the security room, an enforcer watched the estate's monitors while Tony and Bruce scanned the city's feeds.

"Tony," I snapped. "Where are the photos from last night?"

He shook his head with a dumb fucking look on his face.

"The photos from last night? We didn't take any—"

"The photos from the second envelope, goddamn it, Tony."

He stood and held up the yellow envelope.

"Good. Go through them and find the similarities."

I shoved the photos in my hand at his chest.

"These too. Look for minor details that might give us some indicator about the shooter. Not just his identity but his profession, his height, his favorite spot for taking the photos. Anything that might seem remotely relevant.

"And search all images for his reflection. Windows, doors, vehicles. Every-fucking-thing reflective."

Bruce jumped up, the lines on his forehead deeper now.

"Something's up, boss. What is it?"

"The shooter knows Val and Enzo, and he had complete fucking access to them."

SIXTEEN
VAL

Benedetta Capaldo came back into the kitchen to say goodbye on her way out. She didn't hesitate to accept the bag of cookies Enzo had set aside for her.

I'd assumed she would politely decline with an excuse about too many carbs or maybe about fitting into her wedding dress.

She proved me wrong by opening the bag right away, pulling out a cookie, and devouring it.

Surprising move for a woman getting married the next day.

Had she just moaned while chewing the last bite?

"Oh god, how do they taste even better than they smell?"

Enzo put his quick-witted humor on full display for her. "Witchcraft."

Benedetta stared at him for a second, then she burst out laughing as he flashed a huge grin at her.

One day, my son would be a lady killer, likely sooner than later at this rate. There was no stopping it.

Like father, like son, damn it.

"Have another espresso with it. That's the secret," he added.

Mother of Christ, had he just winked at her?

Then he pushed a button on the espresso machine, waiting patiently for the little cup to fill before handing it to Benedetta.

Stefano's espresso machine made an excellent cup. If I could get away with it and didn't have to leave in a hurry when it was time, I would take it along with the robe I planned to steal.

When Benedetta and Enzo's small talk ended, she finished her drink with another cookie, then made her excuses to leave, hauling out with her a bag filled with a dozen cookies at my son's insistence.

He and I would have a talk about older women before long.

His reaction to her, and more importantly, her reaction to him, confirmed for me that Benedetta had nothing to do with the threat against us. She showed the same level of sweetness she had years ago, and I could see it was just as genuine now.

Shifting gears, I began preparing myself for Stefano's impending delivery of the "my fiancée doesn't want you and my bastard son living under my roof" speech.

I knew he had to do it, and I didn't blame Benedetta. Not after what had happened between Stefano and me in his office.

Knowing that speech would come should have thrilled me.

It would make things much easier when it came time for me to escape with my son, making the likelihood of getting out without being noticed higher. Exactly what I'd been hoping for.

Or was it?

The thought didn't give me the relief I had expected. No, a strange hollowness gnawed at my stomach instead.

A familiar sensation, the one I had experienced the day I discovered Stefano's true identity, then again when I realized I could never be with him.

But it didn't end there.

The feeling had returned when my one and only pregnancy

test revealed those two little pink lines. And then again more recently… just the night before when I forced myself to leave Stefano in his office alone.

Maybe five minutes later, he came in wearing black slacks and a dark blue shirt that made his eyes pop. He'd left the top buttons open, revealing some of the ink on his chest.

This man's presence when he entered a room was powerful.

The small smile dangling at the corner of his mouth made me wonder if he knew that, and if he knew how devastatingly handsome he looked.

I shivered.

He waved the yellow envelope in his hand, and I assumed it contained whatever he'd prepared to give me in exchange for taking Enzo and leaving his house and his life forever.

I didn't want his money, but turning it down might prolong the entire situation.

We both needed out.

As Stefano approached the island, he held my gaze, and his eyes grew darker.

"Let's talk," he said.

I smiled, quickly realizing how many times I'd offered the same fake smile to the unpleasant customers at Con Amore. The people I didn't want to deal with.

"Of course, but privately." I turned to Enzo. "Hey buddy, why don't you head to your room and get cleaned up, then watch a little TV?"

My son studied my face for a minute, then hit Stefano with a serious expression that I'd never seen on my baby's face before.

Then Enzo pulled his gaze back to me and smiled.

"Okay, Mama. See you later."

As he headed upstairs, the oven's timer went off, conveniently giving me a minute to gather my thoughts while I pulled out the cookie sheets, set them on the counter, slid the last two into the oven, and set a final timer for baking.

When I turned around, Stefano had started on a cookie while nailing me with a heated but otherwise unreadable stare.

"So when does she want us out?" I asked.

I supposed I could have danced around the subject and extended the fantasy I'd stupidly allowed myself to fall into over the last few hours, but that would just make the inevitable even more painful.

"When does who 'want you out' of where?"

Stefano took another bite of his cookie, his lips lifting into a slight smile as he chewed.

I'd forgotten these were his favorite.

Keeping my eyes focused on the motion of the dishcloth, I wiped down the back countertop.

"Your fiancée," I said. "She's beautiful."

"Is she? I hadn't noticed."

I rolled my eyes.

"Umm, yes, you have. Men like you always notice a beautiful woman."

"I might notice when a woman is attractive, Valerie, but I haven't thought of another woman as beautiful in a decade."

The smoothness of his words made my legs weaken and my heart flutter.

And I hated him for it.

I hated how easily he manipulated me into wanting him.

"Look," I blurted. "I don't know what kind of arrangement you and Benedetta have, and it's none of my business. But I need you to know I will never be your mistress or your whore or the woman on the side, whatever you want to call it. Benedetta deserves better than that, and so do I."

The words tumbled out of my mouth in a heated, slurred mess, and I hoped he understood because I couldn't bear to look up and meet his eyes again.

I couldn't risk him seeing the lie in mine.

After snatching up a spatula, I moved cookies from a baking sheet to the cooling rack, focusing so intently on the task that I didn't hear Stefano come around the island. I didn't realize he stood behind me until he put his hands on my waist and pulled me backward against his chest.

He smelled so good, the rich spice and woody notes in his cologne overlapping but not overpowering his own scent.

I wanted to turn and bury my face in the hollow of his throat and let him hold me. Instead, I didn't respond at all, keeping my eyes on the cookies.

He slid his hands to my hips and spoke close to my ear.

"I need you to tell me about the men in your life."

"Stefano," I whispered. "That's none of your business."

It might have been convincing if I hadn't been so breathless.

I still couldn't hide how his touch affected me.

"I promise you, this isn't about me being possessive, Val. I'm not jealous, and I won't get mad. But I need to know about the different men in your life. All of them."

"It doesn't matter."

"It absolutely matters," he growled. "No one touches you but me. Your body belongs to me, and you will not allow another man to have what is mine."

The liar. He did get jealous and a little angry.

And I liked it.

I had to brace myself against the counter to keep from

melting into him. If I wasn't careful, our desk session would repeat itself right there in the kitchen. Then I would probably have to explain to Enzo why I had powdered sugar in my hair.

"How does your fiancée feel about that?"

If my question wasn't enough to douse us both with metaphorical ice water, I didn't know what else could.

It seemed to work because he stepped back and tossed the yellow envelope around me onto the island.

A cloud of powdered sugar puffed into the air beneath the envelope's weight slapping down onto the stone.

"What's this?" I asked.

"It's why I need to know everything."

I opened the envelope and removed its contents. More pictures like those in the first envelope he'd shown me, but now there were even more. Many included similar shots of Enzo and me walking to school, spending the day at the park, shopping...

Bile rose in my throat as I stared at a new type of photo.

The pictures focused on Enzo and me together or just one of us alone, but they no longer remained purely in public places. No, now I saw images of my son and me on the couch reading or together in the back of the café. Someone had taken photos right outside our apartment.

Someone had been watching us in our home.

One showed Enzo in his bed, where he should have been safe and comfortable in the privacy of his own home. Several other photos had captured shots of me through my bedroom window while I undressed to get ready for bed.

These were intimate, private moments of our lives.

My heart raced.

I had never felt so violated.

"Not just your lovers," Stefano said. "I need to know about

friends, employees, vendors, the men who are regulars at the café. Anyone you interact with frequently."

While trying my best to hold back the tears threatening to spill over, I looked up at him.

"Why?" I choked out.

How could I have failed so miserably and remained so clueless until now?

He pulled me against his body again, as if that might be the secret password to get me to tell him everything all at once.

"Just tell me, Val."

He felt so warm, so safe. I wanted to close my eyes and indulge in the fantasy of this being my life, of this being my kitchen, my home, with my husband holding me and cherishing me while our son was safe and protected upstairs in his room.

Where some psycho with a camera and a rifle couldn't get to us.

I'd been so stupid.

I didn't understand how they observed us so closely and for so long. I should have run the first time I felt the eyes on me. This mess was all my fault, the product of my recklessness and complacency.

Whoever had taken the photos, they found it possible because of me. Because I'd gotten too comfortable in my cozy little life.

Now it was only a matter of time before another someone came to find me and take me back.

Stefano wasn't the only one I had to protect Enzo from... I needed to remember what was at stake, the whole picture. If the other man found me, if he found my son, it would all be over.

I needed to run fast and far.

But would any place be far enough away to keep us safe?

I had no idea. I'd gotten myself in too deep. The whole thing was completely beyond me.

Stefano pressed his lips to my temple for a surprisingly tender kiss, pulling me back into the present moment.

"What are you thinking about right now?" he asked. "When you see these pictures, what name flashes through your mind? There must be at least one."

He wanted to know what my instincts told me at first sight.

There had been a name, but the man that name belonged to couldn't have done this. No, much too sloppy. He wouldn't have allowed that.

If it had been that person, that name, I wouldn't have made it this far. Stefano would have been dead by now, and Enzo ripped from my arms to fulfill a familial obligation. And me? They would have sent me away to repay a debt that ended only with my life.

I had no more power than that in this person's eyes. Just a bargaining chip and a whore, and that was all.

"I don't know," I murmured.

Because I didn't.

The monster I feared more than any other simply couldn't have been the one behind it.

The threat on our lives right now wasn't nearly as big as the threat Stefano posed to my son, but it was still far more dangerous than I could handle.

Then again, whatever Stefano might do to me was nothing compared to the horrors waiting for me in Chicago.

I turned in Stefano's arms to face him, looking into his eyes.

"Tell me why this is happening. I want to know the truth. Tell me what they want."

"They want me to call off the wedding," he said. "They

want to make sure I don't marry Benedetta tomorrow. And they got their wish. The wedding is off."

"Well, that's a nice sentiment, but tell me what you're actually going to do."

I didn't believe for one second he could truly give up a beautiful bride like that, not to mention the Capaldo fortune right along with her.

"That is what I'm doing."

Stefano dipped his head closer, his dark eyes searching mine.

"The wedding's off. Whoever is doing this gets exactly what he wants. I'm going to continue letting him think he has won, that he wore me down, but I'm still going to hunt him down, and when I find him, I'll destroy him—"

"And then you'll marry Benedetta," I finished.

He touched my cheek with the back of his warm fingers.

"No. I said there will be no wedding."

I shook my head and let out a small, nervous laugh.

"You don't have to lie to me. You're not doing that for a woman you forgot about and a child you didn't even know you had. I know you, Stefano. You'll never give up control of the two largest mafia families outside of the Commission."

He gripped my upper arms, pushing me back, and the intensity of his gaze flared to a new level.

"How do you know about that?"

My heartbeat thumped in my throat. My mouth ran dry. But somehow, I shrugged it off and pretended like I didn't know what he was talking about.

"I don't know," I said. "In passing conversation? I've been overhearing a lot of talk between you and your men."

Then I flinched, realizing I'd just made one of the biggest

mistakes of all. I'd shown him a glimpse of my cards, at the wrong time, for the wrong reason.

How fucking stupid could I be, over and over again?

Stefano dug his fingers deeper into my flesh.

His jaw muscle flexed.

"My men don't discuss those details around you, Valerie, and the Commission is the last thing on anyone's mind right now. Because we're focused on finding the son of a bitch who tried to murder you and our son."

He tilted his head and studied my face, his painful grip bruising my arms.

"How do you know so much about Benedetta's family? And how the fuck do you know anything about the goddamn Commission?"

SEVENTEEN
STEFANO

Val had fucked up big time, and I did not appreciate being played. Whatever her game, it wasn't the time for it.

I let go of her and pushed her against the counter with my body, flattening my hands on the granite on either side of her to cage her inside my arms, so she couldn't turn away from me.

A goddamn erection pushed at my slacks.

Not the time for that either.

I knew what Val wanted.

Having power meant there would always be someone trying to take it away from me.

Seemed even Val wanted it.

Nothing attracted people to a man like me more than the desire to feel the strength of his power. Not even money. I had to be on guard all the time, in every situation, including with those I wanted to trust.

Trust had never come easily to me because I knew very well about the dangers of losing it.

My father and my brother had been way too trusting. And in the end, that oversight and their arrogance got them killed.

I wouldn't allow myself to be destroyed by that same shit. If my reactions sometimes bordered on paranoia, so be it.

"Tell me how you know about the families," I repeated.

I didn't want to hurt Val, but maybe scaring her enough to show her how serious I was about getting answers would get her to open up to me.

She shoved at my chest.

"Because I know who you are, Stefano, and I told you I wanted nothing to do with the way you live your life. But I wasn't stupid enough to believe you wouldn't ever come looking for me and find my son, so I've watched your world. To be prepared."

"To be prepared? What the fuck does that even mean?"

"Do you know how many journalists out there walk the streets of New York, searching for the next breaking mafia story? And of course there's social media. You can literally find information about the families on the internet.

"Oh, and what about the low-rent mob bosses constantly brag about their low-level shit on public sites? You should look into that."

I nodded. I would absolutely have that investigated.

"So you researched me? And Benedict Capaldo as well?"

I paused, inhaling her distracting scent while giving her a minute to consider how she wanted to continue responding to my questions.

Christ, why hadn't I ever completed that background check on her? I'd started the process, but something inside me just couldn't do it. I was blind to what I thought was her innocence.

She pushed at me again, gently this time, and nodded.

"Yes, I guess you could call it that. I keep my eyes open. For

Enzo's sake, how could I not? There are thousands of blogs written about New York's mafia dons and countless articles published about the city's wealthiest families.

"God, Stefano, Benedetta Capaldo walked right in and introduced herself to a stranger using her very recognizable name. I can't even tell you how many articles I've seen about her father. It makes sense for someone like you to marry a woman like her."

"Well now I'm not marrying her," I said, staring at Val.

Val's explanation might have made sense, might have been logical, but it didn't feel right in my gut.

Sure, I could successfully threaten the editor of *The New York Times*. But I couldn't shut down the social media giants. I couldn't take down every blogger writing about their mob conspiracy theories. Most of them were full of shit anyway and had zero evidence to support their claims.

Now and then, when one of their claims hit a little too close to home, my lawyers handled those.

Most of those websites didn't report the full truth about mafia life, and Val certainly didn't seem like the type to waste her time with conspiracy theories.

If she had been so worried about me finding out about my son, why didn't she leave the city instead of staying in the same fucking place?

I scoffed at the thought of it all and then narrowed my eyes.

Something still didn't add up.

"Social media, blogs, that's it?"

"That's it," she hissed.

Then, after glancing down at the bulge in my slacks, she tore away from me with a new fire lit in her eyes.

"Are you happy now, Stefano? Did you squeeze all the information you needed out of me? Yes, okay? I spent more time than I should have scanning those ridiculous websites for stories by amateur journalists because I'm afraid. I wanted to know how to keep you from corrupting my son."

"Our son," I corrected.

She pushed out a heavy sigh.

"Are we done now?"

My paranoia had subsided. To be fair, she'd been right about our son, but now it was too late for that.

We still had some unfinished business.

"Not quite yet, Valerie."

She put her hands on her hips and gave me a fake smile.

"Oh, don't worry. As soon as you eliminate this threat against my child, we'll be out of your way, and you can get back to your plans for world domination. You can build your empire as vast and as brutally as you like... just leave me and my son out of it."

Not an option. She had to know that by now. She had to know I would no longer let them go. Didn't matter what I had to do or say to make it so.

She belonged to me. And she would only be safe with me.

No world existed in which I would not be in our son's life.

No reality remained in which she didn't spend all her nights in my bed.

That time had passed.

Val went back to cleaning the kitchen, wiping down the island countertop as I watched and considered spelling out her new reality for her in terms she wouldn't misunderstand.

No, too soon.

She would fight me. She might even do something stupid.

Like try to run.

To get Val to stay with me where she belonged, I had to show her a few things. Enzo would never again truly be safe anywhere but here under my roof. And she couldn't be happy anywhere but here with me. I had to show her what I could provide for her and our son.

In the event she refused to see those things, refused to do the right thing, then I would cross that bridge if we came to it.

The front entrance door slammed shut, something that always pissed me off.

A few seconds later, Tony came into the kitchen carrying a dark red envelope, and immediately I recognized the raised gold lettering on the front.

Fuck. The day just kept getting better.

Without saying a word, I took the envelope from him but didn't bother opening it right there. Everyone in New York knew what this envelope contained.

I'd just received an invitation.

The kind of invitation I couldn't ignore, not yet... but soon.

"We'll finish this later," I said. "I want the names, Valerie. All of them. Make a list while I'm gone."

She rolled her eyes as she offered Tony a plate of cookies that he greedily accepted.

"If you say so," she said.

Her bratty dismissal of me in my own kitchen made me want to bend her over my knee and show her what happened to insolent little girls.

The time would come when she found her place by my side in public, on her knees in private, and in my bed every night.

Soon. The time would come.

I gnashed my teeth as I headed for the staircase, needing to get away from her, needing to clear my head before dealing with what waited for me inside the red envelope.

Upstairs in my office, it seemed lonelier than usual. The energy seemed different. So much had happened in the room over the last twenty-four hours.

After sitting down at my desk, in my father's heavy leather chair, I glanced over at the box holding Val's necklace. It still belonged to her, and one day she would wear it.

I shook my head, pushed my hand back through my hair.

The empty feeling inside would fade away as soon as I got down to business. It always did.

Gripping the envelope, I sliced the fucking thing open.

Edgardo Lordi.

The man who'd had my father killed. And my brother.

Lordi was many things. A brilliant strategist. An ambitious, successful man. A man whose ambition had led him to break with Cosa Nostra code by taking out another boss without having the Commission's permission.

A power-hungry, neurotic fuck yet to be punished for it.

This man viewed the pomp and circumstance of clandestine meetings arranged by secret envelopes as a show of strength.

I saw it as cowardice.

Don Lordi surrounded himself with bodyguards and enforcers and shrouded himself in the mystery of a ceremony because he didn't truly have what it took to protect his empire.

From someone like me.

The invitation served as his demand for my immediate presence. He wanted to talk.

I didn't think it had anything to do with Enzo. That wasn't Lordi's style. He had more wisdom than to hire someone as sloppy as the Con Amore shooter. And if he wanted to take out my son, he wouldn't tell me about it.

Granted, killing the boy in front of me would have been cruel. But showing me that I had a son just to take him away would have made this whole thing very personal.

Lordi always separated business from personal.

Even when removing my father and brother from the equation, it wasn't personal to him. The man's motives had been straightforward. Take my father's power and ensure my brother would never come after Lordi seeking revenge.

What was I to this man?

He had let me live as a show of good will, because I didn't pose a threat to him. More than that, the Commission had left me in place to pick up the pieces of my family. They hadn't allowed Lordi to absorb my men or undermine my authority as next in line to inherit my father's empire.

It all worked out for Lordi. He'd eliminated his competition for the open seat and made me look weak, making my father's connections believe the Vignali organization had become too inconsequential for anyone to worry about.

The last part of his plan didn't work for long.

Lordi was aware of that now. He'd underestimated me.

I dropped the invitation on my desk and texted Tony to let him know we were leaving and to have him tell my driver to pull the car around. Then I went to the armoire to put on one of my black three-piece suits and a dark red shirt.

Once my father's style, now mine.

No one could deny I was my father's son.

Lordi would notice the strong resemblance, and I wanted him to see it. I wanted him to remark on it. I wanted to force him to face the product of his betrayal.

Me.

I doubted it would shake him up, but I wanted him to know he hadn't completely defeated my family.

His men would search me upon arrival. Only a fool would allow a man with a vendetta to enter his establishment and his presence with a weapon.

Didn't matter. I wouldn't go unarmed.

I put a forty-five in my crossover holster, fitted a pistol at the small of my back, and put another in my ankle holster. All uncomfortable and not as practical as the movies made it seem. I hated that misconception.

Then I added two knives, one custom made to slide through my belt loops behind the belt and another in the sole of my shoe. Again, not comfortable. But being within spitting distance of that fucking rat, I would enjoy my discomfort.

Back downstairs, I found Val on her way out of the kitchen. I grabbed her and kissed her hard, showing her one of those things she needed to see, that she was mine.

"I need to go for a sit-down," I said, close to her lips.

She blinked up at me, her cheeks pink, little puffs of breath coming from her pretty mouth.

I had to step back to pull myself away.

"Before I leave, Val, I want to make a few things clear."

"Okay," she whispered.

"Our conversation isn't over. We'll pick it up again tonight, in my room. I'm not going to marry Benedetta. And you are certainly no one's whore."

Then I kissed her again, not allowing her to respond.

This time she tried to fight me, but only for a second, then her beautiful, soft body melted against mine. She kissed me back, pushing her hands into my hair, claiming me just as fiercely as I claimed her.

Val might not have fully accepted it yet, but her heart and her body knew she belonged to me.

FIFTY-FIVE MINUTES LATER

It took nearly an hour in the city traffic to reach the restaurant where Don Lordi waited for me.

As Jimmy pulled up in front of the building, I noted the red brick construction, no streetside windows, a striped awning leading up to the entrance, and potted Italian cypress trees framing the door.

I'd never been inside. It sat too far out of my territory.

"Could this guy be any more of a cliché?" Tony asked.

I double checked the mags in my pistols. Force of habit. They would take my weapons before I got beyond the vestibule.

"There'll be cannoli on the table by his revolver," I said.

We got out of the car, and I headed for the door with Tony covering my back two steps behind and two to the right. He understood the assignment.

As soon as we entered the first set of doors, two of Lordi's men approached with blank expressions. They patted me down first, taking my phone and just one of my guns.

The lazy fucks.

I'd punish my men for that kind of mistake.

Either they were half asleep, or they had grossly underestimated my ability to threaten their boss.

A grave mistake for Lordi, underestimating me.

Tony received a more thorough pat down, getting stripped of his phone and all weapons other than his ankle piece.

Unlike my own men, Lordi's guys apparently received no instruction to check below the knee.

Stupidly satisfied, the two of them led us through a dining room full of red chairs and white linen tablecloths to Lordi's area in the back.

The restaurant echoed with emptiness, of course.

I'd expected a little more class once we reached the back, but it turned out to be just as fucking tacky. Old wood paneling on the walls, seats upholstered in either red faux leather or red velvet, tablecloths draped over three tables. Taper candles shoved into old Chianti bottles.

I never understood bosses like Don Lordi, those who got lost in mafia mystique, making it seem as if they belonged on the set of *The Godfather*.

Why play at being a mafioso when you were one? Why imitate a stereotype when you knew there was more to it?

Then again, maybe stripping away the ambience, the props, and the bad acting might reveal how Edgardo Lordi wasn't all that impressive.

At least the room smelled of good quality tomato sauce.

Well, surprise, surprise. Lordi sat with two others from the Commission, drinking wine and dining on prosciutto.

I approached the table without acknowledging the extras. They weren't important right now. Instead, I stared at Lordi's fat pock-marked face and jerked my chin up at him.

"What the fuck do you want?" I asked.

"Stefano Vignali, my boy, take a seat."

He motioned to the empty chair at the table, a seat lower than the others. A little game to make me feel smaller than him and his companions. Only men who knew their power remained vulnerable stooped to using such cheap tricks.

"I'll stand," I said flatly. "This won't be a long conversation. And I'm not your boy. Now tell me why I'm here."

His lip curled in some deformed version of a sneer. Then he addressed his companions.

"He not only looks like his father, but he behaves like him too, doesn't he, boys? Same arrogance in his walk. Same cock-sure attitude."

The other men chuckled. I ignored them.

My focus centered only on the threat in front of me.

"You should be careful, boy. That arrogance is what got your father killed," Lordi added.

"I disagree. It was his inability to identify a rat," I said.

Although I presented them with an outwardly calm demeanor, my patience crumbled second by second. Before Lordi could respond, I went on.

"He trusted you. But you should know that I do not make the mistakes my father made. So what's this about?"

Lordi put down his glass, sat back in his chair, and moved his gaze up and down, inspecting me from head to toe before speaking again.

"You know, boy, I've known you for your entire life. I've got to admit, I never thought much of you. Neither did your father if you want to know the truth. He always said you would have made a better girl. Because you were too weak to lead, on your own or at your brother's side."

I forced out a dry fucking laugh.

"Funny, he always said you were a loyal friend. My father was a poor judge of character, and we all know that now. I'm still waiting for you to make your point."

"My point is, yes, you proved him wrong. Your father and I both underestimated you. From the moment he bled out in the street, you started showing the families you were stronger than we thought. Certainly stronger than I imagined. I respect that.

"You pulled it together and kept your family's legacy intact with no outside guidance. I admired that in you, boy, for a time. But now your strength and intelligence have drawn more than admiration. It's drawing attention and making waves.

"One might even say you've become a threat to us all, and I think it's time the Commission deals with you."

EIGHTEEN

VAL

The front door closed softly behind Stefano as he left the house with his underboss and his lead enforcer.

I would give it fifteen minutes.

It seemed like the longest fifteen minutes of my life, standing around in the kitchen, my arms braced on the island countertop while I stared at the clock.

When the small hand finally landed on roman numeral three, the silence around the house and outside in the front courtyard convinced me he'd cleared the property.

My opportunity had arrived.

A pain struck me in the stomach.

Still, after all my planning, I had doubts. Because whoever had come after my son remained at large, free as a bird.

I suspected if not Benedetta, then it had to be the Commission. Stefano's marriage to the Capaldo princess would have shifted the power balance in the city, and the Commission would want to stop that before it became a reality.

No other explanation made sense to me.

Even if there was someone else, they got what they wanted...

Stefano did indeed call off the wedding.

Enzo should be safe now, at least long enough for me to get him out of the state.

Time to run.

I left the kitchen, keeping my stride slow and casual, despite the adrenaline rushing through me. I called out to the guys who Stefano left behind and told them the cookies wouldn't be quite as good if they fully cooled down. A lie.

One of the guards thanked me as he and another cohort hurried to the kitchen.

Smiling down at them, I climbed the stairs and headed to our temporary suite. When I opened the door, Enzo lay on his bed with his arms wrapped around the same pillow he rested his head on and watched a Disney movie on the room's large flatscreen TV.

Nervousness kicked into high gear. My hands shook.

"Get up now, Enzo." I said. "Get your shoes. We're leaving."

He stared at me for a minute, then he sighed in a big way that deflated his entire body.

Disappointment. I could handle that.

I knew he liked Stefano's house, even if we hadn't been there for a full twenty-four hours. He enjoyed the big bed and the TV, the space I'd given him, and the idea of having a father around.

Disappointing him was the last thing I wanted to do, but it was necessary. As his mother, I had to keep him safe first and foremost, and seeing my baby's disappointment had to be the price I paid. And because of our dangerous situation, I would pay it ten times over if necessary.

He didn't argue, though. He nodded, slipped on his shoes, and grabbed his book.

After making sure I had everything we needed, I ordered a car to pick us up on the street behind the estate.

We crept down the staircase, careful to not make any noise.

The plush carpets along the hallway muffled the tapping of our footsteps. The challenge was crossing the open foyer to the front door. You could see the front door from the kitchen.

With my back pressed against the wall, I ignored my slamming pulse and the sweat dampening my hair on the back of my neck as I peeked into the kitchen.

The two men still hung around the island, talking loudly as they stuffed their mouths full of cookies. Good. The cookie distraction turned out to be a win.

I turned back to my son, nodded at him, and mouthed the words, "You go first."

Enzo gazed into the kitchen to make sure no one saw him, then he darted over to the front door.

Using only my hands, I signaled for him to stay right there. He understood. Then I waited thirty seconds to make my move, counting them down in my head.

The loud conversation in the kitchen continued on and on.

Why weren't they watching the door? Oh, heads were going to roll when their boss returned.

I stared into the kitchen for a few more seconds. Still clear.

Right now, these trained men working for the notorious Stefano Vignali were more concerned about who could fit more cookies in their mouth.

The nasty part of me hoped for one of them to choke.

With a deep breath and forced courage, I darted across the floor to join Enzo, where he waited for me by the door.

No shouts for me to stop. No running, no footsteps at all.

So, as quickly as we could, Enzo and I slipped out the front door. It seemed way too easy, and that pushed the level of my nervousness higher.

No way would I breathe easily again until I had the confirmation for our airline tickets in my hand, and Enzo and I sat on a moving train headed out of the city.

Strangely, in that very moment as we escaped down the front steps, I couldn't help noticing how the bright afternoon sun warmed up the chilly autumn breeze.

Neither of us said anything as we crept along the cobblestone driveway, ducking behind trees and shrubs, only to run into the huge wrought iron gate holding us on the estate like prisoners. A brick wall stretched along the property on either side of the gate.

There had to be a door somewhere.

Enzo grabbed my arm and pulled me behind a shrub just before the gate swung open and a black sedan passed through it.

Not Stefano's car.

I caught a glimpse of the man in the back through his open window. Much older, smoking a cigar, and his skin appeared an unhealthy shade of gray. He had to be ill.

My first thought landed on Benedetta's father, Benedict Capaldo, but I couldn't be one-hundred percent sure. The man in the vehicle seemed like a ghost compared to the pictures I'd seen online.

As the car made its way up the drive, my son and I used the opportunity to slide through the gates before they closed and locked us in again. We made it just as they shut behind us.

"Run, Enzo," I shouted.

We ran hand in hand until we reached the little blue car idling at the curb, waiting for us. We darted to one side, and as soon as I verified the driver's identification, we slid onto the back seat and slammed the doors shut.

"Lock the door. Push the button on your side," I said.

No one said a word on the drive to Brooklyn, not the driver, not my son, not me.

My mind jumped into overdrive, moving through all my various mental lists of what needed to be done now that we were out of the house and away from Stefano's estate.

We wouldn't be able to use the café's front door, so we would have to use the rear entrance and head straight up the backstairs to the apartment.

Enzo and I needed to each pack a small bag, sticking to only the essentials. I planned to grab our passports and other fake documents quickly, and then we could be back out of there in less than ten minutes.

From there, we would take the second car I had ordered and go to the bank, so I could get everything out of my safe deposit box. Money for the airline tickets. A burner phone for booking flights.

For my son and me, a flight heading west. Maybe Phoenix. Maybe Los Angeles.

Then we would have to ditch our real IDs and get to the train station first before going to the airport.

Four train tickets then... two adults, one child, and an infant. And purchasing them with cash would make it a hell of a lot harder to track down. Whichever train left the earliest. The first one heading south would be the one Enzo and I would travel on.

The driver hit a big ass pothole, and Enzo banged his head on the window.

I reached over and touched his cheek. He hated it when I fussed over those things. He wanted to be tough like his...

No, like himself.

With any luck at all, my son and I would be out of New York before Stefano found out we were missing.

Once he found out, the situation could still get messy.

It would get really messy.

Stefano would track my movements by following the money, or try to anyway. The trail would be easy to follow at first. An Uber to my apartment and then to the bank.

A man like Stefano with vast resources could easily track down the airline tickets purchased under our real names as well.

I didn't have any idea if his reach extended to TSA agents. I knew he could call the mayor. He could bribe someone to put a block on our IDs. Maybe even get us added to a no-fly list.

But none of that mattered.

They would find our seats empty on that flight.

Even if he saw through my fake money trail and checked the train station, no one could tell him about a woman who had bought a ticket for herself and a young boy.

Witnesses would only remember the information I fed them. A young mother trying to keep her cranky toddler happy while her husband changed the baby's diaper in the restroom.

Claiming to be a family of four and making the story easily memorable would make us much harder to track.

Only when we made it safely out of this entire region of the country would I sit down with Enzo and explain everything to him. I would tell him the whole truth. I would finally tell him about my family and Stefano's family.

My son would get the actual story this time.

He deserved that and more. He deserved to know why he could never go back.

But not until we made it safely to our destination.

Finally, after another fucking pothole, we were two blocks away from Con Amore, and I asked the driver to stop. Then my son and I ran the remaining distance to the back of the café.

Even with the colder autumn air, the alleyway reeked of trash and urine, though it smelled more bearable than during the hot summer months.

We dodged broken glass, bags of trash, and stray cats, and when we reached the rear entrance to the café, yellow crime scene tape and a sign posted by the police blocked the door.

"Wait here, Enzo. Stay put for just a second," I said.

"Hurry, Mama."

I broke through the tape and unlocked the door.

An image in my mind of all the shattered glass and furniture hit me. I couldn't bear to see it with my own eyes again, the carnage left behind in the attack. Everything we had, destroyed. I just couldn't do it.

So I didn't open the door between the kitchen and the dining room. Instead, I pressed my ear against it and shut my eyes. Maybe if I listened hard enough, I could confirm the emptiness of the place without looking.

Completely, eerily silent.

I returned to the back door and extended my hand to Enzo. He grabbed on, and we went up the back staircase to our apartment together.

No yellow police tape there.

Either the cops had been too careless to bother coming upstairs or they had considered it and kept it separate from the crime scene.

A comforting thought. A stupid thought.

"Come on, buddy. Change and pack for three days."

I kept my voice at a half whisper.

"Socks and underwear too. Put everything in your backpack. Two books, that's it. Do you understand me, Enzo?"

"Yes, I got it," he said.

I watched him tiptoe to his bedroom. Then I squeezed my eyes shut and prayed I made the right decisions for my child.

In my room, I grabbed a duffel bag from the closet, shoved my bed aside, and pulled up two loose floorboards. In that dark little hidey-hole were stacks of cash, one-hundred and fifty thousand in large bills, ten thousand in small bills, and plastic bags containing our new identities.

I threw it all into the bag and put my clothes on top.

We needed to move freely and blend in, so I unzipped my dress and let it fall to the floor. I shoved my legs into a pair of jeans, pulled on a plain old sweater, and laced up my sneakers.

As I circled back to my bag and double checked everything, Enzo came in and handed me a framed photo of the woman who had taken me in when I arrived in Brooklyn.

My generous, beautiful, loving nonna.

We had our arms around each other in front of Con Amore while smiling at the camera.

Enzo must have gone downstairs very quietly, and the fact that he'd risked himself for that photo made my eyes burn with unshed tears. Tears of love. Tears of fear.

I wiped my eyes.

Swallowed the lump in my throat.

Kissed my thoughtful son on his forehead.

"You ready to go?" I asked.

"Yeah, I just have to put on my good high tops."

"Perfect. Go on, baby, and get them. Hurry."

He ran to his room, and I took a deep breath, slowly releasing it, collecting myself and my thoughts.

Stefano hadn't discovered we were gone yet. He would have been blowing up my phone by now on his way to come and get us if he knew. So far, my plan had worked.

Yes, I was on the run again, but at least I had some experience with it this time, and that should help me keep Enzo safe.

The bell hanging above the door downstairs jingled.

My heart raced, but I couldn't move my feet.

I opened my mouth to call for Enzo. Nothing came out.

Glass crunched beneath heavy footsteps.

Footsteps that came closer and closer to the back staircase.

NINETEEN

STEFANO

I gave Don Lordi and his two companions a bored stare.

I would not be intimidated.

"Good, by all means, deal with me," I said. "You believe my father never respected me and that I've become a threat to the balance of power in New York. Now that we've established your beliefs, why am I really here?"

Lordi flashed a knowing smile.

I wanted to rip his face off. I flexed my fists at my sides.

Heat blasted up the back of my shirt onto my neck.

The smug bastard had racked up an enormous debt with me, and he would settle it in full with his blood and his bones. But not quite yet. It was part of a greater plan.

I met his eyes with mine again, holding his gaze with the same blank stare my father had given me whenever he thought I wasted his time.

"These younger men are always so impatient," Lordi said.

The others laughed into their Chianti glasses.

Christ, it was like watching one of those Broadway mobster

musicals where the fat diva sat in the middle while smaller backup singers flanked his sides to make him look better.

Never trust a man who surrounds himself with yes-men...

One of my first lessons learned after taking over my family.

Those men never seemed to value the opinions or advice of others but instead parroted the words of their boss back at him, like these two idiots at the table were now doing for Lordi.

That made their world very small.

It also made men like Lordi overly confident, a trait that could become a weakness to be leveraged against him.

On the other hand, it also made him a genuine threat. Arrogant. Unafraid. Destructive. Acting like "a bull in a China shop," as my grandmother had always said.

"My impatience has nothing to do with my age," I said.

Then I lowered my voice to signal an impending warning.

He'd deliberately not answered my question again.

"I'm a busy man with important business matters to handle, and this waste of my time affects my patience."

"Ah. Yes, I hear congratulations are in order. Taking the Capaldo girl as your bride is definitely important business. You've managed to grab yourself a fine young woman. Not to mention she comes with one hell of a dowry. Her father's men will be yours within the year.

"We know Benedict Capaldo is a very sick man with one foot already in the grave. Seems the princess's uncles have disappeared, as have her brothers, and all under mysterious circumstances, I hear."

"Is that right?" I asked. "I hadn't heard. The Capaldo family certainly wouldn't be the first to suffer a string of terrible luck."

Almost a confession on my part.

He knew it as well as I did.

Showing my cards? Not at all. I'd just added to the pot.

Lordi shifted his fat ass around in his chair, and his expression darkened.

"Yes, well, that terrible luck means a great deal for you. If you're married to Capaldo's daughter when he dies, you'll be entitled to his empire. How convenient for you."

I offered a halfhearted shrug.

"That's my business, not yours. You still haven't gotten to the point. I hope you do still have one."

"My point, boy, is your wedding. I invited you here to make an offer... let's just call it a wedding gift."

Nothing good could follow that statement.

I stood still with my shoulders relaxed despite my pulse rushing inside my ears. Whatever game this prick had in mind, I didn't like being at a disadvantage.

This rat bastard clearly had a plan.

He wouldn't have called me here if not.

I'd assumed I would have him figured out by this time. Unfortunately, he gave nothing away, leaving me with no idea what to expect.

Fuck. I needed to get out of there.

I brought my expression into check, realizing I'd narrowed my eyes, and went back to my indifferent stare.

"Well, I'm sure Benedetta is registered at Neiman Marcus and Saks. I hear she loves all things red."

The men laughed. I waited for their wine-soaked chuckles to stop. Barely four in the afternoon, and these assholes were well on their way to being intoxicated.

Drinking so early in the day was a rookie mistake, even for someone like Lordi. It made men slow and careless. I could have drawn my pistol and put a bullet between his eyes before the other two realized what had happened.

For a second, I let myself entertain the fantasy. But it would force the other Commission members to retaliate. I would be no better than him for doing the same to my father.

And I had a son to protect now.

I wouldn't be satisfied with just Lordi's corpse at my feet. I wanted them all. When the right time came.

Lordi went on again after slurping the last of his wine.

"No, you misunderstand me, boy. We've done the math and decided you've earned a place at the table. We want you to take your family's seat with the Commission. You've more than proven your worth, even as your father's son. But we won't hold that against you."

More chuckles from the drinkers.

I scoffed without bothering to hide my contempt.

"My grandfather was a founding member of this committee. He drafted the articles that now keep the families from waging war and shedding blood in the streets. Without the Vignalis, the Commission wouldn't exist, and we wouldn't be any better than the savages in Chicago."

Lordi opened his mouth to say something.

I put up my hand to shut him down.

"I have more right to a seat than most of you, so don't fucking insinuate that my family fell out of favor, Lordi. We were betrayed. My father had the right to lead the Commission, and you betrayed him. So why the hell would I want a seat at the table with men I can't trust?"

Lordi nodded as if he were considering my words. His six chins squished together, preventing his head from moving too far forward.

"I understand why you think someone betrayed your father, Stefano. Maybe you're right. But that's for God to decide. The choice I made was based on how unfit your father became to lead the committee. Bad tempered. Shortsighted. All the signs of a weak man.

"You've clearly inherited your father's rage, but unlike him, you've learned to manage it. You shape it into a finely honed blade as another tool in your arsenal, not letting it drive every move you make the way your father did."

"You don't fucking know me," I snarled.

"I know you better than any other living person. I observe what happens when you're angry. I see what happens when you let it go. I know you control it with the strength of a man far older and with far more experience than you have."

This man loved to hear his own voice. He kept going on.

"You know when to use that strength, boy, and when to show mercy. You know how to bide your time to make more strategic moves. A skill your father never quite grasped."

He wasn't wrong.

My father certainly had his faults, his temper worst of all. I realized years ago that his temper and the rash decisions he'd made because of it caused more problems than they ever solved.

But just because I agreed with that one point didn't mean I would overlook what Lordi had done to my family.

"What if I choose not to sit at the table?" I asked. "What happens then?"

"If you marry the Capaldo girl and take over her family without also taking a seat at the table, we'll be forced to act. But I assure you, the last thing we want is a war."

I gave myself a minute to consider the truth in his words and the hidden meaning between the lines. In this situation, and now that the wedding had been called off, the better move might be to acknowledge some middle ground.

"I agree," I said. "War is necessary in some situations, but it's also bad for business."

Lordi's mouth twisted like I'd just made his point for him.

"Your father never understood that."

"That being said, and with all due respect, Don Lordi, I don't do business with anyone who has my family's blood on their hands... with the man who killed my father."

His nostrils flared. His cheeks and neck became blotchy red.

"Your father's actions would have taken us all down."

"And what about my brother? You had him executed without knowing how he would lead or if he would even bring any risk for the five."

Lordi sat back in his chair, calmer now. "True enough."

I shook my head, dismissing him, the conversation, his offer, dismissing every-fucking-thing.

"No, I won't be joining the Commission."

"You're making a grave mistake, Vignali."

"I don't think so. You have nothing to worry about anyway. The marriage contract between Don Capaldo and me was dissolved this morning. I won't be marrying his daughter. That means this sit-down is pointless."

Lordi blinked at me, then lifted a hand as if swatting away a fly in slow motion.

"If that's indeed true, then I guess you're free to do as you wish. But the offer still stands. You would be a welcome addition to this committee. Maybe one day, you'll even sit at the head of the table."

"Don't hold your breath."

I turned to leave.

"If you're not marrying the Capaldo girl," he called after me, "you should find another bride. You need to establish an heir soon, Stefano. Otherwise, why continue building the Vignali empire? Empires are made to outlast a man and live on through his future generations."

I stopped but didn't turn around. I was fucking fed up with him and his hideous restaurant.

"Are we done here?" I asked.

"You belong with us on this committee. We make much better allies than enemies. Something for you to consider."

"I don't need to—"

"No, don't answer until you think it over. Go home and weigh the pros and cons. Look ahead at how things might play out either way. Then, if you change your mind, come back here after closing, and all Commission members will welcome you into the fold."

I looked back over my shoulder at the three men sitting there, stuffing themselves with wine and prosciutto.

Yeah, no thanks.

"Let's get the fuck out of here, Tony," I said.

As we crossed the room to leave, I realized the meeting had been useful.

The Commission wasn't behind the attack on my son. They weren't aware he existed, not yet.

As much as I hated to admit it, Lordi had made a valid point about having an heir. I needed someone to pass my empire to when the time came, even if that looked differently now that Enzo had come into my life.

If I wanted to name him my heir apparent, I needed to make him my legitimate child first.

"This way, sir," one of Lordi's men said.

He flagged us over and returned our weapons and phones, then quickly stepped out of my path with a respectful nod. Tony and I checked our phones, and we'd both missed numerous calls from the house and from Bruce's cell phone.

A sharp pain knifed me in the gut.

Val. My son.

Were they hurt?

Had the shooter found them and gotten past my men?

The second we got in the car, Jimmy started rambling.

I stared at his face, stunned, searching for a clue.

"Spit it the fuck out," I demanded.

"What I'm trying to say is Bruce called and Don Capaldo's at the house again and the girl and your son went missing."

A wash of frozen dread slid down my spine.

My lungs spasmed, making it hard to draw breath.

"What did you just say?" I said, not really asking.

Tony smacked Jimmy on the back of his head.

"What the fuck you talkin' about?" Tony asked.

"Ow. Sorry, boss," the driver said. "She found a way out."

I punched the back of his seat.

"Get me to Brooklyn now, goddamn it! If she's running, that's where she'll go first."

Then I called one of my captains, commanding him to get to my estate and help Bruce and Hastings search Val's personal and business phone records and bank accounts.

"And get Capaldo the fuck out of my house," I told him. "At gunpoint if necessary."

Val had deliberately left my protection.

Anything could happen to her, to my son.

Whoever wanted them dead ran freely around the city.

TWENTY

VAL

The shouting from below held me frozen in place, every muscle locked in fear, my gaze fixed in the direction of Enzo's bedroom.

"I know you're here somewhere, you stupid bitch!"

My heartbeat *whooshed* loudly inside my ears.

Still, I could hear all the things shattering downstairs.

Then a huge *thud* shook one of my bedroom walls. It wasn't a gunshot, but more like the man had thrown one of the heavier tables against the wall below me.

No, it wasn't Stefano.

I knew that right away. The intruder's voice sounded sinister and mocking, like a villain from a Disney movie, like he tried to make himself seem bigger or tougher.

I recognized the voice, so familiar, but I couldn't place it yet.

Definitely not one of my brothers.

This man had a New York accent.

My brothers wouldn't have destroyed my business anyway. They stopped that kind of behavior a long time ago after one stupid journalist compared them to rioters.

From then on, they were careful to maintain a better public image to avoid what my father always referred to as "muddling the message."

Hard to say what happened to the reporter.

When my family sent a message, they made it crystal clear.

Using a quick, panicked process of elimination, my mind settled on the only viable option.

The monster downstairs was the same man who had tried to kill my son.

And I didn't have a way out for us.

"Fuck," I whispered.

My mind raced, searching for possible moves.

The man down there would find the door for the staircase as soon as his destructive tirade moved into the kitchen. And that meant Enzo and I were trapped in the apartment.

All we could do was wait for him to find us.

No, I refused to be a damsel in distress or allow my son to be a sitting duck.

Enzo appeared inside the doorway, his eyes wide with fear.

"Mama?" he whispered.

I put my finger against my lips as he hurried closer, then I hugged him close to me and pulled us together into a crouch.

"We need to be very quiet, baby," I whispered.

I thought I'd planned for everything, but I was wrong.

So fucking wrong.

I loved this little apartment. I had worked hard to make it perfect for us after Nonna passed, creating the warm, comfortable home my son deserved.

Everything from his overstuffed comforter he'd picked out for himself, to the colorful rugs on the wood flooring, to the bookcase wall we'd filled over the years with all the stories he loved so much and couldn't bear to part with.

And a monster took it away from us.

Not Stefano.

I could no longer blame the destruction on him.

The fault belonged to the faceless monster downstairs, destroying everything as he headed our way.

I crept over to the window. A two-story drop onto concrete covered with broken glass. Visible from inside the café.

Dropping two stories into the filthy back alleyway with all the trash and metal dumpsters wouldn't be any safer for my son.

We needed to run, and we couldn't do that if either of us broke a leg jumping out the window.

I pulled Enzo with me into the connecting bathroom between the two bedrooms, then gently closed the doors.

My stupid brain paused for a second to note how odd it had been that our rooms at Stefano's house also had a connecting bathroom.

"What are we going to do?" Enzo whispered.

Yes, what the hell were we going to do? What was I supposed to tell my terrified child? Shit. What was my plan?

"We wait quietly," I blurted.

"Wait for what, Mama?"

I turned off the lights, plunging the windowless bathroom into darkness, and sat on the edge of the tub. Then I wrapped Enzo in my arms, so I could hold him and whisper to him.

"Okay, buddy, here's what's going to happen. Stefano will realize we're gone and come looking for us. If he gets here soon enough, we won't have to worry about the man downstairs. Stefano will take care of him."

I prayed to the Holy Mother that would happen.

"He'll be really mad at us for leaving," Enzo said.

"You let me handle that. You will be fine. He'll be so relieved to see you that he won't be mad at all."

"But what if he is?" Enzo asked. "I won't ever be fine without you."

My heart skipped beat after beat, breaking for him. A surge of overwhelming guilt shot through me. I had put him in a terrifying situation not once, but twice now.

"Listen to me, Enzo. Stefano won't hurt me," I whispered. "I'll tell him we came back for our clothes. You let me handle that part, okay?"

I could only hope things played out that way. If not, well, at least I could soothe my boy's fears now, in the moment, and deal with the rest later.

Another crash downstairs echoed up the stairs and into the apartment, making us both jump.

I held on to my baby tighter.

"What happens if he doesn't get here in time?" he whispered.

I kissed the top of his head.

"We're still going to be very quiet. When that man comes upstairs looking for us, he'll go into one of the bedrooms first. Whichever one he chooses, you and I sneak into the other one, then we run down the stairs as fast as we can and get outside. Understand?"

Enzo nodded.

I hated being helpless and trapped, forced to sit and wait.

The waiting and anticipation exhausted me, and I needed to conserve my energy.

Deep breath in. And out.

"Shouldn't we call the police?" he asked.

"No, baby, not this time. We can't trust the police around here with this kind of thing."

He nodded, locked his arms around my waist, and pressed his face against my chest.

The screaming taunts and crashing and banging continued from the monster downstairs as he destroyed the rest of the café. I tried to tell myself it didn't matter. I'd planned to leave it all anyway.

Just part of an old life. That was all.

But with every crash, something inside me also broke. The last ten years of my life had been poured into this café, and this bastard so recklessly dismantled it all.

I shut my eyes to picture what our new life might look like.

Maybe we would settle in Savannah instead of going west. Winters would be warmer, the everyday pace slower, and while I imagined that would take some getting used to, it might be a better start for Enzo and me.

Maybe we would open a New York style pizzeria or maybe even another cozy café.

But whenever I envisioned something new and far away, my mind shifted the vision to an image of dark blue eyes.

Eyes with the same crease between them as my son's.

I hated how much I craved Stefano. I hated him for it. And that he could already speak so easily with my son and had earned his respect so quickly. I hated how relief had washed over me when he told me he wasn't marrying Benedetta.

And I fucking hated that he'd been right.

I couldn't protect Enzo on my own.

Now, as if proving my point, heavy footsteps climbed the stairs, each thudding hard on the old treads, one after the other.

"Come out, come out, wherever you are, fucking whore."

"Get ready," I whispered to Enzo.

He nodded against my chest before tiptoeing to the middle of the bathroom, getting ready to run in either direction.

I hoped the monster would go into Enzo's room first. My son's bag sat on the bathroom floor beside us, but my bag sat on top of the bed in my room. Of course, I would leave it, but then my plans for a clean escape with the cash I'd saved over the years would go right out the window.

But at least we would be alive.

The lock on my bedroom door clicked.

Oh fuck, he was locking us inside.

He dragged the couch from the living room and shoved it against the door, then he went into Enzo's room.

A cold shudder rippled along my spine.

The man had done his homework. He knew the layout of the apartment. And it hadn't taken him long to figure out my plan and blow it up so quickly.

There was no time. I had to act. I had to do it immediately.

Both bathroom doors could lock.

So I tiptoed over to turn the lock on the door between us and Enzo's room. I led my son by the hand into my room. Then, before closing the bathroom door behind me, I locked it.

I met my son's gaze and mouthed the words "get into the wardrobe" at him.

The stubborn boy shook his head.

I pointed forcefully at the wardrobe. "Now!"

But he still shook his head, mouthing back at me "not without you" as he extended his hand toward me.

With desperate tears stinging my eyelids, I kneeled in front of him and whispered into his ear.

"I need you to hide so you can help Stefano find me. Can you be brave for me? Can you help your father save me?"

It didn't matter whether he and Stefano ever found me. It didn't matter if this man killed me before I got out of the room. I needed Enzo to hide right now. I needed him to be safe.

Stefano would come for our son and fiercely protect him.

Deep down, I'd known all along that if Stefano knew he had a son, he would keep the boy safe. He would succeed where I could only fail.

Enzo nodded, agreeing to do as I asked.

Our attacker broke through the first bathroom door.

My boy scrambled into the wardrobe, pushing his way to the back behind our winter coats and Nonna's old dresses, so even if the doors opened wide, he would be hidden.

As I closed the wardrobe and turned away from it, the second bathroom door splintered and ripped off its hinges, falling into the bedroom.

My heart leaped into my throat, and I darted to the other side of the room, leading the man away from Enzo's location.

I pretended to struggle with opening the heavy old window.

The monster stepped into the light.

He stood there and stared at me, saying nothing at all.

I couldn't believe my eyes.

Shock vibrated through my soul.

I could hardly catch my breath.

"You? Why are you doing this to us?" I cried.

TWENTY-ONE

STEFANO

Panic overwhelmed me. My hands shook. My lungs became dead weights inside my chest, pinching my heart between them.

I pulled out of my jacket, loosened my tie, lowered the car window, and sucked in the cool autumn air.

Tony turned and stared at me from the front passenger seat.

"Still in Lordi's territory, boss. Open window isn't safe."

I nodded and put the bullet-proof glass back up.

Fuck. I needed to get to Val and Enzo faster.

Jimmy did his best to get through the traffic quickly, but it didn't matter how much skill a driver had or how many laws he broke. Manhattan streets were always congested during rush hour, making it impossible to get anywhere in good time.

"How the fuck did she get out of the house?" I asked.

But the real question in my mind, the more important one, remained unspoken.

Why did she leave me again?

She wasn't safe anywhere else or with anyone else. Someone out there wanted to kill her and our son.

Why couldn't she accept the truth and let me protect them?

I had broken my marriage contract, calling off the wedding with Benedetta's blessing, losing the power that came with it... to show Val that I meant every fucking word I'd said.

Val understood the repercussions of the choice I'd made. She knew I had relinquished my best chance to seize revenge for my family, the one thing I'd worked so hard to accomplish. She knew what I'd given up for her and my son.

Still, it wasn't enough for her.

Tony cleared his throat to get my attention, giving me a better outlet for my energy.

Good. A worried mind and a panicked one were useless.

"I know you don't want to hear this, Stef, but Bruce said the men were distracted."

"What?" I snapped.

Anger, I could work with that. Anger got shit done.

I let the rage flow through my body and used it as fuel.

"Distracted by what? And if you say they were watching some TikTok bitch bouncing on a yoga ball again, I'll put a bullet in their fucking heads myself."

Tony cleared his throat again.

"What?" I repeated.

"Fuck," he said. "It's worse than that."

Tony frowned, clearly annoyed with the men, but kept his eyes forward, helping Jimmy look for openings to jump lanes.

Sweat coated the inside of my fists. I clenched and relaxed my jaws. My shoulders carried the heaviness of my rage on them, making the stitches in my arm tighten with a stinging sensation.

Pain could be as useful as anger. It focused my senses and sharpened my resolve.

"Explain," I ordered.

"Valerie told the men they should eat her cookies while they were still warm," Tony muttered. "Then she went upstairs with the boy, leaving them to it."

Red clouded my vision. I pulled breath in through my nose, the ring on my left hand digging into my flesh as I hung on to what little self-control I had left.

"Are you telling me baked fucking goods distracted my trained soldiers?"

"No one thought she would try to leave your house, boss. You laid down the law with her. She had to know it's the safest place for her and the boy. The excuse I'm getting is she behaved very obediently with them, seemed reasonable even."

"You're fucking kidding me, right? So they've never met a strong woman protecting her child? Reasonable doesn't even register. I swear to Christ, if I don't get her back, Tony, I'll kill every one of those lazy motherfuckers."

"Leave it to me, boss" Tony said.

As my second, Tony had the right to demand nearly the same level of respect from the men as they gave me. He trained them and they answered to him, so when they failed, he failed.

"I'll give you one shot to make it right before I step in. One, Tony, that's it. Understand?"

He nodded.

"Good. Now shut the fuck up and get me to Con Amore."

FORTY FUCKING MINUTES LATER

I could have walked faster to Brooklyn.

The second we pulled up in front of the café, I knew something had gone very wrong. The night before, after making sure

Val and Enzo were safe, I called in a few favors to ensure the cops on my payroll helped process the scene.

One of my crews met them and covered the broken windows with plywood. They tacked a sign to the front door telling customers the place was closed for renovations. Some excuse about a pipe bursting and a promise that Con Amore would reopen for business soon.

I planned to rebuild it. I knew how much Val loved the place, how much hard work she'd put into it over the years. More than that, Enzo needed continuity. He needed to have the only home he'd ever known available to him when he needed it.

Hell, I had my own personal attachment to it.

Once the police released the scene, I intended to send my men in to fix the damage and bring in associate subcontractors for the improvements. I wanted to make it the same for Val and Enzo, but better.

More comfortable. Stronger. Safer.

The place needed new ovens, top-of-the-line commercial coffee machines, and solid furniture. I would make this right for her and spare no expense.

But as I stared at the building now, I noticed how the plywood dangled, how the new lock on the front door hung by a thread after likely being smashed with a hammer.

No question, Val hadn't done that.

She'd taken her purse. She had a key for the back door.

"You should stay here. Let me have a look first," Tony said.

"Fuck that. I'm going in."

I got out and went around to the car's trunk. Tony followed and opened it. Then he removed the false bottom to reveal our hidden collection of weapons. I grabbed a couple more magazines for my pistols.

Then Tony pulled out an assault rifle, slammed a magazine into it, and shut the trunk.

"At least let me take point, huh?" he asked.

I gave him a look which clearly said that wasn't happening.

With a sigh, Tony stepped into place behind me and to the right, ready to follow my lead. If this were anything less important, I would have let him take point. Beyond it being his job, he also had the military training I lacked.

Didn't matter in this case.

For my family, no one risked more than I did.

My gaze moved around the shop as we entered. It had been destroyed worse than during the shootout.

Absolutely everything.

All tables and chairs were decimated. Holes punched in the walls. Coffee machines smashed. A destroyed refrigerator door from the kitchen.

"What the fuck," Tony said under his breath.

I carried my gun in the low-ready position while weaving through the rubble and passing through the busted kitchen door. The goddamn kitchen was worse if that was possible.

The gas range stood on its side in the middle of the room.

I pointed it out to Tony, and he nodded before heading that way. He dropped to one knee, sniffed around, then shook his head, letting me know he didn't smell any gas.

The police must have shut off the line running into the building. So no ticking clock counting down to an explosion.

A *thud* came from above us.

Someone moved upstairs in the apartment.

Tony and I pivoted and aimed our weapons up the stairs. The sound continued, another *thud* every few seconds.

My second-in-command stepped forward first to climb the

staircase ahead of me, but I blocked him with my outstretched arm and took the lead myself.

The apartment had received the same treatment as the café. The living room and kitchen had been ransacked from top to bottom. Furniture lay upside down, bookcases tipped over, clothes and personal items littered all over the floor.

Fuck. But where was Val and our son?

"Val... Enzo... Valerie!" I shouted.

More glass crunched beneath my shoes.

Whoever had destroyed my son's childhood home would pay for it with his life.

The bastard's death would come slowly with excruciating pain. The animal would suffer for his crimes against my family. I would make sure everyone saw his lifeless body and understood what happened when you fucked with someone who belonged to me.

After we slid the couch away from the door, I cleared the first bedroom, then moved on to the bathroom. Enough light from the adjoining bedroom penetrated the darkness, so I could check the tub and linen closet.

Clear.

A *thunk* came from the other room.

My gut clenched and knotted.

I motioned for Tony to step aside. Then I pushed through the hanging pieces of the bathroom door and into the second bedroom.

The room wasn't as trashed. The bedside table had been turned over and a door broken.

Another *thunk*. This time, I pinpointed the origin.

It came from inside the wardrobe.

Someone banged around in there, trying to get out.

With my pulse racing, I signaled for Tony to step back. He trained his weapon on the wardrobe as I moved toward the giant piece of furniture. Tony remained focused with his assault rifle as I flung aside a piece of the bathroom door and threw open the wardrobe's double doors.

We didn't see anything but clothing.

I took a cautious step back to get a better angle.

Inside a split second, my son tumbled out onto the floor.

Enzo's arms and legs flailed as I bent to pick him up. He pushed me away and kicked me. His face had flushed with a deep crimson, and his cheeks stained with tears.

Seeing him that way did something painful to me. Something I neither recognized nor understood.

Both heat and cold washed through me at once, like there was too much air, but I couldn't take in any of it. My blood was on fire, my chest housing some frozen foreign mass, and I wanted to tear the fucking world to pieces.

For the first time in my life, I didn't know what to do.

My son.

Someone had done this to my son. Someone had made him hurt this badly, and I couldn't fix it. I was his father. It was my job to fix it, to protect him, to keep him safe and happy.

A father for less than twenty-four hours, and already I had failed my son.

"This is your fault!" Enzo screamed.

His hands balled into tight little fists as he banged them against me. I didn't try to stop him.

I took every hit he had to give until he started hurting himself more than he hurt me. Then I grabbed his arms, drew him in, and held him close to my body.

"Breathe," I whispered in his ear, repeating it over and over.

My mother's words, her whispers.

The soft words she had used to soothe me as a child after a fight with my brother or my father or the bully at school.

Only my mother's voice had helped me rein in my emotions when I became so full of anger and pain. She had taught me the control my father always lacked.

Now it was my turn to help my boy.

His furious shouts melted into helpless sobs.

"Breathe," I said. "Just breathe, son."

Slowly, I inhaled and exhaled with him, for him, until the rise and fall of his chest matched the rhythm of mine. When he calmed down enough, I pulled him back so I could see his face.

"Where is she, Enzo?"

"He took her. He took her, and it's all my fault," he screamed.

"No, this is not your fault. Do you hear me? It's mine."

I brushed his curly locks away from his swollen eyes.

"I should have done a better job protecting her. Protecting you. This is not your fault. But now I need you to help me. Tell me everything that happened, so I can get her back. Who took her? Do you know who it was?"

Fresh tears streamed down his face.

"I don't know... we came in through the back. To pick up some clothes and some stuff Mama had hidden. Then we were going to leave. We were going to go somewhere safe."

"Tell me what happened next," I said, ignoring the sting of his words.

That pain would have to be dealt with later.

"I thought Mama would want a picture from downstairs. Her and Nonna and the café. So I ran down to get it, and... and I think he saw me. He figured out we were here.

"I ran back upstairs, then he broke in through the front door. We heard him smashing everything, screaming, calling Mama awful names. Then he... he came looking for us."

His words muddled as he tried to get them all out at once.

"Breathe," I reminded him. "You're doing great, Enzo."

He took a deep breath. I put his hand on my chest, so he could match his pacing to mine again. It took him a minute, but he calmed down enough to keep talking.

"Okay, what happened after he smashed up the café?"

"He came upstairs. We were hiding in the bathroom. She said whatever room he went in first, we would go out the other one and run downstairs to get away.

"But he... he knew. Like he could read her mind or something. He locked all the doors and trapped us in. So she put me in the wardrobe and said I had to wait for you to find me. Then you would help me get her back."

"I will get her back," I assured him.

He shook his head, his small body trembling.

"I don't think she meant it. I think she just wanted me to hide, so the bad man would take her and not me."

"Your mama is a strong woman," I said. "And she would do anything to protect you. And I will do everything in my power to protect her, too. I will get her back. Do you believe me?"

Enzo craned his neck to gaze up at me, like he wanted to see through me, then he nodded.

"I believe you. But what if everything in your power isn't enough?"

The lump in my throat thickened more tightly with each of his words, but at least he'd given me something I could handle. Doubt rarely visited me, but when it did, I made sure it didn't stick around long.

I couldn't afford to let doubt fuck with my thoughts.

I'd had plenty of practice assuring others about what would happen. I hadn't gotten as far as I had in this life by falling short on my promises.

I nodded while holding his gaze, so he would know how serious I was.

"Let's make sure it is enough. I need to know everything you can remember about this bad man. How he sounded. What he looked like. What he said specifically. What do you remember?"

Enzo's stare grew vacant as he slowly tilted his head.

"His voice... It sounded like someone I know, but it was all wrong. Mama recognized him. I could tell. But she never said his name. I tried to remember that voice, but I just..."

More sobs wracked his small frame.

I pulled him back into my arms.

"It's okay," I whispered. "You did really good. You stayed safe. Now we'll find her."

Tony stepped back into the room.

Only then did I realize he'd left in the first place, but I felt grateful he'd given Enzo and me some privacy.

"Boss. We need to get you back to the house. The doctor's waiting for you and the boy."

"I don't need a doctor," I said. "But I want him to look at Enzo and make sure he's all right."

Tony pointed at my arm with a brow raised.

"Hate to argue with you, but it's best if you both get checked."

I looked down at my arm.

Blood soaked my sleeve. My stitches had likely come

undone. I didn't know if they'd broken apart in the car or if Enzo punched or clawed them open. I hadn't even noticed.

"Fine. Get a crew down here to search this place. If the attacker left anything behind that might lead us to him, I want to know about it yesterday."

"On it."

I straightened, picked up Enzo, and held his lanky little body against my chest as I carried him down the stairs and out to the car.

Once we were both safely belted in, I turned to ask him more questions, but stopped with my mouth open.

His hands were red, bruised, either from hitting me or from trying to punch his way out of the wardrobe. He held them clenched into fists so tightly that his knuckles were white. And the alarming shade of red had returned to his face.

They were wide now, his dark, familiar eyes, as he stared straight ahead without making a sound.

"Enzo."

He didn't so much as flinch.

"Enzo," I repeated, snapping once in front of his face.

Still nothing. No reaction.

I reached over his lap to feel the pulse at his neck. His heart beat a million miles a minute, and he still didn't move, even at my touch. His skin felt clammy.

Terror struck my gut, my chest.

What if something else had happened to him?

Without warning, he sucked in a raw breath and screamed.

I leaned away from him, but he kept screaming. No words, just earsplitting shrieks as he flailed, slapping and punching and kicking against the back of the seat in front of him.

Unfastening his seatbelt as quickly as I could while trying not to take a fist to the face, I pulled him onto my lap and held him. He screamed into my ear because there was nowhere else to scream as he struggled in my arms, kicking out at anything in the way of his feet.

Until we got him to the doctor, I could only just hold him.

Tony had to yell more instructions into his phone, so those on the other end could hear him over Enzo's screams.

I didn't give a fuck.

If this kid needed to yell, if he needed to scream and hit things, then he should do it. I understood the urge, wanting to do the same. But I had to be strong.

For him.

And for her.

When we arrived at the house, I carried Enzo straight to my office, where Bruce and the doctor waited for us.

Even though Enzo had finally worn himself out and now lay like a limp sack in my arms, my ears still rang.

I gently put him down on the sofa.

Doc crossed the room, eyeballing my blood-soaked sleeve.

I pointed at Enzo.

"No, you'll take care of my son first."

"Sir, I need to assess the damage, so we don't—"

"Him. First," I snarled.

Then I turned away from the fussing doctor, moved my gaze around until I found Bruce standing in the doorway.

"You were in charge while we were gone, correct?"

"Yes, sir," he said, his gaze dropping.

"The only way you survive the next twenty-four hours is if we get her back," I said. "Do you understand me?"

His face paled, and he bobbed his fucking head.

"Yes, sir. I understand. I'm sorry I failed you."

His voice carried the slightest quiver.

Good. He should be afraid.

"I don't give a fuck if you're sorry. Valerie is the only thing that matters."

Bruce nodded again as he approached me.

"This came for you by courier. Ten minutes ago," he said.

Then he handed me another goddamn yellow envelope.

TWENTY-TWO
VAL

I didn't know where my kidnapper had taken me.

When I woke, I couldn't see through the darkness, and there wasn't much room to move. It took me a minute to realize he'd put me in a confined space on scratchy carpet.

The small space moved, and I bounced along with it.

Oh my god. He'd locked me in the goddamn trunk of a car.

My head throbbed. Tears stung the backs of my eyelids, and a lump grew larger and larger in my throat.

I wanted to cry. I wanted to scream. Vomit. But I didn't.

No, instead I sucked in the musty air through my nose and exhaled from my mouth, repeating until my nausea and most of the panic subsided. I couldn't let anxiety take me down while my life was in danger.

I had to conserve my energy. To clear my head and focus.

When an opportunity to strike out against my attacker presented itself, I needed to be ready. I couldn't be if I were a panicking, blubbering mess.

The asshole who took me hadn't tied up my wrists or my ankles or bothered to gag me. He had either underestimated me or was in an incredibly big hurry. Either way, it worked to my advantage if I played my cards right.

If he'd had to rush, maybe someone else came along and saw him, or maybe he realized Stefano wouldn't waste any time coming after me and Enzo.

My baby.

I squeezed my eyes shut, my heart breaking again. I wiped at the tears slipping down my cheek.

Stefano found Enzo... I had to believe that.

I kept my eyes shut and listened, tuning in to the vehicle's movements and sounds. Smooth rolling tires over asphalt. A quiet engine. A large, rectangular trunk. No hint of a new car smell. An occasional squeaky brake pad when the car stopped at traffic lights.

An older model sedan then.

I shivered from the cold.

How long had I been unconscious?

I remembered the banging downstairs in the café. The dark bathroom. Doors breaking into pieces. Hiding Enzo inside my bedroom wardrobe. The monster stepping into the light.

Donnie Luka.

Enzo's social studies teacher.

But he'd looked a little different. He seemed bigger. Meaner. His face red with exertion, and his once passably charming smile flashing a cruel grin.

He had carried a crowbar, a hand on either end, holding it diagonally across his body. What kind of man came at a woman with a crowbar?

A weak man.

A fucking weasel.

I remembered throwing a pillow and trying my best to

dodge around him to get to the other side of the room. He'd blocked my way so easily, so I climbed over the mattress and pretended to shove the bedside table at him. But really, I'd pushed it against the wardrobe with a swift kick to keep the wardrobe doors shut.

To lock Enzo inside.

If my son had recognized his teacher's voice, he might have come out. He might not have understood Donnie Luka only ever pretended to care about him.

Enzo had never truly liked the man as a person, but I thought he probably trusted him as his teacher. I couldn't risk letting that fucking monster manipulate Enzo's trust.

I had thrown the lamp from the overturned bedside table at Luka, and he ducked, so it missed his head. Then he backhanded me using his left hand and smashed his crowbar onto the side of my head with his right.

Gently, I probed the area behind my ear where he'd hit me and winced.

"Ow. Fuck," I whispered.

Thick, warm blood coated my fingertips. Not enough to alarm me. The huge lump worried me more. A lot more.

By some miracle, the dizziness I experienced was minimal, and I could control the nausea with focused breathing. I couldn't say if my vision had been affected, not while inside my pitch-dark prison. And I hoped I didn't have a concussion.

Time would tell.

I needed a clear mind if I wanted to make it out of this alive, so I practiced more deep, intentional breathing.

A few sudden bumps bounced me around again. I braced myself against the floor and the roof, so I wouldn't hit my head. I did, however, twist my ankle.

No broken bones. I could still wiggle my toes and flex my foot, though it hurt like a bitch. I couldn't help but question if it even really mattered.

Then the car rolled to a stop just a few seconds later.

My heart stalled. A cold sweat soaked through my clothes.

Donnie Luka the weasel slammed his car door, came around to the back, and opened the trunk.

I wanted to come out swinging, pouncing on him, tearing him apart with my bare hands, but I couldn't get into a position that gave me any leverage.

As he lifted the lid, light flooded the space and blinded me.

His thick fingers dug into my hair and jerked me up.

The pain of being hauled upright by my scalp made me cry out, but then I bit it back, stuffing my cries back down my throat as he dragged me out like a dead carcass and tossed me on the ground.

Gravel stung my palms and my knees as I slid over it, those abrasions temporarily dulling my other aches and pains.

"Stand up," he ordered.

My limbs were too cold and stiff to move quickly, despite the fiery hatred burning inside me. It took me a minute, but after swallowing a surge of bile and forcing my weight upright, I got to my feet. As I faced my attacker, my unstable body swayed.

"Why are you doing this?" I asked.

Luka sneered.

"Shut the fuck up. Here's what's going to happen. You'll pretend to be a well-behaved lady and not the rabid bitch you are. You'll walk quietly wherever I tell you to go. You won't make a scene or do anything to draw attention.

"If you can't follow these simple instructions, I will find

your son and make him pay for his mother's inability to follow my directions."

He bared his teeth like a feral beast each time he spat out those words. And this bastard had the nerve to call me rabid.

I had never liked him, and now I knew why.

He was crazy. My son's teacher was insane.

Even if he wanted to follow through with his threat, he could never again get to Enzo. Not anymore. Stefano had surely found our son. He had to have. I wouldn't accept believing anything else.

Granted, I couldn't be one-hundred percent sure, so I did whatever he said. I walked quietly beside Luka through a well-lit underground parking structure.

That kind of location provided me with no quick escape.

The sick fuck clamped down hard on the back of my neck, steering me like a disobedient child.

The deserted area didn't have so much as another single car on the same level.

Then he forced me into an elevator and jabbed the fourth-floor button, his sweaty right-handed grip on my neck getting stronger by the minute.

It seemed like an eternity before the elevator doors opened, but when they did, I knew exactly where he'd taken me.

My kidnapper knew the layout of Enzo's school much better than I did, but at least I could find my way around. And I knew only one rent-a-guard manned the security office on the third floor.

I had to bide my time.

Make a break for it when the right time came.

Weasel boy steered us toward his classroom, though I didn't

have any idea what the fuck he thought he could accomplish by taking me there or even taking me at all.

When we passed the main staircase, I decided that might be my chance. The security office would be right below us.

I jabbed my elbow into his gut to break his hold on me.

He grunted and grabbed his abdomen in reflex, but then he caught my hair and threw me down on the floor.

My palms squeaked against the shiny marble as I slid over it on my stomach.

When I caught myself and got up on my knees, the mosaic design installed last summer stretched out beneath me. A feature made possible by the money I had helped raise for the school.

Fuckface Luka laughed.

"You really think you're going to get out of this, don't you?" he asked. "You? No way."

He shook his head and laughed again. A more sinister laugh than the last one.

"I just don't fucking understand you, Valerie. You're a beautiful woman. A little thick in the hips, sure, and you need to be taught some fucking manners, but I could have done that for you. Would have raised you up from the gutter.

"You made yourself a whore when you slept with that man. Why would you go back to him now when you could be mine?"

The world around me spun, and I struggled to follow his ramblings. I pushed back another strong urge to vomit.

Luka came closer. His shoe touched the side of my hand.

"But no," he continued. "You turned yourself into another home-wrecking slut with the fucking audacity to humiliate someone so much better than you.

"Have you looked at yourself? You think you could ever

compare to Benedetta? Now there's a real woman. Actual class. Genuine beauty. You're just... average. You have a kid, for fuck's sake. And yeah, I know your little secret."

I tried to focus on Luka's words, to understand what he said while staring at the mosaic on the floor beneath me.

My arms trembled. My ankle screamed. Now that the trunk's darkness and silence were gone, replaced by blinding light and noise, the pain in my head pounded like a jackhammer.

By all means, weasel, go on. Keep talking.

"I've seen the real you," he said. "You know, when you think no one's watching. I see how you pretend to close the curtains at night, but you always leave those three inches open.

"You shouldn't do that. That little pussy boy of yours ruined your body. Oh, your tits are great. But your ass is like a fucking freighter. And the stretch marks? Don't get me started on how disgusting that shit is..."

I could hardly hear him over the pounding in my head.

Again, bile hit my throat, and I swallowed it.

Mother of Christ, this guy couldn't keep his mouth shut. He just kept going on and on. But it gave me a chance to search for something useful, anything or anyone to help me.

I found nothing. No one.

"I wanted to do the right thing, you know, Valerie. I wanted to look past your flaws and take you anyway. We would sell the café, so you didn't have to work anymore.

"You could spend a hell of a lot more time at the gym instead, for starters. And you would show me exactly how much you appreciated everything I would have done for you and your little bastard."

Now he had gone way too far.

I didn't give a damn what he thought about Con Amore or the choices I made.

As for my body, well, I'd seen how Stefano looked at me, with and without clothes. I would believe a man like Stefano any day before listening to this psychotic asshole.

And I definitely wouldn't listen to him speak that way about my son. He would pay for that.

"I would've been a good father to that boy," Luka said. "I would've given him the discipline he needs. Beat that quiet, creepy shit right out of him. Make him better. A people person. Not some fucking freak no one can even stand to look at. Hell, I would've even let him stay once you had my first child."

I struggled to my feet. The room spun.

The vertigo had to wait. I had to kill this man.

"You threw it all away, Valerie. And for what? Just to be a criminal's whore?"

I narrowed my eyes but kept my anger in full check.

"You're wrong," I said. "I didn't throw anything away. I made love to a strong man who knows who he is. The man who will protect me and my son. His son. There's no comparison between you and a man like Stefano."

"You shut your mouth!" he shouted. "You don't have any idea what you're talking about."

"I know I would rather be Stefano's whore, fucking him in his marital bed night after night, than be with you. You are nothing. Benedetta knows about me. She knows about Stefano's son. And even she would rather share Stefano than be stuck with a sniveling little worm like you."

The wedding had been called off, but this lunatic didn't know that. So I baited him, to make him yell, scream, hit something. Anything to get the security guard's attention, so he would come and investigate.

Luka sneered, leaning in as he opened and closed his fists, and his breath came out in small bursts.

"You're going to regret those words, you stupid bitch. Don't you know who I am?"

"I know who you aren't. You aren't the man Benedetta would ever choose. You aren't the man I want or the man I love. At this point, I question if you're a man at all. You talk about me having your children, but are you even man enough to get it up? I bet your tiny little dick can't even get hard."

My grandmother once said if I ever needed to defend myself against a man, go for what hung between his legs.

But since I literally couldn't get there, I applied her advice using verbal assaults instead.

Luka's eyes got wider, his pupils like pin pricks surrounded by muddy irises and red-streaked whites. A deeper flush pumped crimson into his face and neck. Spittle flew from his mouth, not only when he spoke but also with his panting.

He was close to snapping.

I needed to push him a little further.

"How were you planning to get me pregnant? Maybe you expected me to be unsatisfied and run to fuck Stefano? He could get me pregnant again, that's for damn sure. Who knows? It's possible I'm carrying his second child right now."

I touched my stomach, smiling, while the idea took root.

Oh shit. Could I really be pregnant?

"You are such a fucking whore!" he screamed.

Yep. That did the trick.

With another fake smile, I backed a few feet away, waiting

for a door to open or to hear footsteps racing this way after an exclamation like that in the middle of an elementary school.

Nothing happened.

Where the fuck was that security guard?

"I'm not yours," I said. "I'll never be yours. And Benedetta Capaldo will never be yours either."

I could blame the head injury, or the duress caused by the situation, but it really came down to one simple fact...

I had underestimated how unhinged this man had become.

How far he would go.

I hadn't even realized he carried a gun with him, not until he jerked it out of his pants.

"You should've behaved like a nice Italian girl," he snarled.

Then he aimed his pistol at me.

"This would've been so easy if you'd just been nice to me."

TWENTY-THREE
STEFANO

Fuck. Another envelope.

I snapped at the doctor and everyone else.

"Treat my son in his bedroom. And the rest of you, get the fuck out. Give me a few minutes."

"I'll stay with the boy," Tony said.

Good man. I nodded.

"Make sure he gets a healthy dinner and plenty of milk."

Enzo seemed physically weak after what he'd been through. And too thin. His size might have been typical for a boy his age, but I had no experience with children, so I couldn't be sure.

I wanted my son as strong physically as he was intellectually.

Bruce glanced back at me with a remorseful expression.

"You stay. Sit and keep your mouth shut," I said.

He took a seat as I sunk into my father's heavy leather chair with the yellow envelope still gripped tightly in my hand. This one weighed much less than the others.

My gut already knew what waited inside that envelope.

Every cell in my body rejected the idea of opening it. I

couldn't put the truth back inside and forget about it once it came out.

I didn't want to see her that way.

"Where's Mama?"

My head snapped around at the sound of Enzo's voice.

He stood in the doorway, and Tony stood behind him.

The night before, this boy had come to me like a man, so determined, forceful even. He would grow into that man sooner than either of us realized.

But for now, he was still a child who needed his mother.

"Son, you're supposed to be in your room."

Enzo shook his head.

"Not until we know," he whispered.

Christ, how could I say no to him? He had a right to know.

I pointed to the chair closest to me. After he settled on the velvet cushion, I summoned the strength to open the envelope.

One photo slipped out onto my desk. Nothing else inside the envelope.

The grainy image showed Val lying on the ground. A pool of blood surrounded her. She clutched her arm while glaring at the person taking the photo.

He'd hurt her. He'd already fucking hurt her.

I would kill that motherfucker with my bare hands.

"Looks like there's a note on the back, boss," Tony said.

I turned the picture over.

*CALL OFF THE WEDDING OR YOUR WHORE DIES
THEN WE COME FOR THE BASTARD*

I looked at Enzo.

He sat upright in the armchair, his eyes locked on my face.

"Do we know where this came from or the pick-up location?"

"The courier picked it up from a locker at the train station," Bruce said. "We started pulling the station's security footage to find a visual."

"Get back on it. Follow that lead. Get me some answers."

Bruce quickly left my office, then Tony took his seat.

"What's next, boss? How can I help?" Tony asked.

"Start calling in some favors. We need extra manpower to search every inch of the city. Call Lordi's second and relay a message from me. Tell him the Commission's assistance would mean my allegiance."

Tony's eyes widened.

"But Stef..."

"Just fucking do it," I ordered. "Keeping Valerie alive is more important to me than avenging the dead."

With a compliant nod, Tony left the room to make the calls.

I had connections. Good connections inside other families and outside of the business. Men who I'd helped in the past.

I worked hard to rebuild the Vignali reputation. To improve it. For ten long years.

Those debts owed to me needed to be paid now, no matter how large or small. Even if the contributions were small, a few men to help mine sweep security footage or additional soldiers for more boots on the ground, I would take it. My allies had to come through.

Enzo squirmed, cleared his hoarse little throat, and shifted from one side of the chair to the other while continuing to stare at me. The boy wanted answers.

As I studied his face, the way he held his mouth, his eyes, I realized his mind worked like mine. He actively plotted his own course of action to get his mother back.

I couldn't let him do that. I made a mental note to keep him close. His plan would only get him taken away from me, same as his mother. Val would kill me herself if something happened to our son. And rightly so.

The woman had given herself to that animal to protect Enzo, and I refused to let her down by pissing all over her sacrifice.

"Enzo, I gave you my word. We will get her back," I said.

"Why would you help me or Mama?" he asked.

"What?"

He'd caught me off guard. I needed to give him some clarity.

"You're my son. She's the mother of my child. That means everything to me."

"But you didn't know that until yesterday. Why would you care now after Mama lied to you?"

I couldn't stop staring at him, wondering how best to answer his questions. There was no easy way to tell him that I had always loved his mother. No easy way to say I'd only gone away because she made me go before hiding my child from me.

How could I explain myself without making Val seem like the bad guy?

I couldn't.

I wouldn't do anything to affect the way he loved her.

And because deep down, as much as I hated Val for what she'd done, I still understood the fault was all mine.

I had lied to his mother first. I never reached out to her after getting her letter. I never begged her to give me another chance.

What the fuck could I say to him about all that?

Not a damn thing. At least not now.

"Why don't you go back to your room and lie down?" I suggested. "Get some rest until dinner's ready."

With perfect timing for once, the doctor returned and got to work on my arm.

But my son didn't go to his room. He stood in front of me and stared at me.

"No," he said. "I won't let you go get her without me."

"Enzo," I growled.

"No," he repeated.

I shook my head and narrowed my eyes in warning, but that strong, determined boy from the night before had come back.

He balled his hands into fists.

"I'm serious, Mr. Vignali. I'm going with you when you get her back."

I winced.

My own son had called me "Mr. Vignali." We needed to get that ironed out soon. But not without Val.

"Okay, I understand," I said.

And I did. But it didn't mean I really planned to take him along and risk his life again.

"You've been through a lot today, Enzo. I want you to rest right now, so when it's time to leave, you feel better. Can you do that for me?"

He stared at me, his eyes narrowed, mirroring my own as he searched through my bullshit for the truth, but then he nodded.

Good. Some progress.

He left just as the doctor finished bandaging my arm.

"That was a good move," the doc said.

"What was?" I asked.

He snipped the last length of new sutures, then packed his supplies in his medical bag.

"Getting the boy to rest. Physically, he's fine. A few bruises and scrapes. Nothing to worry about. But the emotional toll is much worse. It might take a while for him to shake this off. That's assuming you get his mother back."

"And what if I don't?" I asked.

I had nothing to go on. I didn't have any idea who the fuck had her, where he had her, or even how to tell the man he'd gotten what he wanted, that I'd called off the wedding.

"You cross that bridge if you come to it. That's an important part of parenthood, crossing bridges only when you must."

I nodded, understanding the notion but not liking it. Lying to my son made my stomach turn. But I had no other alternative. I would not fucking tell him that he might lose his mother.

Nor would I admit defeat.

"I hope everything turns out well. I really do," the doc said, shaking my hand. "And if you need anything at all, you know how to reach me. But I would be remiss if I didn't mention my friend at this point. She's a very good child psychiatrist who could help your son process his emotions. Grief too, if needed."

I nodded again and thanked him. He wanted to be helpful, I knew, but I couldn't entertain the idea of failure.

After getting back to my desk, I spent a few minutes really studying the photograph of Val.

It was hard as hell, but I forced myself to focus on more than just her image, the pained expression on her face. I needed to examine her environment, look for clues, a lead, any small detail pointing me in the right direction.

She sprawled across a marble floor. Her feet partially

covered an image or logo embedded into the stone with colorful mosaic tiles, but I couldn't make it out.

I could've had one of the boys try a reverse image search, but that would require uploading this image to the internet, and I couldn't risk putting it out there in the public domain. The last thing I needed was for the FBI to find it and get involved.

I needed to keep this under law enforcement's radar. I needed to be entirely free, beyond legal jurisdiction, when I struck back.

Tony knocked on the door, and I waved him in. He took a seat on the other side of my desk and stared at his feet instead of meeting my gaze.

"I made the calls, boss."

"Tell me."

"The other families won't help. They say you don't have the clout to demand this kind of favor. If it was your wife and a legitimate son, that'd be a different story. Then they'd fight to protect your family.

"But for a mistress and a bastard... no. You'd have pull if you and Benedetta were married, but since that's off the table..."

"If she were my wife, I wouldn't need their men."

"I am aware, sir."

He continued avoiding eye contact, which meant this was about to get worse.

"What else, Tony?"

"The Commission won't help either. Not until you're a member of the committee, and that could take months."

I jumped to my feet and began pacing around the room.

"Fuck! What does that leave us with?"

"Not many options," Tony said. "But we're not dead in the water yet. Bruce and Hastings are working on grabbing the security feeds at the train stations. We're still watching the city's feeds around Con Amore. There's always a chance they picked up something."

I pushed my hands through my hair, pulling it tightly away from my scalp, then let out my breath. Something, some fucking detail, still eluded me. There had to be something I just didn't see yet.

"One more thing, boss. I spoke to Don Capaldo about the announcement to cancel the wedding. Figured if we could at least get word out there for this psycho to pick up, we might buy the girl more time."

I turned on my heel to face him.

"That's a great idea. Why aren't we doing that?"

"Capaldo refuses. He says the wedding is still on, and if you're not at the church tomorrow, he'll kill you himself."

I scoffed at the idea.

"He needs the strength to pick up a gun first."

Still, Capaldo had created another problem. Another threat I couldn't afford to ignore, just not the most pressing threat right now.

I had to be smart about this, think things through.

A few options came to mind, and I hated every one of them.

The other families thought I lacked the standing to garner the type of favors that would help me out of this situation...

Val and Enzo weren't considered my legitimate family, so their well-being wasn't protected under Cosa Nostra code.

If I married Benedetta, I would have the Capaldo men under my control, but not until after the ceremony. Too slow.

The Commission refused to help me with this even after I agreed to sit at their table.

Then again, if I opened fire on the restaurant, killing the whole committee at once and assuming that power, that would get me the respect I needed from the families.

But that forthcoming respect would take time as well.

And the act itself would start a war before that respect came, a war I couldn't win without the Capaldo men.

Killing the Commission members after marrying Benedetta would give me enough men to stop the war before it started. In a single move, I would have my revenge and control of the entire city all at once.

But that option meant losing Val.

I couldn't find her and save her before news of my marriage became public knowledge. Not even the slaughter of the entire Commission would stop that information from getting out.

Being completely honest with myself, I had to admit I didn't want either of those things. I wanted to find Val myself. I wanted to be her hero, to save her, to protect my son, and to murder with my own hands the animal who'd taken her from me.

If I had it my way, Val would be home right now. She would be mine, willingly and without hesitation. Enzo would be legitimized and named my heir, protected for the rest of his life, no matter how involved I stayed in the business after that. Though in this ideal world, of course, I would be involved.

But that would cost me dearly. It would strip away everything I'd worked to achieve.

Either way, the necessity of a sacrifice stared me dead in the face. Not for the first time, claiming my revenge and claiming the only woman I'd ever loved warred with each other for priority in my next decision.

Choosing Val meant losing all the progress I'd gained. The networks. The power. The contacts. Everything.

The fucking contacts. Even without a marriage to make it official, Val was the mother of my only son, and that should have been enough for them.

They betrayed me. And I would not forget it.

It occurred to me that the families withholding their support could have had something to do with showing loyalty to Capaldo. Helping me find my mistress would be a slap in his daughter's face. The families probably assumed Val had been taken by Capaldo himself.

If I chose my revenge, that meant choosing to let Val die. Not only would I throw away such a vital part of my life, one that I hadn't realized was missing until yesterday, but I would lose my son forever.

Enzo understood what was happening. He knew all this had started because of me.

If I became the reason his mother died, he would never forgive me. No matter where he lived, even if I forced him to remain under my roof. No matter what I gave him. No matter how hard I tried to make up for it in other ways.

He would never forgive me, and I couldn't blame him.

Losing Val also meant losing my son. A son I hadn't known I wanted until meeting him.

Now I couldn't imagine my life without him in it.

But how the hell could I choose Val when I still had no clue how to find her?

All my deliberations came back to the same thing.

Pursuing my revenge came much easier to me because I

knew how to get it. I'd been working toward it for so long, and I understood each necessary next step to avenge my family and finally seize the power owed to me.

I might give up everything to receive nothing.

It should have been a no-brainer.

On paper, it seemed simple. I hadn't seen Val for a decade. I should let her die, put my son in therapy to process his grief, and work hard to build a relationship with him while grooming him as my successor. I would have liked him to love me, but love was an unnecessary addition in this life.

He would learn to respect me in time.

I moved my gaze over to the phone on my desk. I only had to pick it up, and I could make that happen.

So why couldn't I do it?

Why couldn't I pick up the fucking phone and tell Capaldo I would be at that church to marry his daughter?

"Boss?" Tony asked.

"I only see one option with any benefit," I murmured.

A pathetic fucking attempt to give me the excuse to do the unthinkable.

"We're not out of time yet, Stef. Let us figure this out. Give us a few more hours."

"Fuck, Tony. We don't have a single legitimate lead. We're grasping at straws. Those cameras near Con Amore won't pan out. They didn't the first time.

"And what's the likelihood of finding anything on the feed at the train station over the next few hours? If I don't act now, I will lose everything, and she will probably still die."

While I paced, Tony's focus remained on me. Neither of us saw Enzo sneak back into the room.

When I noticed his small form hovering near my desk from the corner of my eye, I turned to scold him. But instead, I froze.

Not a goddamn muscle in my body would move.

He had the photo of his mother in his hand.

"Don't look at it, Enzo," I said.

Too late.

He jerked his gaze from the photo to my face.

"I know where this is," he said.

TWENTY-FOUR
VAL

Donnie Luka's bullet hit my right arm.

I sucked air in through my nose and released it slowly from my mouth, fighting to keep my breathing steady and to push past the searing pain. I refused to cry out.

The depraved bastard would never get that from me. I knew what he wanted... to be in control, to have power over me, to feel like a powerful man.

He wasn't strong. Not at all.

Just another sick asshole.

Never would I let him take my power away and own it.

Whatever psychotic bullshit he pulled out of his bag of tricks next, I wouldn't fall for it. He couldn't break me. I would die before giving him the satisfaction of watching me fall apart.

"This is your fault," he hissed. "If you weren't such a stuck-up bitch, none of this would've happened. All you had to do was be nice and know your place."

"My place? You have no idea where that is. You don't even know who the fuck I am."

"But I know what you are," he fired back. "A worthless

bitch who used her body to trap a wealthy man, so he'll take care of you. And you did it only to find out he doesn't want you.

"He wants someone worthy, like Benedetta. You couldn't take it, could you? So you went crawling back and opened your legs for him again."

I clenched my teeth.

"You better hope you're right..." I said, "that he doesn't want me. Because if he shows up, you'll pray for death before he even lays a finger on you. Stefano will rain hell down on you for taking me. And I think you know that."

My arm throbbed, and the bullet hole burned like crazy.

When I pressed on the wound to staunch the bleeding, blinding pain erupted beneath my fingers. My stomach turned, increasing my nausea, forcing me to swallow my vomit. Letting it out wasn't an option. Luka would consider that weakness and be thrilled by it.

The asshole pulled out his phone to snap a photo of me lying on the floor in a puddle of my own blood. The sick fuck would probably masturbate to it later.

I blocked him out and focused on the pain, controlling it instead of letting it control me.

He grabbed my other arm and yanked me up on my feet.

"Get the fuck up, you stupid bitch."

Then he dragged me to the elevator.

I struggled to stay on my feet, the slick marble floor smeared with blood, making it hard to gain any traction. It left a nice trail behind me for someone to follow, though.

I prayed Stefano would find me before I bled out.

My kidnapper moved quickly, his fingers forcefully gripping the flesh of my arm, making it impossible for me to break away.

I thought about screaming for help, but if no one had heard the gunshot, they wouldn't hear me either.

You never knew, maybe the timing could make a difference. What would it hurt if I tried?

"Help! Please help me," I shouted.

Luka stopped and backhanded me across the face, and I hit the floor again with the taste of blood filling my mouth.

Yeah, that was what it would hurt. Me.

This time, when he yanked me back on my feet, he pressed the short barrel of his pistol against my temple.

"If you do that again, I will shoot you in the fucking head. Then I'll do the same to your son."

His pupils were huge, almost eclipsing his irises. Sweat beaded on his forehead and ran down the sides of his face. Not just from adrenaline. He was high.

He must have taken something before getting to Con Amore, and that made him even more unpredictable and dangerous. And a hell of a lot scarier.

I nodded to reassure him that I would keep my mouth shut.

He chuckled.

"See? You can be obedient after all."

After we got back to the parking garage and then to his large sedan, he threw me into the trunk. I landed on my wounded arm and stifled a scream.

I gripped my arm, putting pressure on the wound again. I didn't know if that helped dull the pain at all, but it had to help slow down the blood loss.

He slammed the trunk lid and plunged me into darkness.

A few seconds later, his car door slammed shut, then the engine roared to life. The tires squealed as he peeled away, and then the brakes made a grinding noise when he stopped quickly. More squealing tires. He was in a hurry.

Luka knew as well as I did...

Stefano Vignali was formidable, a notorious mafia boss known for his unwavering resolve, a cruel man who always needed to win.

And he would catch up with us sooner than later.

I believed that in my heart. I felt it in my bones.

Locked inside my kidnapper's trunk again, I could only wait, prepare, and pray.

With my eyes closed, I prayed first to my grandmother. My nonna had saved me from a devastating marriage that would have ended with my death in less than a year.

A long and happy life had never been in the cards for me, not until she risked her own life to set me on a path I might survive. She helped me escape the fate of my father's legacy.

Next, I prayed to the grandmother who had found me, taken me in, and shown me how to adapt to a new life, a free life. My adoptive nonna taught me what it meant to live, to choose, how to say "no" to those bigger than me, stronger than me, in ways that would be heard.

She taught me how to do things I didn't know I had in me.

Before those women passed, they had helped me through the hardest times in my life, holding me up, making sure I never lost my footing. They taught me how to be strong in ways only a woman understood, how to endure things that might break even the strongest of men.

Then, while continuing to take deep breaths, in through the nose, out slowly through the mouth, I prayed to the Virgin Mother. I didn't ask her to help me or save me. I'd asked my grandmothers for that protection. Of the Virgin, I had a much more important request.

To her, I prayed for the safety and protection of my son, not only from his deranged teacher, but also from the horrors of his father's life.

I couldn't bear to think of Enzo being raised by his father and ending up in the Mafia. I couldn't let that happen. Whether Stefano claimed him as an heir or kept him close as a soldier, the result would be the same for my son, and I couldn't let it be.

But I knew.

I knew all the effort I'd made to keep him away from that life had been for nothing. I had failed. I knew the effort I'd made for so long to keep him away from that life had been for nothing. I had failed. The moment Enzo and Stefano laid eyes on each other, my son's fate had been sealed.

Still, I prayed to the Virgin anyway.

I begged for my son's life to be different.

Let him live. Let him be a good man. Let him marry for love. Let him father children he adores. Let him have a long life. A full life. Let him die an old man surrounded by warmth and a loving family. Make sure my son always knows how much I love him.

Oh god, my head spun faster and faster.

My stomach twisted, and bile hit my throat.

I prayed harder.

No, no, no...

Sharp pains struck my temples, and the throbbing in my arm and shoulder intensified.

But damn it, I refused to stop praying, ignoring the pain, the sickness, the fear while pleading for my son's life.

A cold sweat soaked my neck, my back, all of me. My body trembled violently. I was so cold. Pins and needles stabbed at my hands and my feet.

The car slowed, jostled me around over two or three considerable potholes, then rolled to a full stop.

All the energy had left my body. I couldn't lift my head.

How was I supposed to fight back now?

The trunk opened, and bright light filtered in, blinding me. I tried to block it with my hand and get my vision into focus, but everything remained blurry. My eyelids weighed so much.

"Get up. I must get you ready," Luka said.

"Get me ready for what?"

The sound of my voice alarmed me. The sluggishness, the hollow tone, the incoherently strung together words.

"Why Valerie, for our date, of course."

He reached into the trunk, grabbed my arm, and pressed his thumb on the wound.

A flaring burst of pain shot through my entire body.

I squeezed my heavy eyelids shut and groaned while pushing at his hand to make him stop.

A sudden surge of adrenaline rushed through me. I'd heard that great pain and agony could do that. It was enough to wake me. Enough, at the very least, to allow me to think again.

"If you behave, I might even fuck you. Just so he never wants you again. If he ever did," Luka said.

Then the sick motherfucker yanked me out of the trunk.

When my feet hit the ground, I forced myself to stumble and drop on one knee like my legs were giving out. I fell sideways against the rear of Luka's car, bracing myself against the license plate and rear bumper.

By the time he hauled me upright again, I'd gotten a good glimpse of my blood smeared on the license plate.

Several drops hit the crumbling pavement.

As far as leaving a trail of clues went, a smear and drops of blood had to be better than nothing.

The asshole's grip on my arm got tighter as he dragged me to the front of an old single-family home with buckled wooden stairs and chipping paint.

He hesitated at the door, jerking my face close to his mouth.

"I can't wait to see if Vignali finds you in time," he said.

TWENTY-FIVE
STEFANO

I kneeled in front of Enzo and gripped his shoulders, turning him to face me directly. I needed to see his eyes as he told me what he knew.

Not that I thought he would lie about something so important, but he'd given me hope, and I needed to know it was real.

"What do you mean, you know where this is?" I asked.

His expression shifted, becoming more serious, the deep line creasing the space between his eyebrows.

"I mean, I know where this picture was taken."

"How, Enzo? How do you know this location?" I demanded.

I didn't want to scare him, but damn it, we had nothing else and no other leads.

He handed me the photo and pointed at the floor.

"Those tiles there on the floor. I walk on them every day. This is at my school. She's at Saint Christopher."

Fuck. Of course. How else could the son of a bitch have taken photos of him in a classroom with other children? The man I'd been trying to find had access to the school after hours and direct access to my son and his mother.

Val lived close enough to the school, and it wouldn't have been unusual to see Enzo's teachers or other school staff walking around the same neighborhood as they went to and from work or grocery shopping. Some probably frequented Con Amore.

How the hell had I not put all that together?

Schools didn't let just anyone come and go whenever they pleased. Not private academies like the one Enzo attended.

"Who do you think could do this? Think very hard, Enzo. Are there any men at your school who you might suspect?"

Enzo pressed his lips together for a second.

"Mr. Luka, my social studies teacher."

"What makes you think so?"

"He likes Mama a lot. But she doesn't like him back. She's nice when she sees him, but I can tell how hard she's trying. And I don't like him either."

"Why not?" I asked.

He wrinkled his nose as he thought about it, his lip curling in disgust even if he couldn't quite put words to the feeling yet.

"I don't know. He's just not like my other teachers. If you talk in class, he gets really mad, really fast. One time he screamed at a girl until she cried because she laughed at something."

I nodded.

"This is good. Can you tell me anything else about this man? Where he lives? Anything at all?"

Enzo shook his head. Unshed tears welled in his eyes.

"His name is Donnie Luka. I heard him tell Mama to call him Donnie. But I... I don't know anything else."

I maintained our connection for a minute, longer than

necessary, not willing to break eye contact with my son or lose the feeling it gave me to have my hands on his shoulders.

A choice no longer existed. No more fucking deliberating.

I had to act now.

Benedict Capaldo refused to announce that his daughter and I were no longer engaged. So I would make my position clear to him, to the Commission, and to the other families...

Stefano Vignali did not bend the knee to anyone.

I would never let my son see that happen.

What I planned to do next came from instinct, from my gut, and from my heart. I would announce my engagement to Val. Another layer of protection to help me keep her and Enzo safe. She would be furious with me for it, but eventually she would see reason.

Being the object of her fury again would be a small price to pay for securing their protection.

Bellissima diavola.

It had to be done.

I had to take this first step in the legitimization of our child.

Although not the best time for it, I smiled at my son, Enzo Vignali, and kissed his cheeks.

"You gave me a name, son. That's all I need to get her back."

He held my gaze with unwavering determination.

"Good. You're taking me with you," he said.

"Tony," I called out, still unable to look away from the boy. "Get Bruce in here now."

Tony's jacket rustled as he hurried out of my office.

"I can't take you with me, Enzo. It's too dangerous."

He brought his arms up through mine and shoved my hands off his shoulders.

"It's too dangerous not to take me. You don't know my

school or where the classrooms are or which one's his. I do. And it's a big building. You'll just waste time if you get lost in there, so you need someone who knows where they're going. So yes, you're taking me with you."

The way he arched an eyebrow in defiance after his little speech might have made me laugh in any other circumstance.

"If I put you in any more danger, your mother will never forgive me," I said.

My son narrowed his eyes.

"I will never forgive you if you don't get her back."

The control in his voice was remarkable despite the deepening flush on his cheeks and his hands balling into fists. He hesitated for a second. Then he finished his argument.

"What if it's just like this picture? What if you can't find her because I'm the only one who knows where to go? You need my help. I promise I'll listen to you."

The veins in his forehead and neck pulsed as he stared at me. Not once had he raised his voice. Still, he meant every word.

And he was right. I didn't know the school at all.

After studying him a little longer, I exhaled slowly through my nose, then lowered my voice to keep the sense of urgency out of my tone. Then, when I raised my finger, I forced myself to keep it out of his face. I pointed at the floor between us.

"You will stay behind me at all times. You will do exactly as I say without questioning me. And when it's over, we don't breathe a word of this to your mother. At least not the finer details anyway. Deal?"

His eyes widened in surprise, then he extended his hand.

"Deal."

We had an understanding, an important one, and we shook on it. I stood up as Tony and Bruce entered the room.

"Suit up, Tony. We're heading to—"

I glanced at Enzo for the information.

He stared at me again. Was that skepticism in his eyes?

"I already said I was taking you with me, boy. If nothing else, you can trust I'm a man of my word."

That seemed to satisfy him, so then he looked up at Tony.

"We're going to my school, Saint Christopher in Brooklyn."

"Armed to the teeth," I added. "Bruce, I want everything you can find—last known address, car, license plate, hobbies, known associates, aliases, phone numbers, work history, everything. The name is Donnie Luka."

I looked at Enzo, and he nodded. Then I shifted my attention back to Bruce.

"I want the info ready when Tony or I call you. And keep working on the security feeds. We might need them as backup."

"Yes, sir," Tony and Bruce said at the same time. Then they hurried out of my office.

I looked back at my son.

"What are you going to do while we're out there, Enzo?"

"Stay behind you, do everything you say, and tell you where we need to go."

"Good. Do you need anything before we leave?"

He shook his head so hard his curls bounced against his forehead.

"No, sir. Let's go right now."

I appreciated his eagerness, but we had to be prepared.

"Hang on a minute," I said.

Stepping around my desk, I opened the bottom drawer and unearthed a key buried beneath a stack of folders that unlocked a hidden compartment. I pulled out a polished wooden box, set it down and opened the lid with both hands, staring at the small revolver inside.

Nothing too powerful, but the small .38 Smith & Wesson would do a fine job on its own.

While removing the firearm and its five rounds from the box, I began to explain.

"This gun has been passed down through the family for generations. It's the first weapon we all fire. The weapon we use for training. A basic revolver, small enough for young hands."

I ejected the revolving cylinder and slid the bullets into place, one by one.

Enzo watched my every move.

"I'm not giving this to you to keep. Not until your thirteenth birthday. That's when you'll start arms training like every man in this family before you. But I refuse to take you into a dangerous situation like this one unprotected."

When I sat and nodded, Enzo dutifully approached. I took his hand and pulled him to me, positioning him between my knees. Then I turned him around, so we faced the same direction, and I could direct the next steps over his shoulder with my arms around him.

I handed Enzo the revolver.

"It's heavier than I thought it would be," he said.

"Yes, they're very heavy. So is the damage they can do. Remember that. I don't want you to use this. It's a last resort. But if you must, you need to know how."

I quickly but thoroughly ran him through the basics—how to hold the weapon in both hands by its polished wooden grip, how to aim, how to draw back the hammer, and fire if necessary.

"Where do I put it?" he asked.

"For now, just this once, we're going to tuck it into the back of your waistband. When you're older, we'll get you properly fitted for a holster."

I reached into the box and grabbed the switchblade with the matching wood handle.

"Do you know how to use this?"

He nodded, but I had my doubts.

"Put it in your front pocket and don't take it out unless you absolutely must. And remember, we never tell your mother."

Enzo nodded, turned the knife over once in his hand, and slid it into his pocket.

Then I got up and hurried to the armoire to grab a clean shirt and a leather shoulder holster. In the mirror mounted on the inside of the open armoire door, I watched Enzo watching me arm myself. He didn't say a word.

When I finished, I had several firearms strapped to my body and three knives. I didn't know what to expect, so I had to be prepared for anything.

As soon as I put on my jacket, concealing my weapons, we needed to move.

"Are you ready to go get our girl back?" I asked Enzo.

He gave me a small smile as he nodded.

The simple gesture coming from this child, my child, stoked a gentle and unfamiliar warmth in my chest.

I put my hand on his shoulder, and we headed downstairs.

Tony already sat behind the wheel, waiting near the front door. Enzo and I hopped into the back, closed the doors, and then Tony pulled down the drive and passed through the gate.

Rush hour traffic had decreased, so the ride to Saint Christopher Academy didn't take as long as it might have earlier in the day.

"Want me to go in with you, boss?" Tony asked. "Or stay here and keep the engine running?"

"Stay in the car for now. I'll call if I need you."

He nodded, pulled up beside the large concrete stairs leading to the school's ornate front doors, and shifted into park.

Enzo and I got out of the car and shut our doors at the same time, and I headed for the stairs in a heartbeat. Before I reached them, Enzo grabbed my hand and pulled me to the side.

"Not that way," he said. "They lock that door after school, but the security guards leave one of the side doors unlocked. There's always a guard here, even when everything's closed."

I didn't want to think about why my son knew which of his school's doors were unlocked at any given time of day, but that was a conversation for later.

So we snuck around the side of the large stone building, dodging bushes and piles of leaves left by the groundskeepers to get to the small metal side door.

Enzo reached out to open it, but I put a hand on his shoulder to stop him.

"What are the rules?" I asked.

"Fine," he grumbled, stepping behind me.

"Before I open the door, tell me where we're going."

"There's a small staircase to the left. Mr. Luka's classroom is on the third floor."

"Is the mosaic on the third floor too?"

"Yeah, but it's in front of the main staircase. We'll get to Mr. Luka's room first this way. I think it might be better to check there 'cause it's not like he's going to keep her in the middle of the floor like that when a security guard is here."

"Smart thinking."

I grabbed the metal handle and pulled open the door.

Everything looked clear, so we crept left down the marble hallway to the side staircase. The clean chemical smell alone brought me back to my youth.

Was Enzo like me as a student, reserved and serious? Did he get along with the other kids? Did he have a few friends, or was he more of a loner? Someday I would ask him these things.

As quietly as possible, we climbed to the third floor. At the landing, I shot him a questioning glance, and he pointed straight ahead.

Each classroom had a wooden door with a small placard on it showing the teacher's name and the subject they taught. A small amount of light reflected from the rectangular windows above the placards on each door.

When we came to Mr. Luka's room, the lights were off, but I opened the door anyway. Nothing.

"Okay," I whispered. "Where's the mosaic?"

Enzo pointed down the hall and started in that direction.

"Rules," I reminded him sternly.

He stopped, looked over his shoulder at me, rolled his eyes, and circled back behind me.

Sure, I kind of enjoyed pulling the parent card.

Reaching the mosaic erased any doubt that Val and her kidnapper had been here. A pool of blood greeted us there, dark and thick and stained brown around the edges to match the thinner streaks across the floor.

Those streaks trailed off to the side, interspersed with partial footprints and sporadic smears.

When I looked over my shoulder at Enzo, he'd already started to tremble. I could tell he wanted to run down the hallway and follow the trail. So I turned to him, took a knee, and gripped his shoulders to make him look at me.

Only then, as I studied his face, did I realize he shook not with fear but with rage.

"Look at me," I said.

It took him a second, but when he finally met my gaze, it was crystal clear.

"Do you see what I see here?"

He shook his head.

"Look again. It's mostly dry, even where there's a lot of blood. All the smudges? They're brown. That means all this is hours old."

"We should follow the footprints," he said.

"No, let's be smarter than that. What do you see in those footprints?"

"My mother's blood."

"Well, yes, but there's more. Look at these two first, then this one over here. Two sets. That means she walked away."

It wasn't entirely true. The smaller footprints were uneven, partially smudged and smeared, as if she'd been dragged.

Enzo didn't need to know that.

"Your mother walked away from this," I said. "That means when she left here, she was still okay, so we need to be smart."

"How do we be smart?"

"Look." I pointed at the corner of the hallway to a camera aimed directly at the mosaic. "Is there a security office here?"

He nodded.

"We need to look at the footage from that camera. Let's make sure it really is this Mr. Luka. We might even get a clue to where they went from here."

"The security office is right under us," Enzo said.

"Good. Let's go."

This time, we took the large main staircase to the second

floor. The administration office windows faced the hallway, and on the other side sat one security guard. He reclined in a chair with his feet up on the desk, looking at his phone.

"How did he not hear them?" Enzo asked.

I couldn't stop my lip from curling into a snarl.

"I don't fucking know. But we're going to find out."

We pushed into the office.

Startled, the security guard stumbled onto his feet, catching himself on the back of the chair.

"Y-you can't be here. It's after hours," he said.

I didn't have time for his bullshit.

I pulled the gun from under my left arm and pointed it at his stupid fucking head.

TWENTY-SIX
STEFANO

Tears and snot streamed down the security guard's pale face, mixing on his chin.

"Oh shit, oh shit," he cried. "Please don't kill me, man. Take whatever you want. Anything. I won't say a word."

The weak motherfucking pig.

Enzo watched the man with just as much disdain.

"Dude, get it together," my son said. "We won't kill you unless you make us do it."

I blinked down at him. I couldn't have agreed more, but what nine-year-old talked that way?

Enzo flicked his gaze up to me. "Right?"

"Right," I said, then turned to the guard. "Answer the questions, tell us what we want to know, and you'll be fine."

He wiped his nose on the back of his sleeve, then threaded his fingers together in front of himself.

"S-Sure, man. Whatever you need."

"Good. At what time was the girl shot upstairs on the third floor?" I asked.

His brows raised in surprise.

"What? No, no one was shot here. This is a private school. People don't get shot here. It doesn't happen here."

I rolled my eyes.

"It happens everywhere, you stupid fuck. How long have you been on duty?"

"Since the end of school hours. So like half past three?"

Enzo scoffed at the man, then met my gaze.

"How does he not know she got shot right above him? These halls echo. You can hear things even with our classroom doors shut."

"Never underestimate incompetence," I muttered. "If the rent-a-cop here didn't hear anything, we need another way to get the information."

"How?" Enzo asked.

I pointed at the guard's workstation and the line of monitors flashing between views from the different security cameras around the school. Then I leveled my weapon at the guard's head again.

"There's a security camera on the third floor pointed at the mosaic tiles by the main staircase. Find the camera footage from earlier tonight and start rewinding."

The guard burst into tears again as he sat at the computer.

"H-how far back should I go?"

Enzo reached for my free hand and pulled me back a step, his gaze aimed down at the puddle growing on the floor beneath the guard's pant leg.

For Christ's sake.

I moved around the chair and stood by the guy's dry leg.

"Apparently around three-thirty this afternoon," I said.

As he bobbed his head up and down, he moved the mouse around to wake the computer from a screensaver on a fucking loop. He hadn't even watched the feeds at his own workstation.

"How many guards are here?" I asked.

"Just me. Budget cuts, so we work one at a time."

Finally, the man got the right camera up and went back to the time school closed. Seemed like a quiet building. An occasional straggler in the halls, a lone child running from one classroom to another.

Most figures caught on camera were on their way out.

He sped up the video, making the people on screen look like cartoon characters running around. According to the time-stamp, a tall man entered the frame at 5:30 p.m., hauling another stumbling figure behind him near the large marble staircase.

Val.

"That's him," Enzo shouted. "That's Mr. Luka!"

Then the son of a bitch hit Val hard enough to send her flying across the floor. Even before he'd backhanded her, she looked banged up and bruised.

I hissed out a slow breath, my bones quaking with rage, waiting for Val to roll over, so I could see her face. When she faced the camera again, I didn't recognize her expression.

Nostrils flared, teeth bared, fire raging in her eyes.

My sweet little barista had transformed into a fierce warrior ready to take on the world. It showed me a side of her I'd never seen, not even the night we fought so many years ago.

That night, yes, she'd been furious with me, but she still appeared to be the same woman.

In this video, she looked dangerous, like a determined survivor, a strong woman who could stand by my side and hold her own. Not a trophy wife or stay-at-home mom.

This woman could give orders, strategize, and help me run my empire. Fuck. It had to be the most beautiful thing I'd ever seen, despite the circumstances.

The footage didn't have sound, so I didn't know what she said to him, but her eyes told me everything as she stood and squared off against her kidnapper, her stance wide and steady as she spoke.

Whatever Val had said enraged this Luka piece of shit. He said something to her, his shoulders back and chest pushed out to make himself look bigger. He must have been defending himself.

His efforts hadn't worked because Val laughed. Not with a cute giggle or coquettish simper. No, she tossed her head back, her beautiful dark locks cascading over her shoulders as her mouth opened wide and she belted out wild laughter.

She'd baited him. That much became clear through his body language and hers. Val wanted Luka to yell, scream, make a ruckus to get this worthless security guard's attention, so he would get off his ass and go investigate. Anything to give us a better trail to follow her...

Brilliant idea.

But I'd already seen the photo. I knew what came next on the video playback. The tight grip on my heart squeezed hard when Luka drew his weapon and aimed it at her.

I pulled Enzo over to me, pressing the side of his face against my chest, holding him there, so he couldn't see what then played out on the monitor.

"Holy fuck," the guard whispered. "He's one of the teachers here. I know him..."

The man stumbled over his words as he stood, knocking his chair back, and slipping on his own piss without taking his eyes off the screen. He slowly backed away, as if he thought Luka could turn the gun on him and fire through the video footage.

"Explain to me again," I snarled, "how you sat one story directly below that, surrounded by empty hallways and security monitors, and you didn't hear or see a goddamn thing."

The guard looked away from the screen but kept his gaze away from me, lifting a hand to scratch the back of his neck.

"I-I... maybe I was out doing rounds? Or maybe he had a silencer on the gun?"

"There was no suppressor on that gun," I said. "What the fuck were you really doing?"

His shoulders rose almost to his ears, his elbows tucking in against his sides.

"I-I must've been doing my rounds and just didn't hear it. I swear I didn't hear her."

When he stepped back to get away from me, I saw what he'd been hiding. A headset and gaming system laid on the desk behind him.

I looked at Enzo with a raised brow.

"We're putting you in a better school after this."

Enzo shrugged, then narrowed his eyes.

"You just get my mom back first."

TWENTY-SEVEN
VAL

I worked hard to keep my eyes open as we approached the front door of the dilapidated old house.

The overpowering stink of mildew and rot hit me in the face when we crossed the threshold. What had once been a beautiful middle-class Craftsman home had wasted away with filth and decay.

There was so much lovely detail put into the archways and the floors, all of it likely once a gorgeous cherry red, but now scuffed dry, chipped, and buckling in several places.

The armchairs in the living room had tiny cigarette burns on the arms and the cushions. And the couch's backrest looked to be stained by sweat with something darker on the seat.

The leather upholstered rocking chair with antique brass grommets had a cracked wooden frame. A large section in the front had broken away. It probably still rocked back just fine but rocking forward looked impossible.

Luka swept his arm out theatrically in a ridiculous grand gesture to the living room.

"See?" he said. "You could've had all this. You could have

made this house a home for us. All it really needs is a woman's touch. Could've been your palace after we fixed it up together."

The only thing that would fix this home was a blowtorch.

Trash littered every room—food wrappers and beer bottles and crushed soda cans all over the place. Newspapers and magazines stacked so high they almost reached the ceiling.

Whether it was fuckface Luka himself or the previous inhabitant of this house, whoever had lived there behaved like a damn hoarder.

We walked past the kitchen, and it oozed with the stench of rotting food and death.

Bits of fabric hung from a curtain rod over the kitchen sink window. At one time, the lace had been pretty, but now raggedy shredded strips fell off the wooden dowel, half eaten by insects.

An ancient refrigerator sat in the corner, and its door hung wide open with live mold spilling out of the containers inside.

Something about this house made me so sad.

If I looked closely, I could see the details revealing how deeply loved and cared for this place was in its prime. Now it seemed neglected past the point of no return.

For a moment, I wondered if that was going to be me.

Once Enzo grew up, had his own life, his own wife, his own children, and didn't need to be on the run with me anymore, would he forget me like this house? Neglected and abandoned, left to rot away without a family to fill my days with love and light and warmth?

Without a partner to help take care of me.

Stefano's face popped into my head.

I remembered the date we'd had and how we lay in bed late into the night talking about the future we wanted. Growing old together, taking care of each other and our children, visiting our grandchildren.

That dream had quickly died between us.

The memory of us led me to wonder what Stefano's truth really might be...

Was he truly the man I thought he'd become over the past ten years? Don Vignali, someday the king of all New York kings. Or was Stefano-the-mafia-boss the mask he forced himself to wear for the sake of his family? For the code.

Thinking about the Stefano I'd known first, the man I fell so hard for once upon a time, could that have been a mask worn by the mafia monster?

I just didn't know.

Luka's voice startled me out of my thoughts.

"This home was built for my grandmother," he said. "She was like you. A woman who understood her place and took care of the home. My mother, though... she was different. She didn't deserve this house. I'd hoped to bring Benedetta here. But now I realize that's not in the cards for us."

"Because she didn't love you?"

I hadn't meant to say it out loud, but it grew increasingly harder to focus my thoughts or even control which of them came tumbling out of me.

My mind grew hazier, and my body throbbed with pain.

Luka's eyes flashed with rage as he tightened his jaw and swung back a hand to strike me as he had at the school.

I couldn't control the flinch.

When he saw it, he smiled and dropped his hand.

As if he'd won.

Shit. Maybe he had.

"No, that's not it," he said. "It's because her father wouldn't allow her to marry someone she loved. Instead, he sold her like a prized pig. So I moved on, and I thought for a time that maybe you were the kind of woman who could cherish this home.

"You know, as a poor widow with a child, living above a café, I imagined you would appreciate a home like this."

I needed to keep talking, to keep the conversation going, to stay in the present and not lose my thoughts.

"I already have a home," I blurted.

Talking meant I could ground myself, which meant I could stay awake and be alert longer. If I lost consciousness, especially after all the blood I'd lost, I might never wake up.

Although I believed Stefano would take care of Enzo, that wasn't the life I wanted for my son.

Enzo and Stefano knew each other now, making it impossible to put the genie back in the bottle. That had no bearing on my aversion to handing Stefano the reins. He would not be the one deciding how to raise my son.

So I needed to fight.

And I needed to remember who I fought for.

My grandmother had always said, pain reminded us that we were still alive. When we felt pain, we had to remember why we pressed onward, why we continued fighting.

I pressed my hand against the bullet wound on my upper arm, trying to staunch the bleeding again.

And to feel the pain.

The agony came roaring back, and it sharpened my resolve.

If the ensuing adrenaline burst woke me enough to keep my wits about me, I would take as much pain as I could get.

So I kept my hand there, pressing harder when my eyelids grew heavy, or when my vision blurred.

Luka dragged me through the horrible, decomposing house

until he stopped at a wooden door with peeling paint. Once he opened it, that door yawned down a steep staircase, fading into the darkness below.

Goosebumps raised over my skin, covering my entire body as I stared into the abyss.

"No," I whispered.

I tried to back away from the door. I knew what basements meant. People disappeared into them, never to be seen again.

"You don't get to say that to me," Luka shouted.

In the next second, he claimed a fistful of my hair again and jerked me after him down the stairs.

My options were to be dragged down or thrown down, and I didn't need a concussion on top of everything else, though I couldn't be sure I didn't already have one.

I complied just enough to stumble down the stairs.

"What exactly do you want from me, Luka?"

"Only what I deserve. And you'll call me Donnie, you disobedient bitch."

The only thing you deserve is a bullet between your eyes.

I bit my tongue to keep from sharing that one out loud.

"And what do you think you deserve... Donnie?" I asked.

"The same as every man. A beautiful woman to keep my home, warm my bed, raise my children, and serve me. Just like God intended. No more, no less."

Oh, mother of Christ. I prayed Stefano came quickly, so I could escort this spineless coward straight to hell.

I stopped in my tracks. The basement was by far the worst part of the house, and it had nothing to do with the smell.

Photos of Benedetta covered every inch of the back wall. The images ranged from when she'd been a young girl around the age of ten to earlier today as she left Stefano's house in the gorgeous sheath dress she wore that morning.

"What are you, her stalker?"

A sneer marked his lips, his entire face.

"I'm the love of her life," he said. "And she's mine, the Juliet to my Romeo. Which barely makes you Rosaline, doesn't it?"

The last part didn't quite make sense, but I didn't have the patience for fucking Shakespeare references.

But if he thought of himself as a star-crossed teenage boy who would end his own tragedy by killing himself, I sure as hell wouldn't stop him.

"Then why did you bring me here? You want me to... what? Clean the basement for you?"

"You misunderstand. Caring for my home is a privilege reserved only for my wife. You had your chance, but that's gone now. Honestly, I should've taken it from you the second I found out about Enzo's father."

He just kept talking and talking as he trudged across the basement, his fingers still entangled in my hair.

"The second I saw the engagement announcement, it was all right there, staring me in the face. Vignali standing there beside my Benedetta. How much Enzo looks like him. I knew then what had happened, just like I knew you were nothing more than a worthless whore.

"But I'm a decent man. I still gave you a chance. An opportunity to better yourself, to provide a better life for you and your son. You just weren't smart enough to take it."

I shook my head to keep it clear, to keep myself thinking.

"So you brought me here because I wouldn't date you?"

Luka looked at me in surprise and clicked his tongue.

"Really, Valerie? This isn't even about you now. I brought

you here because everyone knows the best way to kill a rat is to lay a trap. And every trap needs something the rat wants."

"So I'm the bait," I seethed through my teeth.

"Something like that."

He yanked me to the back of the basement, spun me around, and shoved me against the wall plastered with photos. Before I could react, he'd pinned me there against the cold concrete with nothing other than his hand on my throat.

I wanted to fight him, but my arms weighed so much. My failed attempt only knocked a few photos off the wall.

Holding me there with one hand, he fished around for something dangling beside me.

Metal clinked near my ear, then a harsh, cold weight settled around my neck with a heavy click. Then my wrists.

I could hardly hold myself up anymore.

Luka stepped back, tilting his head, grinning like a madman as he admired his accomplishment.

I stepped forward to pull away from the wall, but the cold metal stopped me short and jerked me back with clinking and rattling. The back of my head cracked against the stone, rustling more photos as I thumped against the wall.

The sick fuck had chained me to his Benedetta gallery.

His gaze moved up and down my body as he continued patting himself on the back.

"Let's see if your lover is as smart as you think he is. What do you say? Can he follow the clues to find you before it's too late?"

"What do you mean, it's too late?" I asked.

My eyelids fluttered as I struggled against not only the chains, but also my quickly draining strength.

"Too late for what?" I repeated, now slurring consistently.

"Well, for starters, Valerie, you won't be able to put pressure on that wound anymore."

He slid his fingers beneath my sweater and violently ripped at it. The sleeve split, tearing away from where it had stuck to the bullet wound.

I bit back a scream, still not willing to give him the satisfaction of my pain even as I broke into a cold sweat. Hot blood ran down my arm, splattering against my hip.

He tapped his stupid fucking chin without realizing he smeared my blood on his stubble.

"You've already lost a lot of blood. And judging by how much you're still bleeding, I'll give it an hour. Maybe a few more minutes because it's so cold in here and that might slow it down a bit. Do you think he'll get here before you die?"

A dark laugh escaped me.

"Doesn't matter if I'm dead or alive. He's going to kill you."

"He won't catch me. But hey, you know what? Since I'm such a nice guy, I'll give him a fighting chance."

He reached into his pocket, pulled out his cell phone, and showed me the picture he took earlier at the school.

Me, on the floor, glaring at him from a pool of my blood.

"I'm going to print this as a little gift for him. Put it somewhere fun. The courier will have to fetch it first, then deliver it. That could take up to an hour, depending on traffic, I guess."

He shrugged and smiled like the evil man he was.

"So Valerie, is there enough time for him to find you?"

TWENTY-EIGHT

STEFANO

I stared down at the security guard, hoping the lazy asshole didn't piss himself again.

"This was forty fucking minutes ago. There's no way he left this school without being caught on at least one camera. You're going to find every second of that footage. Now."

The man nodded, trembling as he righted his chair and went to work logging the video timestamps.

When he found the footage, we watched Luka drag Val into a service elevator tucked between the maintenance rooms. Then they went down another staircase to the faculty parking garage beneath the school building.

In each frame, Val looked weaker than in the one before, her feet scraping the concrete, her skin so pale. Blood dripped from her arm, leaving a dotted line in their wake.

Her blood loss concerned me. It couldn't be sustained.

"Find the feed for the exterior camera and show me in which direction he drove away."

As the guard worked on finding the street footage, I grabbed my phone and called Bruce.

"Did you get the address?" I asked.

"There's no Donnie Luka in New York or New Jersey, boss. The name doesn't exist in the PD's records either."

I exhaled while pinching the bridge of my nose, restraining my desire to yell at him, and disconnected the call. If Bruce had something worth my time, he would have said so right away. And I didn't have the patience for any more bad news.

I pointed at the guard with my gun.

"You. Where do they keep the personnel files here?"

"I don't have access to—"

"That's not what I asked," I snapped.

"Most stuff should be in the computer system. But I d-don't have admin access."

I aimed the pistol between his eyes and raised my brow.

"B-But the principal likes to do some things old-school. She has some paper files in her office."

"Show me."

"I... I can't. There's a camera in there. I'll lose my job."

Enzo erupted, his face red, his blue eyes turning black.

"If my mama dies, you'll lose more than that," he shouted.

I put my hand on his shoulder, reminding him to breathe.

He wiped at his face to hide the tear rolling down his cheek.

"I'm sorry, Enzo. Follow me," the guard said.

The man got out of his chair and pulled out a ring of keys from his pocket. Then he led the way to the largest of the individual offices along the back wall.

Shaking violently, he failed his first three attempts to get the key into the lock. Finally, he opened the principal's office door and made a beeline to a large filing cabinet, immediately pulling open the second drawer.

"Top two drawers are the teacher files," he said. "But I don't see one here for Luka."

"What?"

I shoved his stupid ass aside, and sure enough, no file for Donnie Luka existed in that metal cabinet.

Fuck. He'd used the name as a cover.

"Luka isn't his real name, and we don't have time for this."

None. So I ripped all the files out of the drawer and tossed them on the floor.

"Look for his picture," I snapped.

As I emptied the top drawer, Enzo and the guard dropped down and searched the records. Each employee file included their photo clipped inside the cover, thank Christ.

Panic rushed through my blood, making my hands shake.

The clock ticked on.

Val wouldn't survive the rapid blood loss much longer.

I kneeled to help move the files they discarded out of the way. My son and the guard knew Luka's face, but I didn't have any idea what the son of a bitch looked like.

With each discarded file, tension gained strength in my gut. It squeezed my lungs, forced my heart to beat harder and faster.

Enzo's mouth suddenly popped open wide, and he stared inside the file in his hands.

"Here it is! This is him! It's Mr. Luka's face, but it says his name is Donnie Cozza."

I froze hearing the name.

The Cozza family once worked for the Capaldos.

I snatched the file and jumped to my feet. The face of the walking dead man who'd taken what belonged to me stared out from the photo. Then I grabbed my phone, snapped a picture, and sent it to Bruce with orders to pull every spec of information on Donnie Cozza and any living family members.

"How often are these files updated?" I demanded.

The guard looked up at me as he wiped sweat off his face.

"Mine's done every year," he murmured.

I tucked the file under my arm.

"Get the fuck up."

He complied as fast as his clumsy, trembling body let him. He stood directly before me with his gaze on the floor.

"Look at me," I said. "I understand keeping your position means you'll have to inform the police that my son and I were here. You'll call it in right after we leave. Correct?"

"Yes, sir."

"Before we go, you're going to erase all security footage with the two of us."

I gestured toward Enzo, then to myself.

"Yes, sir," the man repeated, nodding this time.

"And Enzo's mother with the piece-of-shit teacher who shot her. That's the only way you get out of here alive. Have I made myself clear?"

Again, the guard nodded, then he ran to his workstation.

Enzo and I followed and stood behind his chair. Then my son tugged on my arm.

"Why are we still here?" he asked. "We have the address. Why aren't we going to get her?"

"We have an address, son, but we can't be sure if it's the right one. If his name was a cover, the other details might also be fake. My men are running his real name to get the correct information.

"We're letting the men do their jobs, so when we leave, we

know we're going to the right place. I don't want to waste time driving around the city. Do you?"

Enzo shook his head. His eyes were now half blue, half black and glossy with unshed tears.

I squeezed his shoulder, wishing I knew more about how to comfort him.

"It's done," the guard announced.

"What's done?" I asked, to be clear.

"I erased every file from four o'clock on. It's all gone. And the cameras are off right now. See? The screens are dark."

"Good," I said. "You've been very helpful."

Then I cracked the butt of my pistol against his temple. One swift hit, and he went down, out cold.

Enzo stared with wide eyes at the guard lying on the floor.

"Why did you do that?" he whispered.

"He's not dead, only unconscious for a short time. This keeps him from changing his mind before we're far enough away that it won't matter."

The boy nodded. "Can we go now?"

"Yeah, we can. Tony's waiting for us."

We made our way to the main entrance, both of us deep in our thoughts.

My men would need a few minutes to verify the correct information, and I needed a few minutes to think through what I'd learned.

My son had been attending a school where the principal willingly hired a known associate of mafia families before also hiding his identity.

On the outside, Saint Christopher Academy looked like the perfect school for a young Italian boy, but Enzo couldn't stay.

No fucking way.

He deserved better.

Enzo was strong, willful, with the raw skills, intelligence, and aptitude for success, and I would be damned if I let a second-rate school help shape him into the man he was meant to be.

In that moment, I finally understood my father. I didn't agree with many of the things he'd done, but now I had a better grasp on what it meant to be a parent—what it meant to be angry when things weren't good enough for my child.

To some degree, I also understood my mother. She couldn't bear the pain of losing my brother, not after she'd already lost my sister to a marriage contract.

Still, I would never forgive her for leaving me the way she had, when I needed her the most, but her reasons made more sense to me now than they had previously.

Love, in all its forms, was a powerful motivator...

And a crushing goddamn weight.

My phone buzzed with an incoming text message.

BRUCE

Sending Tony directions now

Rather than replying, I called Bruce to tell him once we had Val safe, once we neutralized the threat, and I killed Donnie Cozza, I wanted the engagement announcement I'd prepared forwarded to *The New York Times* and *The Herald*.

I wanted Bruce to hear me say the words.

I wanted him to hear in my voice how important it was to me for the families and the Commission to see that Valerie Salera belonged to me, that our son would be treated as my legitimate child and heir from this day forward.

When I got into the vehicle, Enzo had already buckled in,

ready to go. Tony had Bruce again, on the Bluetooth speakers, and finished punching the address into the navigation system.

He disconnected the call just as I closed my door.

"Bruce followed up on the addresses," Tony said. "The one in his employee file was old, but we called in a favor and got the address for his mother's house. She died a few years ago and left it to him."

"Are we sure he's there?" I asked.

"Yeah, we've got two men sitting outside now. They say it's quiet inside, but his car's there. There's blood smeared on the trunk and a bloody handprint on the license plate. Want 'em to go inside or wait for us?"

"How far away are we?"

"About three minutes."

"Close. Good. Tell them to keep an eye on the place. Scout the area to be sure no one else is around. But make sure they stay out of sight. I don't want him to know we're coming."

"You got it, Stef. I'm on it."

Tony punched the message into his phone, then tore away from the curb.

"Tell me everything we know about this guy," I said.

"His father worked for the Capaldo family. Some low-level soldier, but he ended up being a favorite. His mother was mentally ill. When he was a kid, the Capaldos took him in, but that ended because of an issue between him and Benedetta.

"Not sure what happened, but Don Capaldo kicked him out, then the guy went to live with his mother. She left him the house. He's behind on taxes. Still has a mortgage. The bank's foreclosing. Several registered firearms. Short rap sheet. Stalking, sexual harassment, but nothing ever stuck."

Tony made a sharp right turn, making the tires squeal.

"False allegations, or a coverup by Capaldo?" I asked.

"Not sure. Bruce will find out."

Fuck. We could use more information than that, but this had to be good enough for now. I still didn't know what we were walking into, or how mentally unstable this guy might be.

We pulled up in front of the house, and two Vignali family soldiers met us at the car.

"It's completely quiet on the ground floor," one said, "but we heard something come from the basement. No windows down there, so we haven't been able to check it out yet."

I gave a clipped nod, got out, and drew my forty-five. The gun's heavy weight always gave me comfort.

Whether due to the weight, the cold steel, or the amount of power, holding this gun made me feel invincible. It always had.

"Tony, stay here with the kid." I turned to the soldiers. "You two go around back and keep watch. The son of a bitch does not leave this house alive. This ends tonight, and with one hell of a message."

"I'm coming with you," Enzo blurted.

I stopped his door from opening.

"No, you're not. You'll stay in the car where it's safe. You'll see your mother when I bring her out to you."

He looked up at me with his pleading eyes.

"But what about you, Mr. Vignali? You need backup."

Pain and joy thumped inside my chest at once.

He'd called me "Mr. Vignali" again, but he cared enough to offer himself as my backup. I reminded myself the name thing would get worked out at another time and shook my head.

"That's not happening. You're a child. Get in the car."

Then I hovered over him, waiting impatiently.

If anything happened to him, I would never forgive myself. I would never willingly put him or any child in this situation.

Yes, I'd already gone too far by bringing him to the school with me, even though he proved himself to be an asset there. But in that filthy, decaying house, where a madman with a vendetta held his mother captive?

Absolutely not.

"I'm going in there," Enzo said. "And if you wanna stop me, you're gonna have to shoot me."

Before his words even sunk in, the boy shoved open the car door, smashing it against my leg, hopped out, and sprinted toward the house.

I bit back a curse and ran after him. My hand came down around the nape of his neck just as he opened the door.

"Get back to the car," I growled.

"No," he said, trying to wriggle away from my grip.

"That was not a request, Enzo."

I wrapped my arm around his middle and hauled him back to the vehicle.

A door slammed somewhere inside the house.

We didn't have time for this argument.

I set my son down on his feet, maybe a little more firmly than necessary, and spun him to face me before pointing at him.

"You and I will have a talk about this later, and it will not be a pleasant experience. For now, you stay behind me at all times. If anything goes wrong, you run. You find Tony. Do you understand me?"

A single nod from the boy.

This was by far the dumbest shit I'd ever done, creeping through an abandoned house with a nine-year-old on my heels and a crazy fucker hiding somewhere inside.

Definitely wouldn't get the Father of the Year award.

But we were truly out of time.

Val needed immediate medical attention, or she would die.

So I led a cautious charge through the open front door with Enzo behind me.

A sharp cry echoed up the basement stairs into the kitchen.

"She's in the basement," Enzo breathed.

I couldn't risk clearing the rest of the house myself.

I texted Tony.

Clear the house now

Then I met my son's gaze.

"Let's get down there and get our girl," I said.

TWENTY-NINE
STEFANO

I drew my forty-five again, hesitating for a second with my left hand on the tarnished brass knob.

Pieces of peeling white paint dropped onto my shoes and the floor as I cracked open the basement door and listened.

Enzo stood behind me. His rapid little puffs of breath against my jacket warmed a small spot on my back.

"I'm going to open it and go down slowly, step by step. You stay close to me, boy," I said.

I glanced over my shoulder, and he nodded his head.

The door creaked open, revealing a narrow staircase leading to pitch darkness. I could only make out three steps before me.

Enzo followed each of my steps with a lighter one of his own, staying on my heels as he'd been instructed. Then he shoved at my back in his desperation to get to his mother faster.

I spun my head and glared at him, raised a finger to my lips before he could complain, then pointed to my eyes and an ear.

We had to be alert and listen for every little sound. I couldn't have him running blindly into the unknown danger waiting at the bottom for us.

When he gave me a second solemn nod, I knew he understood what I'd meant.

Other than my heart pounding against my ribcage, the pulse rushing into my ears, only dead silence came from the stairwell and the basement. The closer we got to the bottom, the easier it was to see a soft glow bending around the corner of the landing.

The last stair tread buckled in the center under my weight and squeaked.

I stopped, listened, held my gun in the low-ready position.

A light flicked on.

The instant glare from the lightbulb dangling from the ceiling blinded me for a second.

My eyes adjusted... and my heart stopped.

Enzo's teacher stood at the far side of the basement, beaming with a manic smile. He gripped Val by the throat with one hand. With his other hand, he pressed a gun barrel against her temple.

Beside them, a section of broken concrete exposed the earth beneath it. There was a hand-shoveled hole large enough for two bodies.

"Well," the dead fucking man walking said, "you surprised me. You got here faster than I anticipated. Still not fast enough to save her. I wanted her to bleed out, but shooting her in the head also works for me."

I took one step forward.

Blood covered Val's right side. She'd lost too much and struggled to keep her eyes open... she would pass out soon.

I. Will. Kill. That. Motherfucker.

But until I could get her away from this sociopathic son of a bitch, I had to keep her calm. I forced my rage back and kept my demeanor as low key as possible. For her sake.

"Val. Angel, how are you holding up?"

She blinked and pulled against the chains holding her there.

The man shifted, placing Val between himself and me.

"Oh, no you don't, Prince Charming. You stay right where you are. And tell this bitch not to fight me," he said.

He pushed his pistol harder against her temple, making an indentation on the side of her face.

Val winced.

I clenched my jaw, gnashing my back teeth.

My father had often said to my brother and me that a man who was talking was a man who wasn't taking any action. I had to keep this man talking.

"What the fuck do you want, Cozza?" I asked.

"Same as you. A warm home, loving family, obedient wife. But you took mine from me."

"I don't even know you."

His crazed eyes reflected the brightness of the lightbulb.

"You should. You know my name, it seems. I'm a fair man, so I'll give you a hint. I'm the man your fiancée really loves."

I jerked my chin toward Val.

"Doesn't look like she likes you at all."

"Not this slut. She was my second choice. Until I realized her bastard was yours. God no, I mean my angel, Benedetta. She was perfect for me. She should have been my wife."

"You'll have to take that up with her father," I said.

"I did. He doesn't care about what's best for his daughter. He doesn't care that I'm the one to love her and give her children. He only cares about his empire. Then you came sniffing around with your disgraced family name, but yours was apparently still better than mine, honor be damned."

He paused, looking me up and down while licking his lips, then he suddenly shrieked.

"You should've called off the wedding, Vignali! None of this had to happen. But you just couldn't do what you were told."

"I did call it off, you asshole. I'm marrying Valerie."

Her eyes widened, and she nailed me with a hard stare.

My timing was shitty as always, but I couldn't stop myself from flashing her a smirk.

Cozza shrieked at me again.

"You lie!"

Then Enzo made a move behind me.

God-fucking-damn it.

Now I had to split my attention between two threats.

I kept my gaze forward, not wanting to alert this fucking madman to my son's presence. As unstable as Donnie Cozza had turned out to be, I didn't know how he would react.

In my periphery, I tracked Enzo's movement as he slipped through the shadows on my right before hiding behind a tall stack of magazines, likely calculating a path to take him closer.

If he'd been anyone else, if he was older and had training, I might have called this a brilliant move.

But this was my child, a nine-year-old boy who had never held a gun before I put one in his hands. He should've been in the car, not trying to flank some psycho to save his mother.

I had to keep Cozza talking.

The good news? Men like this one, who said dumb shit like wanting an obedient wife, all had the same problem. They always thought they were in control.

Whenever someone had to declare they were in charge, it meant they were not. This beta bitch teacher only played at what he thought an alpha male should be.

That made him stupid and easily manipulated.

Any sign of disrespect would drive him batshit crazy.

I remembered the video with Val yelling at him, saying something that had enraged him enough to make him snap. She'd been baiting him... but certainly hadn't intended to get herself shot. Hell, I'd only taken one bullet this week. I could take another for her.

While staring the motherfucker up and down, I grinned, baiting him as she'd done.

"If Benedetta loved you so much, Cozza," I called across the basement, "why didn't you just run away with her? She would've gone with you, right? Because she loved you? Wait. That's right. You weren't man enough to take her like I did."

His lip curled into a snarl.

"You don't know what you're talking about, Vignali."

"Oh, but I do. Benedetta and I had many conversations before our engagement. We talked about what we did and didn't want in our marriage. She said she'd never been in love. That no one had ever made her heart beat faster than I did."

I narrowed my eyes at the pathetic little shit.

"So what happened? She forgot about you? You don't matter to her like she matters to you? Does she even know your name?"

The asshole's face turned fifty shades of red. Sweat soaked his hair and dripped down the sides of his face. Spittle flew from his mouth as he shrieked again.

"You don't know what the fuck you're talking about!"

"I do, but you got what you wanted anyway. You told me to break off my engagement to Benedetta, and I did that. It's not my fault she doesn't know your name while you're waiting by the phone to hear from her. I mean, what makes you think you're good enough for either of these women?"

"Because I'm a real man. I can provide for them. I can—"

He stopped mid-sentence and looked around the space. He'd heard Enzo drawing closer through the shadows.

Fuck. I had to draw the psycho's attention back to me.

"Provide for them?" I scoffed. "On a teacher's salary? What exactly are you going to provide... this rundown old house that should've been demolished years ago?"

His sneer trembled, and I hoped to hell I had him snagged.

"You've seen the way Benedetta dresses," I continued. "You couldn't afford one of her handbags if you saved for a decade."

Now his arms trembled. The pistol in his hand shook.

"You don't know what you're talking about," he repeated. "I work at a prestigious academy."

"You work in an overpriced shithole, where the principal is so underpaid, she took a bribe to hire you. Benedetta needs a king. She would never love a pauper like you."

I shook my head and *tsked*.

"You are no king," I added.

A sound like a shoe scuffing against the side of a box came from the stacks of junk in the corner. Cozza whipped his head in that direction.

Taking a couple of steps forward, I dragged my feet, making a similar noise as I moved.

"And what about Valerie? How are you going to support her and her child, Cozza? You said you wanted more children. So how will you get the money to feed them?

"Both women need a real man. Someone in charge who can take care of them in the way they deserve. You can't even take care of yourself. You don't deserve these women. They're far beyond your means."

"Nothing is beyond my means," he snapped.

"Nothing is within your means," I countered. "Look at this place. It's falling apart all around you. And I know for a fact you didn't pay for this shithole. You inherited it."

He blinked several times like he realized I knew his real identity, that I'd uncovered all his secrets.

But he still hadn't lost it. I had to push him harder.

"And even still," I said, "you're about to lose this house. I know you're behind on the taxes. And you have one month tops before this place goes into foreclosure. Pretty sure the only reason it's been delayed is because the bank took one look at this dump and realized they couldn't even sell it."

"If I had a wife, she would—"

"If you had a wife, she would kill herself," I said.

That one hit a nerve.

"You don't deserve them either," Cozza shouted. "Why don't I just take care of this one for us both right now, huh? Then we'll go find Benedetta and make sure she knows a real man will marry her if you won't."

"And who the fuck would that be?"

"Me," he screamed. "I'm the real man! I deserve her!"

I let out a bitter laugh.

"You have no idea. You think taking sniper shots at a child makes you a man? You think stalking women, hitting them, shooting one because you can't control her makes you a man? No, Cozza. That makes you a sick little bitch."

His hand gripping the gun seemed even more unsteady. It would take only one little jerk, and that would be it.

His grip around Val's throat tightened, his fingers digging

into her flesh, bruising her. Her lips had shifted in hue from their naturally pretty pink to gray. Soon they would be blue.

"Why don't you let the girl go?" I asked calmly. "Then we'll settle this man to man. Come on, just you and me. Right here, right now. We'll find out who deserves what. Winner takes all."

"You don't deserve anything," he spat.

"That might be true. I haven't always been a good man. But I know what you deserve."

"And what's that, Vignali?"

I tilted my head, grinned at him again.

"A shallow grave."

He shook his head and screwed up his face.

Good. Another tantrum.

"Think you can talk to me like that and get your slut back in one go? No! You know what? I think I'll kill her now. Get her out of the way. Then we can settle the rest man to man."

He twisted the barrel into Val's temple, drawing back the hammer this time with a final click.

She let out a low whine.

I reached out with my left hand, like I could stop him from pulling the trigger. I couldn't. Then Enzo emerged from the darkness behind his teacher, with the blade I'd given him open.

In one swift move, the boy crouched and brought the switchblade slashing across the backs of Cozza's legs.

With a scream, the man's knees buckled. His pistol clattered to the ground, and he lost his grip on Val.

Then Donnie Cozza tripped on his own feet in his attempt to spin toward his attacker, which sent him toppling sideways over the broken concrete, into the hole he'd dug himself.

Val fell to her knees, wheezing as she snatched up the gun

into her trembling hands. She crawled to the hole, dragging the length of the chains with her, and stared into it.

The raging scream bursting from her lips coursed through her entire body, making her tremble even more. Before I could react, she fired Cozza's weapon, slapping the hammer back after every shot as she screamed.

Even after the rounds had been emptied from the cylinder, she kept pulling the trigger. The basement filled with empty, hollow clicks one after the other.

Only when she ran out of breath did she stop.

"Mama," Enzo cried.

The revolver fell from her hands.

Stunned, she turned to see her boy, staring at him as if she couldn't believe what her dimming eyes were showing her.

He ran to her.

I ran to her.

We got her up on her feet.

She reached down and brushed her fingers over our son's cheek. Then she whirled on me.

"You brought him here?" she croaked.

Fire flashed in her eyes, and I didn't have a chance to say anything before she shouted at me.

"You brought my son into this hell? With this madman? You gave him a weapon? He's a child!"

Val raised her hand as if she meant to strike me, but then her eyes rolled back, and she collapsed.

I caught her in my arms before her body slumped against the chains.

My men rushed down into the basement, shouting questions, asking for orders.

"Get these fucking chains off her now," I said.

"Is Mama alive?" Enzo whispered, his eyes wide and glossy.

My boy. My heart. Thoughts of my own mother's death.

Goddamn it, I could only give him a reassuring nod.

"She's alive, son," I said. "Let's get her to the doctor."

While Tony removed the second iron cuff, I craned my neck around to see into the hole.

Cozza's shallow grave.

A pile of bloody flesh.

I rushed up the stairs with Val in my arms, shouldering past the men as they pressed themselves against the staircase wall.

Enzo stayed close on my heels.

I shouted at Tony.

"Tell the doctor she needs blood."

A lot of blood.

Then I ran to the car, her body dangling over my arms.

Praying it wasn't too late.

THIRTY
VAL

y weak body trembled with cold. So much cold.

We were moving.

A smooth ride this time, no musty stench, no confinement.

Strong arms cradled me, warming me like a familiar security blanket I never wanted to give up.

I opened my eyes.

Beautiful eyes stared back at me. Not one pair of beautiful eyes but two pairs, so much the same and yet so different.

Dark blue, worried, hardened.

Dark blue, worried, innocent.

A hand pressed down hard on my arm.

Pressure but no pain.

Only cold, cold blood. But without the pain...

Was I alive?

Blurs of light sped past.

My eyelids grew heavy again, so I let them close.

My mind faded back into dark oblivion.

ALIVE

The jostling of my body and my flailing arms pulled me back into a distant awareness again.

I opened my eyes and met Stefano's gaze as he carried me in his arms, holding me against the warmth of his chest.

His breath pumped in and out. He was running.

His woodsy scent with its notes of whiskey and a spicy floral, iris maybe, overwhelmed my senses.

Proof I still lived.

He shouted at someone, his deep timber echoing through me as if he stood at the opposite end of a long, empty tunnel.

I wanted to say something, anything, but I couldn't push out enough breath to form any words.

Then his warmth left me. His eyes. His scent. Gone.

He'd let me go.

Please come back.

Wait. A cold, hard surface—I lay on his desk.

The thought gave me a fleeting moment of happiness.

And then I lost myself to that fucking darkness again.

STILL ALIVE

Searing hot pain burst through my arm, shooting up through my shoulder, and I screamed.

I was still alive, and now wide awake.

The cold left me, everything becoming hot and wet and sticky. Sweat covered every part of me, which kind of didn't make sense because my entire body trembled and shook.

An older man with white hair stood over me, studying my

arm with small magnifying attachments on each lens of his eyeglasses. Stefano's private physician.

"Hang in there, kiddo. Not much longer," he said. "I found the bullet. Now we must get it out."

With great effort, I rolled my head to the side and focused my gaze on Stefano. He sat beside me, holding my hand between his own strong hands.

The tube attached to my wrist with layers of medical tape had an enormous needle going into my arm. Not the normal tubing you would see with a standard IV but thicker, with dark liquid running through it into my vein.

I sucked in a sharp breath and stared at Stefano.

The line in my arm came straight from his.

"You lost a lot of blood," he said.

"Are you... umm..."

I couldn't remember my question.

Haziness muddled my thoughts, like I had to force them through a thick fog before my words could come out.

The one thing that came through loud and clear?

The pain. I would take the pain, though. All of it. Because it meant I had lived to see another day for my son.

Stefano asked and answered my question.

"A universal donor? Yes."

Sweet mother of Christ, was he trying to hold back a smirk?

"Squeeze my hand, Val," he added, "until the anesthesia takes you under again."

I blinked, not able to manage even a nod.

But where was Enzo?

"My son?"

"Our son... is safe in his room, cleaning up. I didn't want him to see this, to see you hurting like this. He'll be back soon."

"Okay," I whispered.

If nothing else, I approved of the way Stefano had handled that part of the whole mess.

I absolutely did not want Enzo to see me like this.

I didn't want to see myself like this.

So I just shut my eyes while the doctor pushed the anesthesia into my arm.

Then I drifted away again.

DEFINITELY ALIVE

When I woke from the anesthesia, Stefano had me tucked into his bed and surrounded with his expensive down pillows and silk sheets.

I didn't know how long I'd been out, but the plush mattress made me want to sink in deeper and go back to sleep.

My arm throbbed like crazy, though, and hunger pangs burned the lining of my stomach.

I needed food and painkillers. And an enormous glass of water. The impossible dryness in my throat brought a new kind of agony, adding to the miserable mix.

With more effort than it should have taken, I wiggled myself to the edge of the bed, got to my feet, and stumbled to the door.

My head spun, and my vision blurred. I braced myself on the doorframe for a minute before I could stand straight and focus my eyes.

Only then did I realize I wore the same Neiman Marcus robe from my first night in Stefano's house. How long ago had that been? Two nights? More?

Gathering myself together, I pulled the sides of my robe around me, tied the belt, and opened the door. Then I made my way down the hallway, keeping one hand on the wall so I didn't fall on my face. Every step made my legs tremble, and the dizziness increased. I stopped several times to catch my breath.

I didn't know how long it took me to get downstairs, but at least I didn't run into anyone along the way. The journey literally left me in worse shape than when I'd started out.

But I couldn't just stay in bed.

When I got to the kitchen, Stefano sat alone at the island, eating the last orange spice cookie while staring at his phone.

"Where's my son?" I asked.

Stefano stood. "Our son... is getting gun safety training."

I heaved a shaky sigh.

"Why are you teaching a nine-year-old to play with guns?"

"I'm teaching a nine-year-old to never play with weapons and making sure he understands why. I planned to make him wait until he turned thirteen, same as me. But after all that's happened, I can see he's stubborn enough to find a gun himself and try to figure it out on his own. Training him now is safer."

"You could just tell him no."

Boss man arched an eyebrow.

"That word means very little to him. I don't know if that's on you or him, but it needs to be addressed. I told him no when he wanted to help me find you. I told him no when he wanted to enter that house with me. I told him to stay in the car. And do you know what your son did?"

I hooked my hands on my hips.

"Oh, so now he's only my son?"

Stefano fixed me with an unamused gaze.

"Come here to me."

Then he lifted me and sat my ass on the countertop. His

hands came down flat on either side of me, caging me in, all the while holding my gaze with his.

"Enzo told me if I wanted to stop him from going into that house, I would have to shoot him first. Then he smashed the car door into my leg and ran past me like a lunatic."

I nodded. "Yeah, that sounds like him."

Enzo had always been so smart. Along with his intelligence came an unwavering concept of right and wrong. He always did what he thought was right, consequences be damned.

With a shrug, Stefano stepped back.

"So he'll learn the basics of gun safety now."

I sighed and dipped my head.

"The boy must learn to be more obedient, Val," he added. "Gun safety alone isn't enough."

If this were any other day, I would have argued with him, but I just didn't have the energy to fight with this man, so I nodded. He was probably right anyway.

"Good. We'll work on it together. Now why are you out of bed?" he asked.

"I wanted to see Enzo and I desperately needed some water and I'm starving."

Stefano went to the pantry, calling out over his shoulder.

"You're hungry... that's a good sign. What would you like?"

I stared at his back, wondering if he actually knew his way around the kitchen as he stood halfway inside the pantry.

"You're going to cook for me?" I asked.

He came back with takeout menus and flashed a wide grin.

A devilishly handsome grin.

The one that made me fall for him in the first place.

Then he slapped the stack of menus down on the countertop beside me.

"Not quite. We'll order something in."

As I sorted the menus, he filled a glass with cold water from the pitcher in the fridge and handed it to me.

"Red meat," I said. "Steak. Or a burger. Something juicy."

"Smart. The iron will help your recovery. Steak it is."

I gulped down the water while he placed an order and sent one of his men to pick it up.

The room spun. I set down the glass and shut my eyes, willing it to stop. Maybe a distraction would make it go away.

"Tell me what happened, Stefano."

When I opened my eyes, he stood right there, studying my face, my bandaged arm, touching my cheek.

"You feel warm. We should get you back to bed. I'll bring the food up to you."

I shook my head, adding to the dizziness, damn it.

"No, tell me what happened. Please, I need to know."

Placing his hands on my legs, he went over his version, filling in some blanks for me. Then I told him mine, starting with Con Amore. I explained how that weasel broke in while Enzo and I were upstairs in the apartment.

"That wall full of Benedetta's photos in the basement," he said. "Some creepy shit."

A dry chuckle slipped out of my mouth.

"That was probably the least creepy thing about the psycho. Where is he? He's been taken care of, right?"

The little line between Stefano's eyes grew deeper.

"What? Val, you shot him," he said. "Several times. You don't remember?"

"I don't want to remember. Not yet," I whispered.

He brushed over my cheek with the back of his fingers, so softly, and gave me a slight nod.

"There are other things we should talk about... for one, you tried to leave me."

"Please, Stefano, not that, not now."

Then I rested my head against his shoulder and opened my legs for him to step in closer to my body. He wrapped his arms around my waist and held me, his heat warming me.

"Okay, not now," he said, "but soon."

"Soon," I promised, pulling him closer.

Under any other circumstances, I wouldn't have pulled him in like that. It revealed too much about my feelings, but just this once I didn't have the strength to resist.

He held me until our food arrived.

Savory aromas filled the room, making my stomach rumble as Stefano pulled plates out and set the table. Then he lifted me from the counter to carry me to the table. When I wrapped my legs around his hips, he stopped for a second.

"Don't do that kind of shit if you don't intend to finish what you start."

We both dropped our gaze, and he put me on the chair.

He sat across from me and piled still-sizzling filet mignon, garlic roasted potatoes, and seasoned broccoli onto my plate. I touched his hand to stop him from adding more.

"Thank you. This looks amazing."

He smiled. "Good. Eat. You need your strength."

If it weren't for the pain and the dizzy spells, having dinner with Stefano in the cozy breakfast nook might have felt like, well, like a date.

We talked about Enzo and what I wanted to do with the café. Stefano mentioned he'd contacted his contractor associate in the city. He'd set a meeting for the following week for the man to assess the damage and quote repair estimates.

"Thanks," I said, "but I can cover it."

He grinned. "Yeah, we found your cash."

I sucked in a sharp breath, almost choking on a bite of meat. "What did you do with the money?"

He brushed off my outward worry with a wave of his fork. "It's safe. That's part of what we'll talk about later."

With a hesitant bobbing of my head, I agreed.

We finished eating in silence.

My mind reeled as I peeked at him from under my lashes, watching him cut his food and chew. I couldn't be so sure about who he really was now.

Still the same man I'd fallen for years ago?

Could Stefano still be the sweet, caring man who liked to laugh at my dirty jokes? The man who had been so gentle with me while teaching me about desire and pleasure.

My first lover. My only lover.

Or had he truly become the Vignali boss? A coldhearted killer who only a few nights before had thrown me around the room and ripped the pleasure from my body like he owned it, like I owed it to him, because he always took what he wanted.

And my god, just who the hell was I?

When I first met Stefano, I pretended to be Valerie Salera, the friendly neighborhood barista. A single Italian girl with no baggage. I wanted to be that girl. But that girl never really existed. She'd been a facade.

Because at my core, in my heart, in my soul, I had always been someone else.

Something else.

A mafia princess from Chicago.

A girl presumed dead.

Me.

Valentina Moscatelli.

A shock pulsed through my blood, forcing my heart to race. I hadn't let myself even think those words, to say my own name, for so very long.

I thought I'd gotten rid of Valentina forever.

But when that fucking psychopath Luka took me, when he shot me, when he chained me to the wall in that basement, Valerie Salera disappeared.

Valerie hadn't been strong enough to withstand the horrors. She wouldn't have known how to push the man to save herself. She wouldn't have understood how badly the bastard wanted to hear her scream.

She wouldn't have survived the trauma.

Valentina had to take over to save me. She was the one with the strength, knew how to use it, knew how to keep going.

I couldn't define the woman who now existed.

Valerie or Valentina?

Which woman wore the damn mask?

More importantly, which one would my son accept as his mother?

And what right did I have to judge Stefano the way I had, to be angry with him for lying about his real identity, when I'd also concealed my identity all along?

I just didn't know anymore.

A knot bunched in my gut.

I had to tell him. And it had to be soon. As soon as I healed a little more, physically, emotionally, when recent events no longer clouded my thoughts.

Stefano touched my hand.

"Val," he said. "Did you hear me?"

I dropped my fork and stared at him as he shook his head.

"I can see you're not all right. Come on, Angel, I'm taking you back to bed."

"Okay," I whispered.

Then he stood and lifted me into his arms once again.

"My room, Val. That's where I want you. I'll still sleep on the couch if that's what you want—for now—but Enzo will go back to sleeping in his own room. He never left you last night."

That knot in my stomach loosened. My heart... I didn't know how to translate the skipping and pounding of my stupid heart into words.

I touched Stefano's face.

"My boys are so sweet."

Stefano's eyes widened, and his lips parted. I guided his face down to mine and put a sweet kiss on his mouth. And then he carried me up to his room, to his bed.

Silence then filled the air between us.

He spoke first after tucking me in beneath the comforter.

"There's a TV if you want to watch something. Or I can have books brought in."

"A movie sounds nice," I said with a small smile. "I can't tell you how long it's been since I've watched something other than a Disney movie or Harry Potter."

Stefano let out a noncommittal grunt while he grabbed the remote. With the click of a button, a hidden compartment inside a cabinet near the foot of the bed slid open, and a flatscreen came up.

"Watch a lot of TV here?" I asked.

He stared at the screen, opening a streaming app.

"Yeah, when I can't sleep."

Then he handed me the remote and went to the door.

But I didn't want him to go. I craved the comfort of his warmth, his presence.

"Stefano, wait. Is there something that needs your immediate attention?"

He stared at me. "It can wait."

"Then will you stay with me for a little while?"

He didn't say anything. Shit. What had I just done? I lowered my eyes to the comforter and fiddled with the edge, scrunching it, and then smoothing it straight again.

"Look at me, Valerie," he finally said, and when I did, he went on. "Depends on what you want to watch."

"What?"

With his stare locked on me, he kicked off his shoes, got on the bed. Then he chuckled and took the remote.

The fucker.

Always the boss. He'd just answered that question.

I curled against his side beneath his raised arm.

"No gangsters and no Disney, please, but anything else is fair game," I said.

Stefano kissed my head while scrolling the options.

The next thing I remembered was his voice, deep but softly speaking into his phone. I didn't even know what movie he'd picked because I fell asleep so quickly.

I looked up at him.

He stared down at me, then tossed his phone away.

Another kind of hunger consumed me. Consumed us.

His kiss, in that moment, it was all I wanted. All I remembered. All I needed to heal.

I lifted my face, pushed my fingers into his hair, and tugged on his neck, asking him to give it to me.

Careful with my arm, he angled himself over me and kissed

me. A tender Stefano Salvatore kiss.

He couldn't be that man ever again, and I knew he was telling me so with that kiss. He had evolved as a man, as a leader, becoming more than he ever had been.

His kiss would also change and evolve.

And it would change me.

Truth be told, I had evolved too.

Valentina Moscatelli was back. She'd always been there, lurking in my soul, waiting for her time, just as the Vignali blood had always been strong in Stefano.

But who we were as individuals, who we wanted to be, that could all wait. I didn't want it to define who we would become together.

"Ace," I whispered.

"What do you want?" he said against my lips. "Tell me."

"I want you. All of you. The man you are now."

He pulled back to study my eyes, like he searched for a truth neither of us had been brave enough to admit.

Then he leaned down, and his next kiss became fierce, rough, demanding. His hand went to my throat, but he didn't squeeze. He understood my pain and the bruising left behind by another man who'd never been worthy of touching me.

Stefano held my throat in his hand, replacing my abuser's touch with his own, erasing the horror from my memory.

His blue eyes darkened.

As he moved his hand down to untie my robe, he didn't do it slowly, didn't take his time to explore my body. No, he took what he wanted, opening the robe with a yank.

His commanding behavior overwhelmed me. It lit a strong desire in me. Slick, beautiful heat built up between my thighs.

He grabbed my hair in his fist as he devoured my mouth

with his rough kiss. With his other hand, he flicked his thumb over my nipples.

A moan escaped from my mouth into his.

Even after everything I'd been through, all the physical trauma, my body responded to him like a starving animal.

I supposed that was kind of what I had become, a deprived animal so desperate for his touch to sate me.

"Do you want me to make you feel better, little girl?" he growled against my ear.

"Yes," I said.

"Yes? Yes what, Valerie?"

"Yes, sir. Make me feel better."

The intense eyes of a very different man burned into mine. The strong man I had always needed. The man I wanted more than anything.

"Only good girls get to come in my bed... and we still have a matter to settle between us."

Another moan conveyed my agreement.

I wanted whatever he had to give.

"You were a bad girl. You tried to leave me."

Those words, the way he said them.

I writhed beneath him, my need getting higher and hotter, but he quickly pinned my body down with his.

I gasped. "Please, I've learned my lesson."

"That might be true, but you haven't apologized," he said. "So now you'll show me how sorry you are..."

And he crushed his rock-hard cock against my stomach.

THIRTY-ONE

VAL

I would never escape from this man, not now that he knew what he wanted and planned to take it.

I would never escape this life again.

Stefano chose to bring our past into the present and stop living for the dead. His kiss and his command of my body made it clear he wanted to live for me, for his son, his own family.

No longer could I cling to my own false pretenses either.

I had to do what Stefano had done. I had to choose to live authentically, to honor my heart, to trust him with the truth.

"Whatever you want me to do, whatever you need to hear me say. I'll do it," I said.

He shifted his weight after realizing he'd been crushing me.

"I want action, not words."

Action, yes. I knew what he wanted, so I reached between our bodies to unfasten his slacks and take him in my hand.

He grabbed my wrist to stop me, then he got off the bed.

A little mewling whine moved from my throat onto my lips.

A cocky smile tugged at his mouth.

"Don't worry, Val. I'm not going far."

And he didn't. He stood beside the bed and stripped off his shirt. Next went his slacks, and just before he stepped out of his black boxer briefs, I totally gaped at the deliciousness of his V-shaped abs and the sexy, muscular grooves alongside his hips.

My breath stopped at the sight of his erection, the sheer size of him. Kind of hard to believe, but he fit inside me.

I bit into my bottom lip.

"Umm... maybe this shouldn't be about rewarding me."

"Nice try, sweetheart. Now come here." He pointed to the floor in front of him. "On your knees. Show me how sorry you are for what you did."

God, the way he ordered me around, how my body instantly responded, proving he was the man for me. The only man I ever needed.

I went to him, raising my arms to wrap them around his neck. I wanted to kiss him, to start at his throat and move down his tattooed chest, to take my time on his tight abs before finally kneeling on the floor to take him into my mouth.

Stefano grabbed my wrists and pushed me back.

"Uh-uh, little girl. I didn't give you permission to do that. I said, get on your knees."

"But... I was just going to... taste you?"

Heat burned my cheeks. Why the hell was I blushing?

Because he liked it, that was why.

He bent his neck, lifted my chin with a finger, then sealed his mouth over mine. His tongue pushed against my lips, and I opened to let him in. He deepened the kiss, a hint of whiskey on his tongue, and I fell into it, losing myself completely.

He broke the kiss way too soon. I wanted more. I lifted onto my tiptoes to kiss him.

"That's enough," he growled.

I squinted. "No, let me apologize. Let me kiss you and get on my knees and worship your cock. I'll do it."

The corner of his mouth lifted into a subtle smile.

"That sounds good, but that's what you want. I'll decide your penance, and now I've changed my mind. You're going to turn your pretty little ass around and lie on your back with your head hanging off the bed. Then do you know what happens next?"

I stared at him.

He stared back at me just as hard. To see if I understood the man before me was the real Stefano. To see if I understood how it would be for us moving forward. And to see if I liked it.

After all, I had asked him for that.

I kept quiet, so he could say the words, so he could tell me what he wanted.

"I'm going to spread your legs and watch how wet you get as I'm shoving my cock into your throat. You're going to take it like a good girl. You're going to suck me like your life depends on it while I decide what I want to do to you."

A wave of adrenaline shot through me.

My heart pumped furiously.

Not fear. Anticipation. The not knowing.

"What are you going to do?" I asked, unable to stop myself.

"Whatever I want. What you should worry about right now is learning how to be my good girl, how to obey when I give you an order. And you should keep in mind that you will not come until I say you can."

I swallowed hard, bobbing my head up and down.

Fuck those romance novels. This man and his kind of control was absolutely the hottest thing ever.

He raised a brow. "What are you waiting for? On your back."

Without another word, I climbed on the bed, lay on my back, and scooted until my head hung over the edge.

"Look at me, Val. You'll need to steel your gag reflex. And if you can't breathe, if you need me to stop, snap your fingers. But if you do, that's it. We're done playing."

"Yes, sir," I whispered.

Then I wiggled to get comfortable, pushing my shoulders over the edge just a little, gripping his thighs, and opened my mouth.

He started slowly, feeding me only the tip first. I sealed my lips around it, darting my tongue over the satiny smoothness to taste him.

It reminded me of a juicy plum, like when your tongue latches on just before your teeth break the fruit's skin.

He pushed in a little at a time. I struggled but did my best to relax into it, to get used to the sensation filling my throat. After a few thrusts, he pushed in more of himself.

My eyes watered. My jaw tightened.

But for him, I ignored the discomfort and sucked. He moved in and out of my mouth, pushing deeper into my throat.

So focused on his cock, I literally jumped when he touched me.

Playing, teasing, groaning as I sucked, he circled my nipples with his thumbs and cupped my breasts.

"They're fuller now," he said, "and very fucking hot."

Stefano slid his hands down my body, to my thighs, and pushed my legs open wide. As he stared at my pussy, I realized how shamelessly wet I'd become. Then he confirmed it for me.

"So wet for me already, Angel."

He dragged his knuckle up through my slit, then stopped to circle my clit with it, and I lost my damn mind.

The ecstasy building inside me whirled around his touch, faster, intensifying with each second.

"Christ, this is still the most perfect pussy. Mine. Have you given my pussy to anyone else, Val?"

Still sucking, I met his eyes and shook my head.

A tear rolled down the side of my face into my hair.

"Good girl," he said.

Then Stefano leaned over my body and slid his tongue over my now hypersensitive flesh.

I gasped around his cock.

When his mouth latched on to me, when his tongue flicked over my clit, my entire body shuddered.

I was so close to coming, but I knew better.

He hadn't given me permission.

I tightened my pelvic muscles, my thigh muscles, everything, hoping to hold it back, and focused on giving him my lie-back blow job. I focused on being his good girl and giving him what he wanted.

I wanted it to be good for him, and I thought it was... until he straightened his back and ripped his cock out of my mouth.

Panting, I lay on the bed with my legs spread, staring at his upside-down frame.

Stefano turned his back to me.

I quickly pulled myself upright on the silk sheets.

Had I bitten him or something?

"Stefano, I'm so sorry. Did I do something wrong?"

"Yeah, you did. Too good for your first time. I was just about to come all over your pretty face."

Turning around with a heated grin, he came to me and

pinched my chin between his thumb and forefinger, tilting my head back so he could look into my eyes.

"I quite like the idea of covering your face with my cum. But not tonight. I'm not finished with your punishment."

Then a cold darkness washed over his expression.

Punishment? What the hell happened to penance?

A chill raced over my naked body, giving rise to goose bumps all over my skin.

"Stand up, Val."

"Yes, sir," I whispered.

When I got to my feet, he grabbed the back of my neck, spun me to face the bed, then bent me over it. He grabbed a pillow and slipped it under the side of my face.

"Put your hands under the pillow and keep them there."

He hesitated for a minute.

"Does this hurt, Val? I don't want to hurt your arm."

Funny how the timing was utterly stupid, but I couldn't help comparing our gunshot wounds. They were identical in location, but mine was more torn up from the close range.

"No, I'm good," I said.

That was the last nice thing he said to me.

In the next second, his open hand slapped down on my ass.

I jumped right out of my skin.

"What the fuck, Stefano!" I shouted.

Another hard slap on the other side of my ass.

"Are you going to sneak out of my house again, Valerie?"

"No, I won't do it again," I said, holding back a whimper.

I agreed with him, so he wouldn't spank me again, or so I thought. But sweet mother of Christ, I had underestimated him. A third slap came down on my ass.

That one stung the most.

I squeezed my eyes shut, thinking this man, this mafia king, would never be underestimated by me again.

"Are you going to refuse my protection again, Valerie?"

"No," I whined.

"Are you going to try to leave me again?"

Then he forced my thighs open wide, and another slap came down. Perfectly angled, this one landed on my wet pussy.

"No, sir," I said with a little moan.

I might have been a damn masochist, but the sting felt exquisite. The perfect blend of pain and pleasure. I could hardly hold back the orgasm about to rip through me.

After pinching my clit, the fucking sadistic tease, he dragged a trail of wetness up between my ass cheeks, and I moaned again.

"Are you going to obey me at all times, Valerie?"

His choice of words and his lowered voice warned me that I should be careful with my response this time. He'd given me a move to make, and it had to be the right one. It would set the tone for us.

"That depends," I blurted through a breathless pant. "I'm not a fucking dog."

Beneath the pillow, I gripped the sheet, bracing for another spanking in case I'd said the wrong thing.

It didn't happen.

No, Stefano bent over me instead, his breath warming my shoulder. Then he growled the words "that's my good girl" against my ear.

"Good girl," he repeated. "I don't want an obedient bitch. I want a woman who can fight me, challenge me, and make me a better man.

"But the next time your insolence puts my son's life at risk, or your own, I will show you what a proper punishment is. I will spank your ass raw, and then I'll take it in every way, with very little prep. Do I make myself clear?"

Again, he dragged his knuckle through my slickness and up between my ass cheeks.

My thighs shook with the need to come.

"Yes, sir," I breathed.

The more he touched me, the more I wanted him. I wanted all of him in any way he wanted me.

"Tell me you belong to me now. Tell me you're going to stay here, under my roof, in my bed, where you belong. Where I can keep you safe."

"Yes," I whispered like a prayer.

Like a promise.

I wanted to be there. I wanted to be with Stefano. I wanted him to give me more children.

Stefano was my future, just like he was my past, and I didn't want to fight it anymore.

"Good. I think you've finally learned your lesson. Now I'll let you come in my bed... and it'll be so hard you'll scream my fucking name."

Then he made love to me in his bed.

But he was sweeter about it, almost gentle as he trailed hot, lingering kisses down my body, careful to avoid the bruises and cuts and my patched-up wounds. There was no more force in his touch. No demanding pleasure from my body. He coaxed it out gently instead.

While I wouldn't have called that pleasure more intense than when he fucked me on his desk, it satisfied me more than anything I'd ever experienced.

The first time he made me come, he sucked on my clit with

two fingers buried in my pussy and another circling my asshole, pushing in just a tiny bit every few passes.

It felt dark, different, forbidden.

It felt like Valentina.

And I loved every second of it.

The second time, he'd insisted I sit on his face. The orgasm was fantastic, made even better when I realized I could lean down over him and suck him while I rode his mouth.

It didn't take me long to come—and scream his name—then I slid down his body, lowered myself slowly and achingly onto his cock, and rode it.

He pulled me into his arms, on our sides, my back against his chest, and kissed my neck and my shoulder as he pushed back inside me, turning my head with the lightest touch to look into my eyes and whisper his promises until he roared through his own climax.

Being with Stefano felt inevitable, like I'd belonged there with him all along.

I'd been born for this life, and with him it would be perfect.

Sure, we would fight often, but that only meant we would fuck just as much or more to make up for it. As soon as my wound healed, I intended to start a fight in the middle of the day, in his office, until he bent me over his desk again.

Then we would rebuild the café and christen every surface before its grand reopening.

I wanted to start each morning with him inside me.

Lying naked with him, inside the warmth of his arms, I wanted to make this life work, the three of us together as an actual family.

Enzo deserved that.

Stefano deserved it.

And so did I.

"Valerie."

I winced. I wanted to hear my real name on his lips. The name my mother had given me. Before that could happen, though, I had to figure out how to tell him the whole truth.

We had so much to talk about, and we would soon. But in the moment, he was the only thing in my life that had been missing, and I couldn't stand the idea of losing him again.

"Stefano?"

"Marry me."

"Yes," I hoarsely whispered.

The easiest answer I'd ever given.

He leaned over me and grinned.

"I'm glad you said yes. Our engagement announcement came out while you were sleeping."

I froze.

He kissed my neck, the side of my face, and then my lips while my stuck mind processed absolute shock.

And fear.

Oh god, no. No, no, no.

My breath got caught in my throat.

My hands trembled.

I pushed myself away from him using his chest.

"What the hell did you do, Stefano?"

THIRTY-TWO
STEFANO

Val pushed away from me.

"What do you mean? What engagement announcement, Stefano? It came out where?"

I hadn't planned to ask her to marry me right then.

I had planned to tell her about the announcement, and once I explained how it made Enzo safer with my rivals and that no other immediate options existed, I thought she would get on board with it.

If only for our son's sake.

Val would do anything for her boy.

Did I want a fake marriage?

Fuck no.

My plan had been to win her over while we nursed her back to health, to show her the three of us could be a family.

A safe family. A happy family.

The words "marry me" had slipped out in the heat of the moment, like an involuntary reflex after making love to her.

She'd said yes without hesitation.

Christ, she'd even accepted my punishment before that.

But when I mentioned making the announcement, her face paled, her voice trembled, and her hands shook.

Val feared something more than just a public declaration.

Instinct kicked in, and I wanted to protect her from whatever had scared her. I wanted to protect her from every-fuck-ing-thing. I touched her warm cheek with the back of my fingers.

"I blindsided you… I'm sorry. But for the sake of our son's safety, you must not fight me on this."

"What did you do?" she whispered. "Show me, Stefano."

I grabbed my phone and tapped open the Weddings & Engagements section in the app for *The New York Times*. It only took a few seconds to find the article.

Prominent Manhattan Businessman and Brooklyn Barista Celebrate Caffeinated Reunion

The headline was polished and harmless on the surface. But anyone who understood power would read between the lines.

Val took my phone with apprehension when I offered it, then she thumbed the screen, not stopping to read anything before closely examining the photos.

Three photos.

An image of me from some business meeting or something I didn't remember.

The picture of Val came from Enzo. The second he'd shown it to me, I made my own copy. It made my heart ache, and it seemed perfect for the announcement. A candid shot of her in the kitchen at Con Amore, wearing her baking apron and an authentic smile. Pure happiness.

I could almost smell the cookies she'd been making.

Enzo had given me the third picture as well. One she always kept close, he'd said.

The one she thought he didn't know about.

It showed the two of us soon after we first met, young and completely enamored with each other. This one gave legitimacy to our relationship, creating added protection for her and for our son.

I thought she might be thrilled with the photos.

She was not. She wouldn't even look at me.

"Talk to me, Val. You're clearly very upset. What is it? Why isn't this okay?"

She swung her legs over the side of the bed, turning her back to me, then stood after a minute of silence.

"Because it's not, Stefano. The fairy tale's over, and it's time for us to leave. Enzo and I need to get to the train station before it's too late. We're starting over somewhere new, like I've planned all along."

My chest constricted as she rambled on about a new life. She wanted to leave me. Without an explanation or as much as a bullshit excuse.

I had her back. I had my son.

And I would destroy anyone who tried to take them from me.

I grabbed her arm. "You're not going anywhere. You know my reach by now. You'll never outrun me again. So tell me what you need, Valerie, and I'll take care of it."

"Stop calling me that," she snapped.

Then she ripped her arm out of my grasp, snatched up her robe, and ran into the hallway.

I grabbed my robe and raced after her, shouting, demanding that she stop running the fuck away from me.

Enzo's bedroom door banged open.

He'd heard us.

Val ran into his room.

"Pack up your things, buddy. We're leaving, and we're not coming back. Do it right now, Enzo."

I grabbed her shoulders, spun her around to face me, and backed her up against the wall.

"I said stop, goddamn it. Tell me what's happening. What are you doing?"

Tears rolled down her cheeks, one after another. She finally made eye contact as she touched my face.

"You should know... I love you, but that'll never be enough."

My blood boiled. My heart pounded like a motherfucker. I punched the wall beside her head, the crack of bone against plaster barely registering.

Enzo charged at me and grabbed my arm. I shoved him back harder than I meant to, and he hit the floor.

"You said you would stay," I snarled. "I won't let anyone hurt you again if that's what this is about."

Her lips curved into a small, sad smile.

"I let myself get caught up in a fantasy, and I lied... because I never intended to stay with you."

A heavy thud hit the front door.

I ignored it.

Nothing mattered but Val.

Holding on to her, not letting her leave me, keeping her from walking out on us again, that was my entire existence in that moment. My only reason to live.

A male voice shouted for me to open the door.

Valerie's eyes widened. She stopped breathing.

I studied the fear and confusion in her eyes while holding her chin between my thumb and finger.

What the fuck was happening to her?

Then she pulled my mouth to hers, kissed me, whispered against my lips.

"I'm so sorry, Ace. I'm leaving you."

Another voice echoed through the foyer.

Thick. Familiar. Chicago.

"Your boss has something that belongs to us."

"Fuck you," I heard Bruce say.

The clicking of a revolver's hammer echoed next.

Again, that stupid fucking accent resonated.

"Don Moscatelli wants the girl back. Tell Vignali to hand her over now, or his kid dies."

Chicago had just declared war on the wrong man.

READ THIS BOOK NEXT

Wicked Villain was only the beginning.

They came for the woman Stefano claimed.
Rival families close in, and every threat against Val is
met with calculated retaliation.

He has already lost her once.
He will not survive losing her again.

Continue the dynasty with Savage Enemy.
Get it here: **geni.us/savage-enemy**

ALSO BY KELLIANN NELSON

CRUEL KINGS

Book 1 – Wicked Villain

Book 2 – Savage Enemy

Book 3 – Cruel King

DYNASTY OF OBSESSION

Book 1 – You Belong Here

Book 2 – Never Let You Go

ABOUT THE AUTHOR

Kelliann Nelson writes dark romance defined by obsession, power, and unwavering devotion. Her stories follow sovereign men, dangerous dynasties, and heroines claimed at the heart of empires built by men who will burn the world to protect what is theirs. Her novels deliver emotionally intense arcs, calculated dominance, and loyalty that does not bend.

For reading order, exclusive newsletter updates, and content notes, visit **kelliannnelson.com**.

instagram.com/kelliannnelsonbooks

facebook.com/kelliannnelsonbooks

pinterest.com/kelliannnelsonbooks

tiktok.com/@kelliannnelsonbooks